THE MAGICIAN
Killer

JEWELED DAGGER PUBLISHING

Designed by Sergio Sandoval

First edition
ISBN ---The Magician Killer eBook 978-1-946146-21-2
ISBN— The Magician Killer Paperback 978-1-946146-20-5

Acknowledgment and a huge thank you to

Barbara Woods: Editor
Sergio Sandoval: Book Designer
100 Covers: Cover Design

I wish to dedicate this book to all those who
cheered me on over the years, as well as those
who told me I could actually be an author and
publisher, and have it all.
As a woman, it is often our lot to take a back
seat to our dreams and to serve others before
ourselves. But I have taken the bull
by the horns and followed my dreams.
A special thank you to my husband, Dave, for
supporting me and for being in my corner
even when it wasn't very profitable to do so.
A special shout-out to my kids and
grandkids. Always know that I love you
beyond the moon and stars and then some.

THE MAGICIAN
Killer

CHAPTER ONE

A New Trophy

T HE NIGHT AIR WAS CRISP and there were currently no clouds in the sky to obstruct his view of the clearing. A light breeze blew softly and rustled the surrounding leaves and branches as he sat high up in the tree stand meant for hunters.

He was waiting for that inevitable moment when his victim would suddenly realize that there would be no escape—no last-minute reprieve by some unknown rescuer. He breathed in and out slowly, trying to regain control of his racing heart.

This one had been relatively easy, he congratulated himself. He'd shown great restraint, simply observing her for eight long weeks before making his move. Timid little Amy had been nothing like his first victim, the only one that got away from him. Just thinking about that first time caused him to grow hot inside and break out into a cold sweat. She'd surprised him—getting the upper hand as she fought back. The memory made him cringe, and his hand unconsciously went to his neck where he fingered the ring he wore on a chain. Her ring.

She'd kicked him in the solar plexus, knocking the air from his lungs. Then she began screaming at him like some crazed banshee. But even then, he hadn't been deterred by her fighting spirit. In fact, it had excited him all the more.

Now his hand involuntarily went to his face as he felt the permanent marks scarring the left side. This is what caused him to back down those many years ago—her clawing his face, raking her fingernails halfway down the side of his cheek, nearly blinding him in the process. He'd retreated back into the shadows of the alleyway and ran away, shocked and humiliated.

That was ten years ago, and he would never make that mistake again. He'd learned a very valuable lesson—one that he would not forget: Know your prey well before you strike. Since that day, he'd always taken precautions, planned everything out to the last detail, and learned to be patient.

Shaking his head to dispel the negative thoughts, he looked out at the clearing to where his latest victim lay unconscious, still unaware of her fate. She was stripped down to her undergarments. Thick rope tied her legs and wrists to the four wooden stakes he'd pounded deep into the ground. There would be no opportunity for escape.

This one he'd doused in coyote blood. But sometimes he would use honey or salmon guts. It all depended upon the carnivore he wanted to attract.

Then he would take something from them: a ring, a necklace, maybe sunglasses or earrings—something unique to remember them by.

In his pants pocket, he fingered her pendant and chain. It was a gold locket in the shape of a heart, with a tiny diamond in the corner. The back was engraved with *Love always, Mom and Dad.*

A stray cloud shifted in the sky, partially covering the full moon, dimming his pristine view of the scene. Soon Amy would awaken from her drug-induced slumber and discover her unfortunate predicament. That's when the real fun would begin.

He felt the first stirrings of excitement as he noticed Amy twitch just as the clouds began to clear away. She tried to pull her right arm in and then her left. Suddenly her eyes opened wide and she shook her head to clear her mind of the last vestiges of the drug that left her brain feeling foggy. Amy began to shake, then thrash, tugging frantically at the ropes that constricted her. Then she began to scream for help.

With her shrill shrieks of panic, his excitement skyrocketed. He could smell the acrid stench of fear even from this distance. He smiled with satisfaction as he felt himself begin to tingle all over. His manhood suddenly hardened and he knew that ultimately his release was not far off. The pure emotion he cognitively experienced from his victims was the only way that he was able to achieve this form of ecstasy.

"And it begins, my little bird," he said out loud, raising his voice so that Amy could hear him below. Placing his earphones in, he pressed play on his Walkman, nearly caressing the machine he had carefully preserved since his early teenage years. The grandeur of Beethoven's *Symphony No. 5* came to life and he waved his arms in the air like he was conducting the orchestra. "Sing louder, little songbird, sing!"

Amy craned her neck, trying to pinpoint the voice from the trees. "Please, help me! You don't have to do this. Please..." she begged.

"Soon they will come."

"Who...who will come? Please...untie me. I beg you. Let me go," she whimpered.

The man laughed demonically.

It didn't take long before a timber wolf crested the hill. The man had made sure that he'd staked her down near the wolves' den for optimal carnage.

Putting its nose into the air, then sniffing, the large gray wolf smelled the blood left behind for him. Two more wolves crested the hill, nipping at one another as the alpha male took a few steps closer.

Utter terror filled Amy as she heard the wolf pack leader howl. As she lifted her head, locking eyes with the large grey wolf for an agonizing moment, she felt unable to catch her breath as the massive beast slowly proceeded down the hill toward her.

Her calls for help were momentarily stifled as she froze, trying to remain completely still.

"You are probably thinking that this is all just a bad dream, sweet Amy. But let me assure you that this is no dream." The man laughed again.

No one heard her cries for help, nor the screams of agony as she was torn apart, piece by piece, by the wolves. No one, that is, except for the man with the steely-blue eyes staring down from his front-row seat, high in the tree line of the deer stand.

CHAPTER TWO

Hiking Boots

S AM STEVENS SAT AT HER DESK, COMBING through another cold case, when she thought she saw her first name appear on the page before her: *Samantha*. She wondered why that name had suddenly popped into her mind after all these years. No one had called her Samantha since she was nineteen.

Pinching the bridge of her nose, Sam felt a headache coming on as the words on the page started to blur. Closing her eyes and massaging her temples, her mind wandered.

Special Agent Sam Stevens was known to some of the other agents as "The Robot," a nickname she picked up in Quantico and disliked with a passion. In fact, the only people who dared to call her The Robot to her face quickly learned to keep it to themselves when she humbled them—men and women alike—on the sparring mat during routine training sessions.

Her fellow agents often wondered about Sam—who she was and what she did for fun—since she didn't talk about her weekends or fraternize with them outside of work.

As far as her coworkers were concerned, Special Agent Stevens was a nun. She'd never mentioned a special man, or a woman for that matter, in her life.

Working out of the FBI's Washington, D.C., office as one of the finest investigative profilers in the Behavioral Science Unit, she managed to quickly move up the ranks because of her work ethic and her innate ability to compartmentalize her emotions.

Sam approached each new case in the same analytical way and could survive on very little sleep and food for days— hence, her nickname seemed to fit. It was easy for her to focus on her career since she didn't have any family. Nor did she allow friendships to get in the way. She didn't even own a houseplant. She was no longer the carefree and chatty girl she had been in high school. So much had changed since then.

Sitting at her desk, analyzing a file she had pulled from the cold cases box, Sam jumped when her boss, Supervising Special Agent Tom Hagen, bellowed, "Stevens! My office. Now!"

Sam pursed her lips together, wondering what he wanted with her so late in the day. She marked her spot in the file with a sticky note that read, "More info is needed." Then she stood up and pushed her chair in.

"What do you think that's all about?" her only friend, Thea, asked, chewing vigorously on a piece of mint gum. She was deep into a case file and gum always helped her concentrate.

Thea Thompson was a bright, effervescent individual and two years younger than Sam.

In a conspirator's whisper, Sam said, "Your guess is as good as mine."

"STEVENS!" Hagen yelled again, with even less patience.

"It appears that my presence is urgently needed," Sam said, grabbing her black suit jacket from the back of her chair, quickly putting it on over her white blouse, and buttoning it up. Then, smoothing out any wrinkles with her hand, she said, "Wish me luck."

"You won't need it. You're the golden girl," Thea replied as Sam headed to Hagen's office.

Feeling someone watching her, Sam looked around the room and noticed the new guy tracking her movements.

"Eyes on your own work, Agent Trainee, before I assign you to clear the files in the basement. There's nothing to see here," she said dismissively.

Flushing red, the trainee quickly turned away and shuffled paperwork around his desk, attempting to look busy.

Giving a cursory knock before stepping into her boss's office, Sam stood at attention, waiting for an invitation to be seated.

Hagen ignored Sam for a full five minutes while he continued to read the papers in front of him, then scribbled his signature on several documents. Sam knew this was retribution for making *him* wait. Annoyed, she shifted her weight from one foot to the other. Hagen finally put down his pen and magnanimously waved her toward the chair in front of his desk.

"Special Agent Stevens, I bet you are wondering why I called you to my office today."

"Yes, sir, the thought had crossed my mind."

"I have a very special assignment for you," he said with what could only be considered a half smile. "One that I have no doubt will be right up your alley. Do you own hiking boots?"

"Ah, yes...yes, sir, I do," she stammered, momentarily caught off guard by the odd question, "Why do you ask?"

"You are from Alaska, correct?" he asked, sitting back in his chair and clasping his hands together like a teepee under his chin as he studied her reaction.

"Ah...yes, sir, I am. But—"

"I have a situation that has been brought to my attention, and I need someone with your particular skill set to go out there and take a look," he said, not yet divulging that her presence was explicitly requested from someone in the Seattle office. Then, leaning forward in his chair, he splayed his hands upon his desk. "We may or may not have a serial kidnapper and killer. No one can seem to get a handle on what the hell is going on over there. Now, don't give me that look, Stevens."

"What look, sir?"

"I've read your file several times. And I understand your lack of enthusiasm to return to your home state. Hell, we all dread going back home. But this request comes from the top. It seems you have an admirer, and your services were requested."

"I'm flattered. But, sir—" she began, only to be interrupted.

"That's why I'm supportive of you for this assignment. If you do well, perhaps you can move up, but don't get any ideas about my job."

"No, sir, I wouldn't—"

"I'm just pulling your chain. Relax."

A feeling of dread washed over Sam. That's when she noticed that her left hand was trembling. It had been five years since the last time this had happened. She quickly tucked her hand into her suit jacket pocket to hide it from Hagen's keen eyes.

She forced a smile to her lips, trying to pretend that everything was normal. But everything was *not* normal. Sam bit down hard on her tongue to refrain from saying out loud, "Send anyone else but me. I'm the absolute wrong person for this assignment!"

Oblivious to her sharp reaction, Hagen held up a file. "This is everything we know about the missing girls," he said, and then dubiously added, "It's a bit thin, but I have every confidence that you will make sense of it in record time and return back home to civilization, ASAP."

Sam took it, fingering through the paperwork as she turned, ready to leave, but then stood in place a moment longer. Inside, the file only included five missing person flyers along with seven pages of official reports. *Who in the world had put this together? What analyst had looked at these five random flyers with their flimsy reports and decided, "Hey, these cases look like they go together?"* she thought to herself, feeling annoyed.

"Is there anything else I need to know, sir?" Sam turned back around, wanting to hand the file back to him as if it were a hot potato.

She felt her pulse racing and cleared her throat when he didn't immediately answer.

"No, that will be all, Special Agent Stevens," Hagen said, dismissing her. "See Maggie regarding your travel arrangements." Then he gestured with his head for her to leave his office quickly.

As she reached the door, she heard Hagen clear his throat before he added, "Oh, one more thing, Stevens. For this case, you'll be teaming up with another agent."

"Oh? Who's going with me?" she asked.

"You misunderstood me," he said, lifting another folder off his desk. "Special Agent McLeroy from the Seattle office will meet you in Anchorage. Here's his dossier."

Halfway to the door with both files now in hand, Sam turned around to propose another agent take her place.

Before she could open her mouth, Hagen looked up. "And Stevens?"

"Yes, sir?"

"Try to get along with this guy. I understand he's good at what he does."

"Why, whatever do you mean, sir? I am the most easygoing—"

"Go on, get out of my office," he said, allowing a low chuckle to escape under his breath. She turned at the door and noticed that he was removing his glasses to pinch the bridge of his nose as if he felt a headache coming on.

"Well, what did he want?" Thea grilled Sam the moment she returned to her desk. "Spill all of the details."

"He's sending me on assignment and I'm not happy about it," Sam explained.

"Where to?"

"You'll never guess."

"Just tell me. Come on, really, what's going on?" Thea laughed, then became serious again when she noticed the strange look on Sam's face. "Is everything all right? You look distressed."

"That's because I am. Hagen is sending me back to the one place I swore I'd *never* go back to again if it were the last thing I did." Sam retrieved her FBI-issued handgun from the top right-hand drawer of her desk and fastened it to her belt. "The Last Frontier."

"Nooo!" Thea said too loudly, looking around to ensure she hadn't attracted any unwanted attention before lowering her voice. "No."

Noticing a toy wind-up robot sitting on her desk, Sam picked it up and then looked around the office to see who might have left it behind for her to find. "Did you notice anyone pass by my desk while I was with Hagen?"

Taking the toy from Sam's hand, Thea said, "This one is rather cute."

Snatching it back from Thea, Sam held the toy in the air and raised her voice just loud enough for everyone to hear. "You would think that in a room full of highly intelligent agents, the lot of them could be a little more original." Then, she tossed it into the drawer with the other discarded robot toys.

"They're just jealous because you have an exemplary record and a brilliant mind."

"I would settle for being normal or even a little less me right about now," Sam grumbled under her breath.

Thea was a beautiful woman of color from the bayous of Louisiana and Sam's only real friend. She was tall and thin with shoulder-length, bobbed hair of rich reddish-brown hues. Thea had worked hard to lose the thick accent of her home, but it would surface any time she was angry. She was also the only person Sam had ever let close enough to confide that she came from Anchorage, Alaska—and *why* she hoped to never see the state again.

"I'm really sorry that you have to go back there, Sam." Thea was very protective of Sam and her feelings and didn't want to see her get hurt.

Pursing her lips, Sam nodded while gathering some paperwork together. "It looks like I'm headed on assignment to Alaska whether I like it or not. Pray for me. And I remember you saying that your granny practices Voodoo. Maybe you could ask her to cast a spell of protection over me."

"Yes, I can do that. Oh, Sam, I'm so sorry. Who's going with you?"

Opening the bottom left drawer of her desk, Sam paused momentarily to decide what to take from her emergency stash. Retrieving a bag of Fritos corn chips and closing the drawer, she sighed deeply before answering, looking directly into her friend's eyes. "I'm meeting up with an agent from the Seattle office."

"Sam, you know I'm just a phone call away. You can call me day or night."

"I know. That means a lot to me, and I might call you in the wee hours of the night so you'd better answer. But for now, I've got to run. We'll talk later."

"Do you mind if I grab something from there?" Thea gestured towards the drawer. "I skipped lunch today and could use a little pick me up."

"Sure. Take what you need. Just make sure that it's replenished before I return from my exile. I wouldn't want to run out of any of my valuable food groups."

Thea peered into the desk drawer filled with snack-sized bags of chips, assorted candy bars, and two power bars for emergencies before selecting a full-size peanut butter cup and closing the drawer. "You know this drawer is a cry for help."

"I will have you know that I have survived more than a few late nights with the help of that drawer."

Casually changing the subject, Thea lifted her eyebrows in a pleading gesture. "Say, a few of us are getting together tonight after work for drinks. Do you want to come?"

Shaking her head, Sam smiled sadly. "I don't think I can make it. I told Hagen that I had hiking boots, so I need to find a pair before I leave tomorrow. Catch me next time. I promise I will try to make it."

"You know, Sam, one of these days you are going to have to let someone into your life."

"I have let someone into my life."

"Besides me," Thea smiled.

"We both know I have serious trust issues."

"And for good reason." Thea knew that it was unlikely Sam would ever let her guard down with the other agents, let alone join them for a night out for drinks. But Thea knew she would never stop trying to get Sam out of her shell. "Thanks for the snack. I'll be sure to get in touch with granny tonight."

Retrieving the paperwork from her desk, Sam stuffed everything into her leather messenger bag, slung it over her shoulder, and left the office to see to some last-minute shopping before she went to her apartment to pack. Like it or not, she was headed home.

She wondered if she still had an old prescription for tranquilizers lying around anywhere, just in case she needed it.

Getting To Know You

T HE NEXT MORNING, Sam was on a 7 a.m. flight from Dulles International Airport to Seattle, where she would catch her connecting flight to Anchorage. She was dressed in dark blue jeans, a white button-down blouse, and an emerald green wool jacket. She was already regretting wearing her brand-new hiking boots. A blister was already forming on the back of her left heel, but her other shoes were packed in her checked luggage.

The flight attendant came around the cabin offering refreshments and earphones for the in-flight entertainment, but Sam was lost in her own thoughts. Her boss was correct when he'd told her the case files were thin; there wasn't even enough to make up a full profile about a possible perpetrator who may or may not have abducted these women. The missing five women were all between the ages of nineteen and twenty-three. Each had brown hair and brown eyes, except for one, whose eyes were naturally blue, but she occasionally wore brown contacts. The one definitive thing they had in common was that they were all employed as waitresses when they went missing. *Perhaps there is some merit in grouping these cases together, after all,* Sam thought. She began to make notes inside the folder, underlining interesting facts before adding the question, "ARE THERE MORE VICTIMS?" in all caps.

Next, she decided to read up again on her new partner. "Might as well know who I will be working with," Sam muttered under her breath.

After some time, the pilot came over the cabin speaker to announce that they were preparing to land in Seattle. Pulling out her itinerary, Sam noticed that the connecting flight would be tight, so she gathered her things together and walked quickly to the next gate.

Afterward, Sam boarded the next flight and began pouring over the files once again, but she felt her eyes getting heavy. Thinking about the long day she had ahead of her, on top of the eleven hours it was taking to get from Dulles to Seattle and then to Anchorage, she placed the files back into her leather messenger bag, shoved everything under the seat in front of her, and decided to grab a quick nap before they landed.

She felt as if she'd just closed her eyes when the pilot's voice came over the cabin speaker and startled her awake from a disturbing dream. Attempting to slow her breathing and her heart rate, Sam heard the pilot announce that they would be landing in Anchorage in the next twenty minutes.

Taking a deep breath and blowing it out slowly, she looked around to make sure she hadn't made a complete and utter fool of herself. That is when Sam reached for her phone and turned it back on to check for any important updates before they landed. She saw a text from her friend Thea that read: *You got this. I believe in you.* The words of encouragement made her smile.

Just landing, Sam texted back.

Immediately, Sam's phone chimed with a new message before she could slip it back into her pocket: *How is the new partner? Cute or some old grump?*

Sam laughed and then replied: *Haven't met him yet. Just getting off the plane. Honestly, you need a boyfriend or a life. I'm not sure which. Will share more later.*

To be honest, she was grateful for the distraction as she waited for the plane to empty before gathering up her things to exit. After collecting her suitcase from baggage claim, she followed the arrows to the exit and rode the escalator down. Ahead, Sam observed a tall, striking man standing by the exit door with a large German shepherd by his side. The attractive man held up a large, handmade sign that read: Sam Stevens.

Sam didn't immediately recognize the agent because his dossier picture was very different from the man who stood before her now. He was about twenty pounds thinner, his hair was slightly longer, and it looked as if he had spent time in the sun. Taking note of these differences, her analytical brain surmised that he must have recently gone through a life-altering event. That was usually the reason for a person's drastic change in appearance. But his faithful partner standing guard by his side was a dead giveaway. Apparently, from the information in his dossier, the two of them were paired up four years ago, and they hadn't been apart since.

As Sam got closer, she also noted that Special Agent Nicholas McLeroy, at six-foot-four, appeared even taller than she had expected and his eyes were more appealing than she had imagined. There was a handsome scruff of whiskers on his face as if he hadn't shaven in a couple of days. His hair was a combination of brown and blond tones, most likely bleached from the sun. He looked as if he would be very comfortable on a surfboard.

The dog obediently sat on the man's right side, watching everyone who walked by with intensity. He would jump up and stand at attention whenever anyone came within his protective radius or stepped too close to his man.

Sam approached while respecting the boundaries of the dog. "I believe you're waiting for me," she said, giving the pair the once-over as she studied their posture and body language closely. She couldn't ignore the fact that his well-worn blue jeans fit him in all the right places. A navy T-shirt, hiking boots, and a pair of aviator sunglasses tucked just inside the front collar of his shirt completed his look.

Giving a command to his partner before extending his hand in greeting, the man introduced himself. "I'm Special Agent Nicholas McLeroy, but everyone calls me Nick." He gestured to his four-legged companion, "And this is Officer Murphy."

She shook Nick's hand and said, "I'm Special Agent Sam Stevens, but you may call me Sam or Stevens. I will answer to either." She furtively glanced down at the dog. He didn't seem aggressive, but large dogs still unnerved her. "Is your dog going to bite me?"

Nick shook his head, reaching down to give his companion a loving scratch behind his ears. "Nah. He usually only attacks on command. You will see that Murphy here has a very gentle soul. He also has a particular set of skills that may come in handy on our case."

"Oh, and what is that special set of skills your dog possesses?"

"*Officer Murphy,*" he corrected, "is a highly decorated officer of the law." He pointed out the two gold stars sewn into the dog's vest that covered his vital organs and doubled as a harness. "He's trained to sniff out both cadavers and drugs. Why, he can sniff out the place where someone was murdered even if they were later moved," Nick declared proudly. "Here, let me get that bag for you."

Sam put up a hand to stop him. "I can carry my own luggage, I'll have you know, Special Agent McLeroy," she protested.

"Nick, please," he said, backing away from her suitcase. "All righty then. If you follow me, I will show you to our car, and we can be on our way. We have to take another plane to a remote location."

Moments later, Nick gallantly opened the passenger door rental Jeep for Sam, but Murphy immediately jumped into the front seat ahead of her. Nick pointed to the back seat, "Platz, braver hund," he ordered.

The dog quickly jumped through the two seats into the back, turned his back to them both, and stared out the window. It actually looked like he was pouting.

"I would like to apologize for my ill-mannered partner. He isn't used to sharing me with others," Nick said.

Murphy seemed to turn slightly to give Nick a glare before turning back around.

Sam climbed into the Jeep as Nick hoisted her bag into the back next to his bag and Murphy. Ten minutes later, they arrived at Lake Hood, where a floatplane was moored at the dock.

Nick parked the Jeep, grabbed both bags from the back seat, and sat them on the pavement before tucking the keys under the front seat. "I made arrangements with someone from the rental car agency to pick up the Jeep later today," he explained when Sam looked at him strangely.

Murphy jumped out of the Jeep and stood at Nick's side. Tiredly stepping out of the jeep, Sam rubbed the sore spots on her back before pulling up on the handle of her bag, then waited for Nick to lead the way.

The familiar combination of fresh air and the smell of briny seawater stirred a flood of memories for Sam, and her mind went back in time to when she was eight. Her mother, father, and she had taken a trip by seaplane to the interior of Alaska, and had flown back to this very inlet on their way home.

Lost in thought, Sam stood frozen in time as so many memories washed over her. "Come on, slowpoke, we need to catch the updraft while it's good," Nick called out, shaking Sam out of her melancholy thoughts. Suddenly, she was grateful for Nick and his four-legged partner's distraction.

Sam hurried to catch up to Nick, who was standing in the middle of the dock waiting for her.

"I noticed that you aren't wearing a wedding ring," Nick said casually, bringing Sam back to reality. "Have you ever been married?"

"Now, who is showing poor manners? And what an odd question to ask of someone you just met," Sam said, gazing out at the water before them.

Murphy ran ahead of them toward the small plane. "Marriage is a lifelong feat of practiced diplomacy. A balancing act, if you will," Sam said with a sad smile as she turned back to face Nick. "As you may have already guessed, I'm not very diplomatic or good at the whole balancing act thing."

"I'll take that as a no," he teased and smiled.

"Did your dog just open the plane door?" Sam asked, her tone reflecting her complete shock.

"*Officer Murphy*," Nick corrected again. "And yes. He can pull the door open. But to be fair, I did leave it unlocked for him."

When they joined Murphy at the plane, Nick attached a safety leash to his partner's harness. "In case of turbulence," he explained when he noticed Sam looking at him. "He can't hang on. He has no thumbs."

Sam turned around to fasten the belt across her chest and lap with shaky hands. She didn't like flying much and she especially hated small planes.

Nick started the engine and then stepped outside to untie the plane and push it away from the dock before climbing back inside. Giving her a reassuring smile, Nick handed Sam a pair of earphones so they could communicate while in the air. The noise from the engine could be deafening.

Next, he began the preflight checks, ensuring the gas tank was full, the tail fin responded, and the wing flaps moved properly before announcing, "Ready for take-off," giving Sam a thumbs up. That's when he noticed her white knuckles gripping the armrest of her seat. "I've logged over two thousand hours on this bucket of bolts, and I've not even had a close call once," Nick assured her. "You're safe with me."

Forcing a smile that she knew was not convincing, Sam said, "I'm fine. Let's just get this bucket of bolts, as you call it, up in the air. The sooner we get there, the sooner we will know if we have a bad guy to catch."

Checking the wind sock blowing in the breeze, Nick slowly pulled away from the shore and into the middle of the lake. Expertly navigating the plane into the wind, he accelerated until he had enough speed to lift them off the water and into the air as he pulled back on the control wheel while adjusting the throttle.

Sam held her breath, keeping her eyes tightly closed. She didn't want to see the crash coming if they were going to die.

"You can unclench now," Nick said. "We are in the air. And I didn't even hit a tree this time."

Sam's eyes immediately popped open. "What?" she yelled.

"Relax. I was just joking with you."

A derisive scoff escaped her lips. "Well, it wasn't amusing," she said, giving Nick a dirty look. "And neither are you."

"All right, all right, so you don't like my jokes or my flying—"

"No, I don't," she insisted, facing forward in her seat and staring straight toward the horizon line.

Nick thought that Sam would be so much prettier if she would just learn to relax a little. Everything about her seemed tense and uptight, like a piano wire.

"Then we should talk about something else. You know, to get your mind off the fact that you're up in the air, in a plane, with a complete stranger. Why don't you show me what you've got? I hear that you are an incredible profiler. So, profile me."

"No, I couldn't. I've been told that it's incredibly rude to profile someone you just met."

"But you do it anyway, right?"

"Of course not," she said, turning to look at him.

"I think you just lied to me," he said with a wide grin. "You know you want to do it."

"That is a rather impertinent thing to say to a total stranger," she replied, looking out the window.

"Come on, it'll be fun to hear your take on me," he persisted. "I've even heard that you're somewhat of a savant when it comes to profiling people—like one of those mystics at a Las Vegas show people pay to see."

"No, really. I just met you less than an hour ago. It truly would be rude, don't you think?"

"I knew they were all lying to me about you," Nick said, attempting to goad her into it.

Pricked by his insult, Sam took a deep breath and let it out slowly to slow her racing heart. She began with her usual once-over, looking him up and then down. "You were the first-born child and, if I had to guess, the only son. You had siblings that looked up to you?" She deliberately posed it as a question, gauging his reaction before continuing. With a confident smile, Sam said, "Two younger sisters that idolized you, I'd bet. I will take your silence, and that look on your face as a yes. Your parents were baby boomers, very traditionalists. Your mother stayed home and took care of the children and household, volunteering at school, and running you and your two sisters to activities. She baked cookies for the bake sales and—"

"Nice guessing," Nick cut in.

"Oh, I'm not guessing, and I would buckle up because I'm just getting started, Special Agent McLeroy." She gave him a lopsided grin. "Besides, you know what they say. It isn't guessing if you're right," Sam added, with just a hint of superiority. "Your father was a professional. I'm guessing a stockbroker or a…" She pondered a split second, giving him another once-over as she changed her mind. "No. Attorney? Yes, he was definitely an attorney."

"How did you do that?" he interrupted again.

"Stop trying to break my concentration," Sam scolded. "You asked me to prove my abilities, and I intend to give you what you requested. Now, be quiet so that I can concentrate. You made friends easily and had a natural athletic ability. Captain of the football team?" Sam again gauged his reaction to her guess. "Yes, definitely the quarterback."

Nick gave her a sideways glance and then pursed his lips together to prevent himself from interrupting her again.

"You did well on tests in school and scored high on your SATs, but only because you received extra tutoring from one of the smarter kids—most likely a cheerleader who had a crush on you," she mused out loud before making it a definitive statement. "Yes. Definitely, a cute cheerleader who was crushing on you."

"How in the world could you know any of that?" Nick questioned. Then, looking straight forward, he chuckled to himself. "I think you're enjoying this a bit too much."

Sam was enjoying the satisfaction she felt as his eyes bugged out of his head when her words hit too close to home. Nick had a tell. To be fair, most people had a tell—a pulse that beat a little more rapidly in their neck, pupils that dilated slightly, and so on.

"All right, you win," he said, holding up one hand to signal his surrender. "So, they were right about you after all."

"Did I say I was finished with you, Special Agent McLeroy? I was just hitting the highlights." Sam gave him a wicked smile before continuing on. "Married once, no children. The divorce was not recent, but you didn't remove your wedding band until a few months ago. By your accent, I would say that you grew up on the East Coast and—"

"What accent?" Nick protested. "I don't have an accent."

"I detect a twinge of Maine, maybe Rhode Island area," she continued as if he hadn't said anything. Cocking her head to one side, she looked at him again. "But you have spent a lot of time most recently on the West Coast."

"How the hell did you..." he began to say, looking at her with astonishment. "And you could tell all of that about me in thirty minutes?"

"I could tell most of that about you within the first ten minutes, Special Agent McLeroy," she added smugly, flashing Nick a brilliant smile.

There was no reason for him to know that she had reread his dossier on the plane ride out and that whatever wasn't in his files, she'd guessed at. She knew his type all too well because she had been the cute, nerdy cheerleader crushing on the handsome jock, both in high school and college. It had always ended the same way—with her getting her heart crushed. Call it her little revenge upon the jocks of this world. Sam would let him stew in his thoughts for a while and then tell him the truth later. Maybe.

"You make me sound so broken," Nick groaned.

Not wasting a moment, Sam gave him a bit of her philosophy on life. "Most people are broken in one way or another, Agent McLeroy. It's just some of us hide it better than others. And if you are lucky enough to find someone whose broken pieces fit with your own—well, that is truly lucky."

"Please, I insist that you call me Nick. McLeroy makes me sound like my father. Have you ever found someone with the right broken pieces yet, Agent Stevens?"

"Sam, or just Stevens. Never mind. Sam might just be easier. And no, I have not been that fortunate yet, Nick," she admitted.

"Hey, by the way, I'm sorry if I came off too harsh earlier. I mean, I don't usually lay out someone's life like that," Sam continued, glancing over at Nick. "That was harsh of me."

"Honestly, don't give it another thought. I did ask you to read me, and I got exactly what I asked for." Nick smiled and shook his head. "You really are as good as they said you were. Maybe even better than I'd imagined in my head."

"You flatter me, Nick," Sam chuckled, then looked out the window. "I'm just cranky from the long day of being shoved into a sardine can and flown out here. I never thought in a million years that I would be called on assignment to this god-forsaken place of all places," she said, as her mind drifted off to long-ago thoughts of her childhood in Alaska.

As her mind wandered, she gazed out the window at the landscape below her. From the lush tree-topped peaks that seemed to reach up to the very sky itself to the glistening lakes and pristine streams running through the valleys, the expansive scene below her took her back in time. *What could be more glorious or peaceful than this?* she absently wondered to herself. *Why would anyone ever want to leave all of this behind?* Just for a moment, her heart was light, and her mind was lost in the abundant beauty below her. But then darkness managed to creep its way into her quiet reflection, and she had to shake her head to dispel the uncomfortable thoughts. *Not here. Not now.* She would not let the darkness overwhelm her now.

The two sat in companionable silence for the rest of the flight. Sam began to feel a wave of fatigue come over her as the effects of the lengthy flights to Alaska mixed with the drone of the plane. She had just yawned when Nick came through the comms to tell her they'd arrived at their destination.

Misgivings and Fears

LANDING IN THE LYNN CANAL AT JUNEAU, Nick stepped out to tie off the floatplane to the dock as Murphy began to bark, anxious to relieve himself. Popping back in, Nick quickly untethered Murphy from the seat and watched as he ran toward a nearby grassy area.

Sam climbed out of the plane on her side and walked around the dock, only to see Nick had grabbed both of their bags and was walking toward the parking lot.

"Do we have a car?" she asked.

He raised his arm and pointed out a black Jeep in the adjacent parking lot. "Your chariot awaits. Murphy, come!" he commanded.

Murphy immediately jumped to attention and, falling in step, glued himself to Nick's right leg.

"He's very obedient," Sam observed. "I noticed you sometimes give commands in what sounds like German. Does he always listen to you?"

Looking down at his partner, Nick smiled. "When he feels like it. Dogs have a mind of their own and sometimes they like to show their independence. He was trained using both German and English commands. This is done so he will listen to his handler, but he will also obey another authoritative voice when the commands are given in German."

"I've never really been around dogs much. I used to be scared of them."

"I would never have guessed," Nick said, with just a slight tone of sarcasm. "You can touch him. He won't bite. We are going to be spending a lot of time together. You might as well take the plunge and make friends with him."

Looking down at Murphy hesitantly, Sam shook her head. "Maybe later, when Murphy and I get a little better acquainted. I wouldn't want to invade his space too soon."

Nick began to laugh. "Are you still afraid of dogs?"

"No," she said, dismissing his accusation a bit too quickly and sounding defensive.

"You *are* afraid of dogs. Why, Special Agent Stevens, I am shocked and surprised by that. Murphy, what do you think?" he asked, looking down at his partner.

Murphy barked as if he understood what was being discussed.

Looking at them both, Sam admitted, "I'm not going to lie; I'm feeling a little ganged up on right now. Where are we off to first?"

"Are you changing the subject?"

"It's called deflecting," she said. "And no, I'm not. Well, maybe I am."

Nick clicked the key fob to unlock the black Jeep and the three of them climbed in. "We are headed to the Juneau Police Department to speak with Police Chief Ted Mercer," Nick said, driving the Jeep out of the parking lot.

They arrived twenty minutes later because the entire town wasn't very big at all when you compared it to Washington, D.C. Climbing out of the Jeep, Sam removed her jacket. It was the end of June, and the weather was unusually warm, even though the afternoon hours waned towards evening. Slapping at a mosquito on her arm, she asked, "Did you happen to bring any bug spray?"

With a shake of his head, Nick placed Murphy back on his leash. "We'll have to wait to stop at a drugstore before heading to our hotel later tonight. The mosquitos here are as big as condors. I mean it. Yesterday, one landed on Murphy's head, and I thought he would fly away with my partner."

Sam chuckled at his exaggeration. "If you think these city mosquitos are big, wait until we go into the backcountry. They are even larger there."

"Really?" he asked.

Sam just laughed. "City boys are so gullible."

Knocking on the chief's door, Nick, Murphy, and Sam were waved into his office as he hung up the phone.

"Welcome, welcome," Chief Mercer said, gesturing toward a couple of chairs. "Please, take a seat. So, you're the two FBI folks I was told about."

"Yes, sir. I'm Special Agent Nicholas McLeroy, but you can call me Nick. This four-legged beast is Officer Murphy."

Presenting her hand to the chief, Sam leaned over and said, "And I'm Special Agent Sam Stevens. I'm a criminal profiler."

"It's a pleasure to meet the three of you," Chief Mercer said. "Let me show you where you will set up your command post."

The chief led them to the station's conference room and had one officer fetch coffee for everyone. Sam strategically placed the five flyers of the missing girls on the long table. "As you can see, I've laid them out chronologically from when they went missing—oldest to most recent."

"So how do we know they are all victims? Or that their disappearances are even connected? Any one of these girls could have taken off. Hell, at least one of them could be down in Florida, enjoying life in the sun," Chief Mercer pointed out.

"You do have a point there, Chief. But we feel that there is a pattern here," Nick said, turning to Sam as if to say, "Take it away."

Sam had been absently tapping her pen on the table while she studied the pictures sitting side by side. There was a similarity in the facial features of all five women. "I think we can see that this is not a random occurrence. Nor do I believe that these are all our possible victims," she said, catching both men by surprise. She looked around the room, searching for something. "I need some tape, please."

Chief Mercer walked around the large table and reached down, opening a drawer. After sorting through some push pins, dry-erase markers in three different colors, and random pens, he handed Sam a roll of clear tape.

"Thank you." She taped the first flyer on the glass wall that looked out onto the precinct floor. Several officers stopped what they were doing to look at her. Ignoring them, she continued, explaining to the chief as she went along. "There is no rhyme or reason to this timeline. There are too many holes." She pointed to the flyer she had just placed on the wall.

"Let's start with the latest disappearance, Amy Mathews, here on the far right. She was taken on June 3, 2024, after her shift at the Sandpiper Café here in Juneau." Leaving a wide space to the left of the first flyer, Sam hung two more right next to each other.

"Kristen Keller disappeared on June 6, 2019, after her shift at the restaurant where she worked in Fairbanks. Crystal Morgan disappeared eight weeks later on August 8, 2019, after her shift at the bed and breakfast where she was waitressing and occasionally working as a cook in Delta Junction."

She hung another missing person flyer directly to the right of the Morgan flyer, leaving a gap between it and the 2024 flyer taped up first. "Kate Dillon disappeared on August 16, 2020, sometime after her shift at the McKinley Chalet Resort in Fort Yukon, Alaska. She was just nineteen. She is the only one of the five victims with blue eyes. But, interestingly enough, she often wore brown contacts. We call that an outlier."

Placing the fifth and last flyer to the far left of all of the flyers, leaving space between it and the rest, she continued, "And that leaves us with Tess Ashton, who disappeared after her shift at the Fisheye Café on June 1, 2017, in Sitka, Alaska.

"If this is truly the work of a serial kidnapper and or murderer, there would be a pattern. We see gaps between the 2017 and 2019 missing persons. Then another wider gap between the 2020 and 2024 flyers. I believe there are more victims," Sam concluded, turning to gauge the reaction of the two men in the room to her theory.

"But how do you know all of these disappearances are even related?" Chief Mercer asked. "They are all from different parts of the state."

Sam pointed to their facial structure and hair. "Just look at them. They are all very similar in age, coloring, and occupation. This is a *pattern*," Sam insisted.

"What Special Agent Stevens is trying to say is that we simply have a working theory at this point, and we need more input to be *certain*." Nick cleared his throat, trying to defuse the tension that was building in the room. "But she's right," he added. "We need to send out feelers into the surrounding territories to see if we get any hits. Meanwhile, Special Agent Stevens and I will set up our home base here for now and see what pops."

Suddenly looking down at his watch, Nick smiled and reached out his hand to the chief. "It's good to be working with you, Chief Mercer, and we will be in touch. Right now, though, we have an appointment to speak with our last victim's employer at the Sandpiper Café. It should be nearing the end of their dinner rush hour by the time we arrive."

"Of course. Don't let me keep you," the chief said, shaking Nick's hand. "Meanwhile, I will send out an all-points bulletin for missing girls that fit our description."

"Make sure you go back ten to fifteen years," Sam said. "If our UNSUB has been doing this awhile, he's gotten good at covering his tracks."

"Of course," Chief Mercer said, walking the two agents out to the front door.

Walking into the Sandpiper Café, Sam was instantly taken back in time to when she worked in a little diner just like this one. The mixed aromas of fried chicken, mashed potatoes and gravy, and the unmistakable smell of strong coffee, paired with the sound of ambient chatter and silverware clinking, caused her to momentarily pause inside the doorway. Her left hand began to shake uncontrollably as she quickly shoved it into the coat pocket of her jacket.

It felt as if she had stepped into a time warp. She'd been working to earn money for the next year's college expenses and was a fresh-faced, nineteen-year-old preparing for her first year away at college. She had just learned that she'd been accepted into the college of her dreams and was so happy and excited that nothing had bothered her that day—not even the extra special orders or complaining customers.

"Sam, you coming?" Nick called to her.

Sam shook her head to clear the memory from her thoughts. She was here to solve the disappearances, not relive her past.

"Are you all right, Sam?"

"Yes. Of course. I'm fine," she insisted, sounding a little too defensive.

Nick made a quick mental note of her reaction to the diner, then took the lead, asking to speak with the owner, Carol Southerland.

Tall and thin, with angular lines, Carol was an amiable-looking person. She stood in front of the two agents, her apron stained because she had been filling in for the missing girl, Amy. It was high season with all the tourists in town and the diner looked super busy. Sweat beaded on Carol's forehead as she smiled at them.

"Mrs. Southerland, I'm Special Agent McLeroy and this is Special Agent Stevens. Is there someplace quiet where we might talk?" he asked, flashing his credentials.

Looking at Nick and Sam with a blank stare for a moment before wiping her hands on her apron, Carol flushed with embarrassment. "Yes, of course. Where are my manners?" she said, shaking Nick's hand as her eyes landed on Murphy. For a moment she looked as if she would object to his presence in her café but then quickly changed her mind.

Showing the two agents to her office, they walked through the kitchen to a small room at the back of the café. "I'm sorry to be so scattered. It's been very hectic ever since Amy went missing. She was one hard-working girl and I can't tell you how much I miss her right now," she said, grabbing an extra folding chair and setting it up in front of her desk. The office was cramped and there was paperwork strewn across the desk. "Why is the FBI looking into Amy? You are here about Amy Mathews? Is she all right?"

"We would like to ask you what you might recall about the day Amy went missing," Sam said, without answering Carol's question.

There wasn't much that could be said since there wasn't any news on what might have happened to Amy after she disappeared. She instinctively knew that the moment she said anything about the missing girl, or what might have happened to her, Carol would fall apart. She had a sixth sense about people, and this one definitely looked like a crier. Sam wanted to get whatever information she could from Carol before the tears started. Pulling out a small pad of paper and a pen that she always had on her, Sam was poised to take notes.

"It was a busy day," Carol began, "Amy was in good spirits, joking with the regulars like she always does."

"Was there anyone you didn't recognize?" Nick asked.

"This is Juneau, at the beginning of tourist season," Carol added matter-of-factly. "There are always strangers milling about."

"What Special Agent McLeroy meant to say, Carol, was whether anyone in particular might have stood out to you?" Sam said, giving Carol a reassuring smile.

"No one that I can think of," she said, pondering the question further. "But as I said before, it was busy that day. People were waiting for tables and milling around waiting for their pick-up orders."

"So, what you're telling us is, it was a typical workday for tourist season?" Sam clarified.

"Yes," Carol said, looking Sam squarely in the eyes. "I can't think of anything that happened that day that wasn't routine, except for the women's bathroom toilet overflowing. I assigned Janet the task of getting a handyman out here to fix it. It seems these things never happen when we're slow."

"Who is Janet and can we talk with her?" Nick asked.

"She moonlights as a waitress and takes care of our books at the end of the week. She's the one who keeps the tax collectors away from my front door," Carol groaned before stepping to the office door. "Jose, can you tell Janet I need her in my office?"

With a nod of his head, Jose hit the bell twice, signaling Janet to the kitchen window.

Sam momentarily jumped, startled out of her daydream as she looked around to see if anyone noticed. Taking a deep breath to soothe her jangled nerves, she began writing down a few notes.

The three of them waited a couple of minutes in awkward silence before Janet appeared. Carol made the introductions.

"Janet, we won't take up too much of your time. We would like to ask you a few questions," Nick said. "The day your co-worker, Amy Mathews, disappeared, do you remember seeing anyone unusual hanging around the diner?"

With a shake of her head, she said, "No, not really. But we were really slammed that day."

"Can you tell us about the handyman you called out to fix the plumbing?" Sam asked.

"He was someone we had used before," Janet said, looking up toward the ceiling as she tried to recall his name. "His name is Jim. No, Joe... something."

"Was he someone fairly new to you?" Sam asked.

"Oh, no, he's been in and out of town for years now. He comes and goes as he pleases, but I still like to use him when

I know he's in town. I think he said he has a sick mother that he takes care of, so he's in town every four to six weeks. He travels around a lot. A real free spirit. That's it. His name is... *Joe Smith*. He does odd jobs for people around town all the time."

"Would you, by chance, have a number or address for this Joe Smith guy?" Nick asked. "Maybe even a business card."

Shaking her head, Janet smiled. "Old Joe doesn't have a business card or even a regular business or anything like that. He does odd jobs for us when he's in town. The guy is nice, but I think he lives hand-to-mouth."

"Why do you say that?" Sam quickly asked.

"Because he never seems to have much money in his pocket. But he always stops by when he's in town, asking if there are any repair jobs we need help with."

"So, you're saying you pay him under the table." Sam's voice was flat. "And there is no receipt or record."

Looking at her boss with a sheepish grin, Janet shrugged her shoulders. "I feel sorry for the guy. Besides, I figure one less person on welfare is a good thing."

"Would you know if he's still in town? We'd like to ask him a few questions about that day," Nick said, giving Sam a side-long look.

"He isn't in any trouble, is he?"

"No, miss. We just want to ask him a few questions. That's all," Sam said.

"I haven't seen him around for a few weeks."

"Would you say that you haven't seen him since the day Amy went missing?" Sam asked, somberly.

"No, I saw him once after Amy went missing," she said, looking up at the ceiling again as she thought about the question. "It would have been, maybe, two days after Amy disappeared. Yes, definitely two days later. I'm sure of it."

"And why are you so sure that it was two days later?" Nick asked.

"Because he came into the café and sat in Amy's section. Then when I came over to take his order, he asked me where Amy was."

Nick and Sam looked at one another, and then Sam asked, "Can you give us a description of this Joe Smith?"

"Of course. He's tall, about six feet...maybe six-one. Average build. Not fat or skinny, but average. Gray hair, blue eyes, and he has terrible acne scars on his face." A bell rang twice. "I've got an order up. Do you need me for anything else?"

"We may need you to sit down with a police sketch artist later. We'll let you know," Nick said.

"Sure. No problem. Sorry—I've got to get an order out before it gets cold and I have unhappy customers."

"We'll be in touch if we need anything further, miss. Thank you for your time," he said. Then, turning to the owner, he asked, "Do you have any cameras?"

"None that have been working for the last two years. I just haven't gotten around to fixing them."

"Thank you for your time. We will be in touch if we can think of anything else," he said as he turned to leave, taking a few steps before he stopped to wait for Sam.

Sam felt oddly cold all over. *Was it this town or being back home in Alaska that caused every nerve in her body to vibrate?* she wondered.

"Are you all right, partner?" Nick asked. "You look a little pale."

"It's been a long day. The flights really took a toll on me, I'm afraid."

"As long as you're sure that's all it is."

Giving him her best-practiced glare, Sam shuffled past Nick, "I'm sure."

CHAPTER FIVE

A Bottle of Wine

AFTER STOPPING BY THE STORE TO GET SNACKS, water, dog food, and bug spray, Nick and Sam took their bags up to their dog-friendly, two bedroom, extended stay hotel suite and settled in for the night. Then, borrowing a rolling whiteboard from the hotel conference room, they went to work, setting up a workspace in the living room.

Sam had made copies of the flyers and the seven papers that made up the files for their case.

Murphy came out of the kitchen area, licking his chops, having just finished a large bowl of dog food. He sat down near Sam's feet and placed his head on his paws.

At first, Sam didn't know how to react. She was tempted to reach out and pat him on the head, just to see if she had the nerve to do it, but then thought better of the idea.

Stepping up to the whiteboard, Sam began by placing copies of the missing girls' flyers in the same order she had at the police station, held in place with tape. She would add information and notes below each picture as it became available to them.

Under Amy Mathews' picture, Sam wrote, "Handyman Joe Smith?" with a big red question mark and his general description. "I think that we need a more definitive picture of this Joe Smith character, Nick."

"I agree. That's why I just sent a message to Chief Mercer asking him to get a sketch artist together with Janet from the café." Nick got up and stepped over to the board to stand next to Sam, staring at the girls' pictures as if answers would come to her if she just looked hard enough. "As a profiler, do you have any insight into the mind of our UNSUB yet?" he asked.

"It's not that easy, Nick." She sounded tired and exasperated. With a heavy sigh, she paced the floor. "We don't know anything about him yet. Hell, we don't know for sure that any one man has even taken all of these girls."

"But you told the chief that you were certain that the cases were linked." Nick ran his hand through his hair in a gesture of frustration, taking a seat on the couch.

Plopping down on the couch next to Nick, Sam explained, "I know what I told him. My gut tells me they are linked and there's a pattern here. But, as you well know, gut feelings don't close cases or win arguments in a courtroom, Nick. Facts do."

"So, why tell Chief Mercer all of that—"

"I told him what he needed to hear to enlist his cooperation." Sam's frustration was quite evident in her tone. Tipping her head back and closing her eyes, she continued. "We needed to start someplace and Juneau is as good a place as any." That's when she stood up and walked over to the minifridge to see what there was to drink.

"Do you want one?" Sam asked, offering Nick the small bottle of whiskey she'd pulled from the refrigerator door.

Shaking his head, Nick said, "Put it back. You know those things cost a fortune, and they won't even get the job done. Why don't you let me buy you a real drink downstairs at the bar?"

After two rounds of drinks and a proper meal, Sam gazed out the window and took a deep breath. "I'd forgotten how light night was here during the summer," she reminisced.

Interrupting her reverie, Nick said, "Sam, I need some clarification, but I also need to know that you won't bite my head off when I ask."

Looking up at Nick with a smile, Sam took a deep breath and sighed. "I do get rather hangry when I'm tired and hungry," she admitted. "I don't want to fight with you either, Nick. Ask me anything."

"If you were to make an educated guess about who or what we are dealing with, would you say that we are dealing with a serial rapist?"

Putting her hands together under her chin, Sam pondered the question a moment before answering. "First of all"—she held up a finger—"we don't have all the facts. Second, we don't know what happened to the girls after they were taken, or even if they were taken. And third, we don't have a motive for the abductions yet. Do you see where I'm going with this?" Sam smiled indulgently. "Until we can fill in all the blanks, I can't come up with an accurate profile of our UNSUB. Does that make sense to you?"

Nodding his head, Nick reached over, patting Murphy on the head. "Got it. Facts first. Then profile to follow."

"Now you're catching on. I think this is the beginning of a beautiful partnership."

"Now that is funny. And they told me you didn't have a sense of humor."

"Who told you I didn't have a sense of humor? I want names."

Standing up, Nick picked up Murphy's leash. "I'm going to take Murphy out for an evening walk so he can do his business before we turn in. Want to come along?"

"I think I'll pass," Sam said, looking down at Murphy, who seemed to be looking up at her expectantly. "I just realized how exhausted I am and that I've been awake for over twenty-one hours, counting the time zone change from this morning in D.C. I'm also feeling very grimy from the long day of travel and really could use a shower. I just hope I don't fall asleep while the water is still running over me."

"We won't be long."

"You two take your time. I intend to take a *very long, hot* shower."

Nick attached Murphy's leash, "You enjoy that long, hot shower, Sam, and we will see you in the morning."

Sam made her way upstairs and showered before turning in. She was feeling quite jet-lagged and fell asleep immediately when her head hit the pillow. She never heard Nick or Murphy return from their walk.

Hours later, Sam woke with a start, a scream caught in her throat. Placing a shaking hand over her rapidly beating heart, she rolled over to see the time on the bedside table clock. It was 3:52 a.m. Kicking the covers off, she flipped on the light and padded across the floor to her adjoining bathroom to splash water on her face. Looking in the mirror, the memory of her nightmare still lingered at the back of her mind. Splashing more water over her eyes before drying her face with the hand towel, Sam returned to bed. But she was unable to shake the terrible thoughts that kept going through her mind as an involuntary shiver shook her entire body.

Crawling beneath the covers, Sam turned her television on and the volume way down. Flipping through the channels, she stopped when she found an old rerun of *The Brady Bunch*. It reminded her of a simpler time when people were kind and decent to one another. Plus, the light in the room helped ease her old fears that had suddenly resurfaced.

Early the next morning, Sam grabbed a power bar from her bag and ate it as she prepared for a morning run. Tying her shoes, Sam stretched, then tucked some money and her room card into the pocket of her jacket and zipped it up.

Coming out of the door of the hotel, Sam ran into Nick and Murphy on the front lawn. Nick was stretching his legs on a nearby bench as he, too, prepared for an early morning run.

Murphy gave two sharp barks when he saw Sam. "Fancy meeting you here," Nick called out. "Going for a run?"

Inwardly Sam groaned before turning toward Nick with a smile on her lips. "It helps clear the cobwebs out of my head," she answered.

"Mind if Murphy and I join you? I like running with someone else," he explained. "Murphy likes to set the pace but if I have someone else around, he usually lets them decide."

Looking down at Murphy she said, "Do you think you can keep up?"

He barked two more times and stood next to her. "Hmm. I think he likes you," Nick said, amused by Murphy's sudden attachment to the pretty agent.

"Are you saying he's not usually so friendly?"

Looking down at Murphy, Nick admitted, "Actually, he's not," while narrowing his eyes at the dog standing between them. "Ready to go?"

"I am if you are," Sam said before taking off at a moderate pace with Murphy and Nick following.

The three of them ran for forty minutes before Sam slowed down and came to a stop, checking her pulse on her neck. They were both sweating and a little winded as they stopped in front of a local coffee house.

"I'll buy you a coffee and Murphy a water," she offered, not knowing if he'd thought to bring money with him.

With a dramatic hand flourish, he answered, "You are a true champion of the lowly and downtrodden."

"College drama class?"

"How did you know?" he asked with a smile.

Giving him a wink and a knowing look, Sam held the door open. She ordered a café mocha with no whipped cream. Nick ordered a double espresso with extra milk along with a bottle of water and a bowl for his partner.

When Murphy had his fill of water, they made their way back to the hotel to take showers and get cleaned up. Sam put on a pair of fresh jeans, a Rolling Stones T-shirt, and hiking boots. She figured that she would blend in and not draw attention to herself with her usual outfit. Nick put on the same jeans as the day before and a fresh T-shirt.

They grabbed breakfast on the way out, arriving at the police station by eight-thirty with little expectation of any new information. But as they walked into the conference room, they saw a stack of missing person flyers lying on the table—at least thirty of them.

Chief Mercer entered the room shortly after their arrival. "Well, it seems that you were right, Special Agent Stevens. All of these came in late last night and early this morning."

Sam picked up the pile and started going through the flyers. After studying the women for some time, she made two separate piles. When she was finished sorting, she attached another six victims to the rolling whiteboard Chief Mercer ordered for the room so they wouldn't need to continue taping flyers onto the glass walls.

"We are possibly going to need two more boards, Chief," Sam said, looking at the new victims she'd just posted. She began pulling the flyers from the night before off the glass wall and attaching them to the whiteboard with magnets. Sam arranged them in order of date and stared at the pattern she saw emerging. "I believe there are still more victims," she asserted.

"I won't ask you how you know that there are more victims, Special Agent Stevens. Hell, at this point, I'm starting to believe that you're some kind of fortune-teller. I will leave this matter in your capable hands. Murder, abductions, and kidnapping are bad for business. So, try to keep this thing under wraps. I will leave you both to it," he said, walking from the room.

After the chief left, Nick turned to Sam. "Enlighten me. What makes you feel that we still have more victims?"

She drew his attention to the dates. "There are still holes in the timeline. There seem to be *years* missing. You can believe me when I say there are still more victims out there. I would guess another five or six, maybe more, depending on how far back this goes."

Murphy jumped up from his relaxed position next to Nick's chair and began barking. An officer he didn't recognize walked into the room. Freezing in the doorway, the officer took a step back. Nick gave a command and Murphy relaxed again.

The officer looked uncertain as he left the requested additional rolling whiteboards near the door and pinned a flyer to one of the boards with a magnet. "Ma'am," he said, turning around and quickly leaving.

Sam studied the new flyer for a minute and gave Nick a look before placing it between two other victims. Then she began distributing all of the flyers across all three boards, leaving gaps where the dates had gaps. Stepping to the door,

Sam called out to a passing officer, "Can we get another whiteboard and a corkboard with a large state map attached to it?" Then, calling out to his back, she offered as an afterthought, "Please!"

"This is unbelievable," Nick said under his breath.

"This is the makings of a serial kidnapper and likely a killer, depending on what happened to the girls once he was through with them." Sam looked at the board again. "We need some of those colored pushpins from that drawer over there." She pointed behind her without taking her eyes off of the boards.

"You mean now?"

"Yes, right now. We need to come up with a pattern. And there is *always* a pattern, even if the UNSUB doesn't realize it. Perhaps we can anticipate his next move." She took in the entire sequence of events. "As far as I can tell, there appear to be two victims each summer, and we have maybe four or five weeks before he strikes again. So, we don't have a minute to waste."

"How do you know it's a man?" Nick asked, retrieving the pins from the drawer.

"This kind of crime against women is almost always perpetrated by men. It would be an anomaly if it were committed by a woman."

"Of course. You would know. You're the expert in all things deviant. What was I thinking?" he said, sounding apologetic.

"Indeed. What were you thinking?" Sam added blandly. "I need coffee. And not that sad excuse for coffee they serve here. I need the good stuff, with a shot of espresso. Better yet, if you can find an IV of coffee, you might just want to put it straight into my veins. This is going to be a long day."

"I'll see what I can find." Nick headed for the door. "One intravenous coffee with a shot of espresso coming up," *he* called over his shoulder just before walking out.

CHAPTER SIX

The Difference between a Psychopath and a Sociopath is a Very Fine Line

THIRTY-SIX HOURS went by as more flyers came over the line. Sam sorted through each of them, weeding out the missing persons that didn't fit the criteria. When they were all up on the boards, they had eighteen victims in all that perfectly fit the profile. The timeline went back ten years.

Sam absently scratched her head. Her mind took her back in time as she remembered that same year when her family moved away from Anchorage. Those were some dark days. So many things changed between her and her parents that year. Her mother became very quiet and withdrawn while her father became angry, finding comfort in the bottle, any bottle. Everything quickly fell apart after that.

56

Her left hand began to shake uncontrollably.

"What are you thinking about?" Nick asked, holding up a fresh cup of coffee prepared just the way Sam liked it. "You looked far away just now," he said, walking into the room.

Shoving her hand deep into her pants pocket, Sam tried to brush it off. "Nothing really," she lied, taking the offered cup with her right hand. She gave him a brilliant smile before taking a seat in front of her laptop. "I don't know about you, but I'm getting hungry."

"Well, I should hope so. It's nearly four-thirty and you skipped lunch," he said, pulling a granola bar from his pocket and placing it on the table in front of Sam. "I brought an extra one, just in case."

"Thanks," she replied, sipping her coffee while taking several deep breaths between swallows to try to calm her frazzled nerves and push her earlier thoughts out of her mind.

A few minutes went by before she suddenly stopped typing on her laptop. "I just can't figure out what happened to the girls once they were taken," she mused out loud. "What bothers me is these girls have disappeared without a trace. But where did they go? What happened to them when the abductor was through with them?"

As Sam turned to gaze into Nick's eyes, she suddenly realized they were a hypnotic blue-green color and quite lovely. Unnerved by this realization and the fact that he'd been studying her, Sam quickly turned in her chair to present her back to him. It had been a long time since any man had turned her head or gotten under her skin. The scent of his aftershave filled the room, but not in a bad way. It was simply...distracting. An errant finger tapped on the tabletop over and over again—a nervous habit she'd picked up in her youth.

"Where are we with locating Joe Smith, the handyman from the Sandpiper Café?" she asked, knowing that it would assuredly break the spell between them.

"Turns out, Joe Smith isn't his real name." Nick's tone alluded to the fact that he had never expected the man to turn up under that name. "We have an APB out for his vehicle. His real name is Joseph Hughes, and he has a record for spousal abuse and a few minor offenses."

"Surprise, surprise," Sam responded sarcastically, looking up at Nick.

"Are we any closer to coming up with a profile on our UNSUB?"

"It's a little more complicated to come up with a profile on an unknown UNSUB than it is sitting down and writing a dissertation on the differences between a sociopath and a psychopath," Sam said, looking down at her laptop again as she began to type.

"Aren't they essentially one and the same?" Nick asked, snapping his finger and pointing at the ground as he gave Murphy a silent command.

"Hollywood would like you to think so, but there are a few distinct differences," she answered without looking up from her work.

"So, educate me," Nick asked, sitting down next to her, sipping on his coffee, and looking at her over the rim of his mug. "I'm always willing to learn something new."

"For real?" she said.

"How else are we going to get ahead of this crazy unless the two of us share information and understand how crazy thinks? But I must warn you, I may need you to use small words. I really want to understand the subtle differences between the two personality disorders."

"Duly noted. Well, sociopathy is an informal term that refers to a pattern of antisocial behaviors and attitudes, including manipulative and deceitful behavior, often arising from environmental factors. Sociopaths may be difficult to identify until one is very familiar with their behavior." Sam paused, looking at Nick, and waited for him to nod for her to continue. "Sociopaths are manipulative; they lie frequently and lack empathy. They have a weak sense of conscience which allows them to act recklessly or aggressively, even when they know their behavior is wrong."

Nick put aside his coffee. She had his full attention.

"While the terms 'sociopath' and 'psychopath' are often used interchangeably and refer to similar behaviors," she said, "it is generally agreed upon, by those in my field, that there truly are subtle differences. Sociopaths are individuals whose callous, deceitful behavior is shaped by environmental factors, such as childhood abuse and exposure to disturbing behavior. Psychopathy is considered inborn and immutable;

hence, it is classified as an antisocial personality disorder. Because both conditions can lie on a spectrum, and the origins of their disorder are murky, it can be difficult to know whether someone displays sociopathic or psychopathic behavior because sociopathy is not an innate characteristic of an individual. Sociopaths are considered amenable to behavioral change and rehabilitation, while psychopaths are not." Sam paused. "So, have I made the differences between the two conditions a little more clear for you yet?"

"Yes, I think so," Nick said, looking very serious. "One can be rehabilitated, but the other one cannot."

"In layman's terms, sure," she frowned, "but it goes much deeper than that."

Chief Mercer poked his head into the room at that moment. "Where are we with this investigation? Have we profiled this psycho yet?"

Nick turned around, giving the police chief a grimace. "It's funny that you should ask that particular question, Chief Mercer. Special Agent Stevens and I were just discussing that very subject. Why don't you come in and join us?"

Stepping into the room, Chief Mercer took a seat across from the two agents. "Sure, why not? I have a few minutes."

"I was just explaining the difference between psychopathic and sociopathic behavior. I'm not saying that we have pinned this guy down yet, since we still don't know what drives him to do what he does," Sam explained, taking a sip of her coffee. She saw a shadow of unease pass over the chief's face.

"Aren't they the same thing?" Chief Mercer said.

"*Thank you*," Nick said, looking from Chief Mercer to Sam. "I just said the same thing. I'm glad I'm not the only one who thinks like that."

"Well, after all, crazy is crazy, right?" the chief said.

"The persistence of the terms sociopath and psychopath reflects the need for a better understanding of subtypes when it comes to psychopathic personalities," Sam said. "Some would like you to think that the label sociopath is a less severe form of a psychopath. But they would be wrong. Both sociopaths and psychopaths have a pervasive pattern of disregard for the safety and rights of others. Deceit and manipulation are central features in both personality disorders and, contrary to popular belief, both psychopaths and sociopaths are not necessarily violent people. Yet, in extreme cases, either condition can trigger violent tendencies."

As a way to help the two men better understand the difference between the two terms, Sam took a marker and wrote SOCIOPATH and PSYCHOPATH on the board. Beneath them, she began by listing their similarities. "The commonality of a psychopath and sociopath lies in their shared diagnosis or antisocial personality disorder. They are both defined by having three or more of the following traits: Many regularly break the law, constantly lie, and deceive others. They often are impulsive and don't plan ahead. They can both be prone to fighting or other aggressive behavior. They frequently have little regard for the safety of others and are irresponsible and unable to meet their financial obligations. Another frequent commonality is that they don't feel remorse or guilt for their actions. In both cases, some signs or symptoms are nearly always present before the age of fifteen. Either of them is well on the way to becoming either a psychopath or sociopath by the time he or she is an adult."

Sam waited to see if the two men understood what she was saying.

Nick and Mercer looked at one another with a puzzled, confused look on their faces. "So, are they the same thing or not?" Chief Mercer inquired.

Taking a deep breath and pinching the bridge of her nose, Sam sighed heavily before responding while writing the differences on the board at the same time. "Psychology researchers generally believe that psychopaths tend to be born that way—it's likely a genetic predisposition in the brain. It's as if they are hardwired to kill, yet not all will act upon those impulses. On the other hand, sociopaths tend to be made by the environment in which they are raised—neglect, abuse, witness to abuses or atrocities, and so on."

With a half-hearted chuckle, Chief Mercer grinned and said, "Well, why didn't you just say that in the first place? Even an old relic like me can understand the differences when you put it in layman's terms!"

Getting up from his chair, the chief left the room. Sam groaned inwardly and put her head in her hands, mumbling derisively under her breath, "Neanderthals, the lot of you."

"Well, I, for one, enjoyed your explanation, and I will never again get the two terms confused," Nick said, getting up from his chair. "Thank you, Sam, for taking the time to explain the differences to me. Is there anything I can get you?"

"Perhaps a little peace and quiet so that I might finish my work."

Knowing when his presence was not required, Nick nodded. "Sure thing. Murphy and I will run over to the Sandpiper Café and interview the rest of the staff who were present when Amy went missing but weren't there the other day we stopped in. Who knows, maybe someone will have remembered something."

Nodding her head, Sam looked down at her laptop and began to type the day's report. "I'll be finished here in an hour. And McLeroy?"

"Yes?" he answered, stopping in the doorway to look at her.

"Tomorrow, *you are* doing the paperwork."

Saluting her before walking out the door, Nick knew enough about his new partner to not argue.

CHAPTER SEVEN

A Slice of Pie

IN HIS WELL-WORN JEANS AND "I ♡ ALASKA" T-SHIRT, he blended in with every other tourist visiting the quaint little town of Skagway. Keeping his head down and his hat and sunglasses on, he ordered coffee, eggs, bacon, hash browns, and a slice of cherry pie while he stalked his next victim during the early morning rush at the Sweet Tooth Café.

He'd been watching her for four weeks now and felt that he had a good understanding of who she was and what her usual routine consisted of.

Lucy Jones was twenty years old and home from college for the summer. She was going to be a veterinarian.

Lucy delivered his breakfast to him and smiled brightly, pouring more coffee into his cup. "Is there anything else I can get for you, sir?" she asked politely.

Momentarily glancing up at her before reaching for the cream and sugar, he shook his head and watched her glide away to check on the next table.

The cook hit the bell three times, signaling to Lucy that she had an order. Quickly finishing the order she was writing down, she walked over to pick up the plates and delivered them to a table a few booths away.

She was sheer poetry in motion, he thought, as he watched her gracefully move about the little café like a hummingbird in flight.

Her type was his favorite, so bright and friendly to everyone. She was innocent and sweet and she didn't have a violent bone in her body.

He had a special treat planned for Miss Lucy. The thought made him grin before shoveling the last bite of pie into his mouth and washing it down with coffee. "So special," he murmured to himself.

Special agents Sam Stevens, Nick McLeroy, and Murphy had fallen into a comfortable morning routine. Normally, they would take a thirty-five to forty-minute run, stopping at the same coffee shop to fuel up before returning to the hotel and cleaning up. Then it was off to the police station.

But today they decided to visit the hotel gym and get a little training in. Sparring was an excellent way to keep their reflexes sharp, and they didn't want their hand-to-hand combat skills to get rusty.

Murphy found a comfortable corner to lie down, resting his head upon his paws as he observed Nick and Sam. Except for his tail wagging back and forth every so often, his eyes were all that moved as he tracked their movements.

"I have to warn you," Nick said, "I was all-state in wrestling, two years in a row."

"Well, then it's a good thing that we won't be wrestling or I might be in a bit of a jam," Sam smirked. "Same rules apply as at the academy."

Giving her a sidelong look, Nick said, "What, no MMA or Cage Fighting?"

"I'm game if you are," she challenged with a confident smile. "No holds barred then?"

Nick felt a moment of trepidation as his mouth made promises that he couldn't afford. "All right then. No holds barred," he agreed, wanting to see what his new partner was made of. "But we need a safe word. Mine is 'uncle.'"

"We are sparring, McLeroy, not practicing S&M. Safe words are for lightweights." She threw out the taunt with a well-practiced wink.

"All the same," Nick said tilting his head to one side, "I don't want to be accused of throwing my weight around and injuring you."

"What makes you think I will be the one getting hurt?"

"Okay then, Stevens, show me what you've got."

Sam began to bounce around on her toes, getting into a defensive position and putting her hands up. "Come at me," she said, motioning with her hands for him to make the first move.

Nick tentatively lunged forward with his hands up, ready to block the anticipated punch. But he was completely unprepared for the speed at which Sam attacked, kicking him in the right and left side of his ribs nearly simultaneously. Then, spinning around, Sam performed an axe kick at Nick's head, missing on purpose as he jumped back quickly and nearly tripped over his own feet.

"You missed me," he taunted with a broad smile and a deep sigh of relief.

"That was just a warning shot, McLeroy. I didn't want to knock those pretty little brains of yours around on the first strike."

"Trash talking," he fired back, kicking his leg up to catch her on her right side, which she easily blocked. Sam then struck him on the opposite side with another kick that came so fast he didn't know he'd been kicked until he was set back a couple of steps.

"Its only trash talk if you have nothing to back it up with," she countered while quickly sweeping his legs from under him before he could say another word.

Lying on his back, he looked up to see his opponent offering him a hand.

"That was a sweet move. Where did you learn to do that?" he asked, taking the offered hand and jumping up quickly.

"Years and years of Taekwondo classes in my youth," Sam replied with a smile, bouncing from foot to foot.

He nodded. "That takes a lot of dedication. I can respect that," he said before ending up on his back on the sparring mat several more times. "So, how did you earn the nickname, The Robot?" he asked innocently.

The smile instantly faded from Sam's face—her easygoing attitude was suddenly gone.

"Sorry. Did I say something wrong?"

"I don't like that nickname," she stood up, trying not to lose her cool. "It's meant to be derogatory."

"Honestly, I think it's pretty badass."

"Well, if you know what's good for you, you will never bring it up again," Sam warned.

Taking a deep breath, Nick nodded his head. "Consider the matter dropped. I will never mention it ever again. Cross my heart," he said while drawing an imaginary cross over his heart.

They took turns being the perpetrator and attacking each other. They were well-matched when it came to hand-to-hand combat because Sam hadn't used her secret weapon yet: Jiu-Jitsu.

Sam was playing the victim while Nick was the attacker. He grabbed her around the neck and simply picked her up and tossed her to the mat, pinning her there. For a moment they were both breathing hard from the exertion when their eyes locked. There was no denying the spark that passed between them as Nick pressed his advantage a moment longer than necessary.

Murphy began to bark loudly, coming over to sniff Sam near her head. She stiffened slightly and froze when Murphy stuck his nose in her face.

"He won't hurt you. He's protecting you," Nick assured her, still holding her in place.

"I've already told you that I'm afraid of dogs and still you allow him to get that close to me when I can't defend myself," she whispered in a low growl, keeping an eye on the dog.

Nick felt her shudder and suddenly felt a pang of guilt for causing her discomfort.

Giving the command, "Murphy down," Nick continued to look directly into Sam's eyes when they darted back to his. "Murphy, kisses."

Upon command, Murphy began to lick Sam's face a couple of times before he stopped and pulled back. Sam closed her eyes tightly out of fear and held perfectly still.

Slowly, Nick let Sam go, but he still hovered over her a few inches. "He's a loveable dog, Sam. He won't hurt you."

With her eyes still tightly closed, Sam whispered, "I can feel him breathing on me. Make it stop, please."

"Do you trust me?" he asked.

"What?"

"Do you trust me?" Nick repeated. "It's a simple question."

"Are you serious?" she whispered, barely moving her lips as she squeezed her eyes shut.

"Answer the question, Agent Stevens," he said, bringing Sam back to the fact that she was a decorated field agent for the FBI and not a scared little child.

Slowly opening her eyes, Sam let out the breath that she'd been holding.

"Yes. I trust you, Agent McLeroy."

"Then give me your hand," he insisted, taking a hold of her hand without waiting for her to give it to him.

Nick held her hand and gave the command, "Murphy, kisses." This time, Murphy licked the back of Sam's hand and she fought the urge to yank it away. The feel of Murphy's tongue against her skin was not unpleasant, and she slowly relaxed.

Sam came up onto her elbows.

"You need to face your fellow agent."

Sam sat up, crossing her legs while facing the dog, and straightened her back just a little more than she would have had she been completely relaxed.

Taking Sam's hand again, Nick told her to make a fist and then placed it in front of the dog's face to allow him to smell her. "This is how you get to know a new dog. Then, when they accept you, then and only then do you reach up and pet them on the head," he said, bringing her hand to Murphy's head.

Murphy crawled on his belly, getting closer to Sam. It startled her a little and she pulled back slightly, then froze.

"What's he doing?" she whispered, afraid to speak too loudly for fear of startling him.

Getting closer to her, Nick held her in place. "He just wants to get to know you better. Stay calm. I swear that he won't hurt you. Murphy here has entertained classrooms full of children, and he's never bitten anyone who wasn't a criminal."

Looking over at Nick, Sam was trying to determine if he was joking or not. "Do you swear?"

"I swear it," he said, placing his free hand over his heart. "So why don't you tell me when you developed this unhealthy aversion to dogs?"

Swallowing the lump in her throat and letting out a big sigh, Sam looked down at Murphy. His tongue was hanging out of the side of his mouth as if he were smiling up at her. Hesitantly, she began to speak.

"When I was five, our next-door neighbor had a huge Doberman Pinscher named Hercules. That dog was always getting out of his yard and terrorizing the neighborhood. One day I was cutting through the field to my house with my best friend Mary when Hercules came running out at us from nowhere. I froze, but Mary managed to get away. She ran for help while I was stuck there, unable to move with that vicious dog's rancid breath in my face. I swear, I can still smell his foul breath when I close my eyes, and still to this day, I remember that moment in time like it was yesterday," she said with a shiver.

Taking Sam's hand in his, Nick gave her a sad but reassuring smile. "That must have been terrifying for you."

"I had nightmares for months. My father filed a police report. The neighbor simply paid the fine and was told if it happened again there would be criminal charges filed."

"So, what happened?"

"Hercules got out two weeks later and attacked another dog, killing it and injuring the owner in the process. The police came and took the dog away and arrested my neighbor, but it didn't matter to me because the damage was already done. I still woke up screaming at night. So, as irrational as it sounds, I am still terrified by large dogs."

"I hope that we can change that for you," Nick said, getting to his feet and pulling Sam up next to him. "Murphy, heel," he commanded. Murphy obediently stood up and stepped to Nick's right side.

Nick attached the leash to Murphy's harness and handed it over to Sam. "You walk him up to the room," he said, "and get that look off of your face. He won't hurt you."

Sam looked down at Murphy with trepidation before gently pulling on the leash. He stepped to her side and waited for her to take a step forward before he moved. Murphy was in perfect sync with Sam as they walked out of the room and into the elevator.

She still felt a slight tremor race up her spine when they stepped into the elevator after the doors opened. Sam told herself, "This is nothing more than irrational fear," as she pushed the button for the third floor.

Looking down at Murphy, she murmured, "Well, boy, it looks as if we are going to have to learn to get along if we are going to work together. I got your back if you have mine." Then Sam brought her eyes up as the doors opened. "Look at me, talking to a dog. I must be on the brink of a nervous breakdown," she said, stepping off the elevator. "A full-blown padded cell and straight jacket," she muttered under her breath as the two of them walked down the hallway and stood in front of the hotel room door while Sam dug the keycard out of her pocket.

CHAPTER EIGHT

Naming the UNSUB

T HEY WERE JUST ABOUT READY to head to Skagway, a forty minute flight away, to interview the owner of the Chilkoot Café, where twenty-one-year-old Mallory Hopkins worked before she disappeared on June 5, 2018.

As Sam and Nick understood it, Mallory had worked part-time at the Chilkoot Café as well as part-time at the West Mark Hotel. The two establishments were part of the same building. Mallory grew up in the small town of Skagway and was home for the summer to earn enough money to follow her dream of going to Hollywood. Mallory was a pretty girl, modeling where she could, and taking acting classes at the local college.

Nick and Sam intended to visit the individual places each girl worked before going missing in order to get a better picture of why these particular girls were targeted.

But before heading to Skagway, they needed to drop by the police station's conference room for a few minutes. That's when Chief Mercer stepped out of his office door. Deep lines etched Mercer's face and he looked as if he couldn't wait to speak with them.

"A Ranger found a deceased gray wolf not too far from here," he said the moment Sam and Nick entered his office. "And you are never going to guess what they found when they opened her up."

"Well, don't keep us in suspense, sir. We have a busy day ahead of us." Sam leaned up impatiently against the nearest chair.

"Sorry, sir, Sam is cranky because she hates flying in small aircraft," Nick said, giving Sam a sidelong look.

"Well, I may or may not have a bit of helpful news for you." Mercer gave them both a somber look.

"If anyone could use some helpful news, it would be me, Chief. We really need a break. Spill it."

"When they did an autopsy to figure out what had killed the animal, they found the remains of a human hand inside the intestines. Well, most of the hand. A few digits were missing."

"Do we know if it is our missing person, Amy Mathews?" Sam asked, then continued to muse out loud. "I'm sure the hand has been partially digested by now. I doubt if they can get any usable fingerprint." Then, looking up at the Chief, she asked, "Were they able to get any usable DNA?"

"We turned it over to the forensic team. They are analyzing it now. I put a rush on the lab results," the chief said.

"Can we visit the spot where the rangers found the wolf?" Sam asked. "Maybe Murphy can determine the actual crime scene."

"I was hoping you'd say that," Chief Mercer said. "I have a car waiting to take the three of you there now."

"Aren't you coming with us?" Sam asked.

"Unfortunately, I have reports to finish."

Nodding her head, Sam turned back around and hurried to catch up with Nick. "It looks like our plans for the day have changed," she said as she reached Nick, matching his strides.

"Yep. Are you ready to name this case or the UNSUB, yet?" Nick asked Sam.

"I don't want to jinx our case, but I think we may have just caught a break."

They drove for forty-five minutes, with the SUV's tires now rolling over dirt, having left the main road fifteen minutes earlier. They were met by two rangers sitting in their truck. Stepping from the vehicle's cab, the rangers looked uncomfortable, even a bit pale. Introductions were made as the five of them walked to the spot where the dead wolf had been found. Cones and yellow caution tape cordoned off the area.

"We came back out here to tape everything off and close the road as soon as we found out about the hand," the younger ranger spoke up.

"We saw another ranger truck about a mile back. Good job, gentlemen," Nick said, giving the pair a reassuring smile. "We are hoping to pick up a trail and find the original crime scene."

Murphy put his nose into the air and began sniffing. "You smell it, don't you boy?" Nick patted him on the head.

Coming to a stop just off the dirt trail, the first ranger pointed to the area. "We found the wolf over there."

Nick gave Murphy plenty of leash and the command, "Seek, boy." It didn't take long before Murphy caught a scent and was off, dragging Nick quickly behind him. Everyone ran to keep up with them, following the two as they made their way through the woods and down a well-worn path made by elk and wolves. When they came to a clearing, Nick carefully maneuvered around to preserve any and all evidence from being destroyed.

"Be very careful here," he called over his shoulder. "Look for footprints, human and animal. Maybe tire tread or anything that looks like a vehicle tire."

A few minutes later Murphy stopped, sniffed the ground, and sat down to indicate they were at the spot.

"This is it," Nick called out.

Sam came over to stand next to Murphy, scanning the surrounding area. Beyond the clearing was a border of trees.

It only took her a moment to spot it—the camouflaged hunting blind. Slowly, she walked toward it, never taking her eyes off of that one spot.

"Nick, send somebody back to the car for gloves, an evidence kit, a black light, and whatever else they may have in their cruiser. And while I'm thinking of it, get them to bring the rig closer," Sam called over her shoulder.

"What do you see, Special Agent Stevens?" he asked, taking on a professional air with the other officers standing beside him.

"Just do it!" She barked the command at him, lost in the moment and instinctively knowing what they had just stumbled upon. Her gut was speaking to her loud and clear. *This is where it all happened. A young woman lost her life in this very place. In this very spot.* Sam could feel it.

She heard Nick giving orders to the two officers, who were only too glad to leave the area to retrieve the needed items.

Stepping closer to the tree, Sam tuned everything and everyone out. She had to think like the killer. To do that, she closed down certain senses while opening up the others. She studied the area around the tree before slowly climbing up the rough boards nailed to the tree. When she reached the platform, she knew that he had stood here, in this spot. Stepping onto the platform and then to the front of the hunting blind, she gazed out over the area before her. She could see Murphy sitting atop a mound of dirt. Carefully, she looked around, making sure not to disturb or touch anything at her feet. She could imagine the entire gruesome scene playing out in front of her eyes, as if he, the killer, stood at her side. An involuntary shiver crawled up her spine.

Sam took several deep breaths to steady herself and come back to reality. She focused her attention on the here and now as she pulled a hair tie from her wrist and twisted her hair up on top of her head. This would prevent cross-contamination until Nick could return with the kit.

A few minutes later, Nick climbed up the ladder behind her with a forensic kit hanging off his shoulder. "What do you see, Sam?" He stopped short when Sam put her hand up to halt him from stepping onto the platform. Her face looked ashen and pale. "Are you all right?" he asked respectfully. "Do you want to trade places?"

Silently, she shook her head, taking the kit from him mechanically before opening the case and taking out the black light to shine it on the platform.

Nick whistled between his teeth as the small space lit up like a Christmas tree. "Oh my God," he exclaimed as Sam took out several swabs to gather DNA evidence. She placed them into evidence bags, sealing them up tight and placing them into her official FBI windbreaker.

Using a flashlight, she took a closer look around for any more evidence, but there wasn't anything else except the semen left behind by the killer. He had taken great pleasure in this killing. With wobbly legs, Sam climbed back down from the platform, swallowing several times to keep the bile from coming up and contaminating the crime scene. Blinking away the tears forming in her eyes, she walked up to where the one officer and two rangers stood and pulled out her phone to record her thoughts.

"This is a preliminary profile on our male UNSUB, who is likely between the age of thirty to forty-five. He is strong. Strong enough to overpower the young women and carry them to a place like this." Sam spoke with complete authority. "I would say that he is awkward with women and has the need to dominate them. He also has a flagrant disregard for human life.

"Our UNSUB was most likely abused as a child—I'm guessing by his mother—who made him feel useless, inferior, and even demeaned, but it could be someone else close to him. He may or may not have been sexually abused by that same person. He strikes back at women to show his dominance over them, but they are merely proxies for his anger toward his mother for not protecting him.

"His sheer brutality and power over these women are also what gets him off sexually. Evidence indicates he is likely a sexual sadist. Asserting power and instilling fear into his victims is what gets him off. He is motivated by a desire to humiliate these women.

"He is also, most likely, a grandiose narcissist. He might be engaging, but most likely, he has a sense of entitlement, which drives him to destroy the happiness of others. He is convinced that his actions are justified."

She handed off the bagged samples to the officer. "See that these get to the lab ASAP. They belong to our UNSUB." With a sweep of her hand, she added, "And cordon off that hunting blind and this mound of dirt Murphy is sitting on. I would say that he most likely buried whatever was left of his victim after the animals did their job. I will be in the vehicle if anyone needs further assistance." Without a backward glance, she walked back down the path to the SUV.

Nick stayed behind to help secure the area and wait for the forensic team to arrive. Then he made his way back to the SUV to check on Sam.

"Hey, are you sure you're all right, Sam?" he asked as he opened the door, ushering Murphy in first. "You looked like you were going to hurl or pass out."

"I nearly did both, but I'm fine now," she answered, laying a hand across Murphy's neck. "The scene just caught me by surprise. You are a good boy, Murphy. You found her." Sam smiled down at the dog.

Nick placed a hand over hers and gave a gentle squeeze before releasing her. He had no words that would comfort her.

"I do not usually like giving our UNSUBS nicknames because it makes them feel entitled. But since our guy has an already inflated ego, I say, why the hell not. We are calling this UNSUB 'The Magician Killer,'" she announced.

"It has a nice ring. But what's with the name?"

"Because he makes his victims disappear—seemingly without a trace. He might even fancy himself a bit of a magician." She gave Nick a sad smile. "I feel that we have just glanced behind the curtain and discovered a few things about this magician's magic tricks. Nick, we have to stop this guy."

"I know—"

"No! I mean, we really have to stop him!"

"And we will."

"There's something so inherently wrong with this one."

Nick placed a hand on Sam's shoulder and waited for her to look at him. "We'll get him, Sam. I promise you. And for the record, there is something very wrong with them all."

Old Nightmares Come Home to Roost

ONCE BACK AT THE POLICE STATION in Juneau, Sam began working on the paperwork while Nick went into the chief's office to tell him what they had discovered. Chief Mercer entered the conference room a few minutes later, followed by Agent McLeroy. "So, what's our plan of attack, Special Agent Stevens?" he asked, sitting across from her.

Officially filing her report to headquarters by pushing the send button, Sam took a deep breath before she stood up. Without looking at the chief, she walked over to the white-boards. "After graphing the dates and locations of the missing women, I believe that our killer will strike again, sir, and soon."

"How soon?"

"We are still early in our investigation, sir, but if he follows the same pattern, and if all of these missing women are his victims," she continued, turning to look at him while pointing at the board, "I believe we have between four and six weeks. It would seem that he takes his time hunting his victims. He kills in June and then again in August. As you can see by the graph, his pattern holds true, going back at least ten years to August 2014."

"Yes, but he only killed once that year, in August, and not at all in June. How do you explain that?" Mercer pointed out.

"One time that we *know about*, sir." Sam swallowed convulsively as a scene of her fighting for her own life in an alley in June of 2014 suddenly flashed through her mind. She was paralyzed with fear and her eyes glazed over.

"Agent Stevens, are you all right?" Chief Mercer asked when he noticed her face go pale.

"Sam?" Nick said, jumping to his feet.

It took Sam a moment to recognize that someone was talking to her. "Yes, of course, I'm fine. I'm—I'm sorry. What was I saying?" she stammered, trying to quell the racing of her heart.

"You said that there was just the one victim that we know of in August 2014," Nick answered, looking at his partner carefully before taking his seat again.

"Oh, of course. Sorry, I don't know what happened there." Sam shrugged, trying to laugh it off. But she knew exactly what had happened. "There could potentially be another victim that we missed. Perhaps this was the beginning of his career, and a traumatic event triggered his killing spree.

"There are too many variables and not enough information yet. Or, perhaps, he was perfecting his technique." She pointed at the first victim before quickly placing her shaking left hand into her pocket. "Molly Cooper appears to have been his first victim on August 19, 2014, but perhaps there were earlier ones we aren't yet aware of."

Nick slowly got to his feet and turned to the chief, "Chief, do you think we could have a few minutes to discuss all of this? I promise to keep you in the loop. I just think my partner, Agent Stevens, needs a coffee and a bite to eat to refuel. It has been a long morning, and we both skipped lunch," he said, sounding perfectly reasonable while walking Chief Mercer to the door.

"Of course. I'll have one of the officers run out and get sandwiches right away. I have work to finish in my office, anyway, so I'll leave you to it."

"That would be truly kind of you, sir. We aren't picky. Whatever you order will be fine with us." Nick smiled before shutting the conference room door.

Then, without missing a beat, he turned to Sam and said, "Why didn't I see this before?"

"See what?" Sam asked, trying to keep her voice from cracking and hoping she looked convincingly bewildered as she turned around to look at the board again. "Did I miss something?"

"You sure the hell did!" Nick's voice jumped up an octave. "What year did you say you left Alaska? Because you resemble these victims, almost to a tee."

"I don't believe I mentioned the year to you, and now you are just being ridiculous. The victims are all between the ages of nineteen and twenty-two. I do not fit the criteria."

"The hell you say," he choked out. "They could all be your sisters. Every last one of them."

His words cut through Sam like a sharp knife. It was as if a large, unhealed wound had suddenly opened up inside of her. *It's not possible. It's really not possible,* she thought. As if flipping a switch, she compartmentalized her emotions.

"Again, that is ridiculous. It is not possible..." Sam took a closer look at each victim's face on the board. "The resemblance is merely coincidental and completely beside the point. Half the women in the United States have brown eyes and hair." She clenched her trembling hand into a tight fist and stuffed it deeper into her coat pocket before continuing. "We need to focus on the facts here, Nick. My incident may have been similar, but it wasn't this one. It couldn't be the same. The odds of that would be astronomical."

Sam's mind began to spin a hundred miles an hour. Long forgotten memories of that terrifying evening bubbled to the surface, cracking wide open and flooding her mind all at once.

Sitting down heavily in the nearest chair, she clenched and unclenched her left hand, trying to make the shaking stop. But it didn't. Her hand continued to shake uncontrollably. She swallowed hard to dislodge the lump that was now obstructing her throat, like a scream that wouldn't come out.

Of course, she knew that it was all true. Sam had put two and two together, maybe even before her plane landed in Alaska. She'd merely been pushing the uncomfortable thoughts as far down in her subconscious as possible, hence the return of her nightmares.

Seeing her distress, Nick poured her a glass of water. "Here, drink this," he insisted, placing the glass into her hands.

Robotically, she did as she was told and drank it all down. Then, looking up into his compassionate eyes, Sam took another steadying breath. "Thanks," she murmured as the memories flowed out from their hidden depths.

She had just turned nineteen that summer in Anchorage. It was the day after she'd received her college acceptance letter. Her thoughts were racing with emotions. She was thrilled and elated with the anticipation of what lay ahead.

"It was June 8, 2014," Sam said, her voice barely a whisper as she began to speak. "I was working in a small diner near my home in Anchorage over the summer while I prepared for my move to Charlottesville, Virginia, in the fall."

Nick took the glass from her hand and poured more water before handing it back to her. She looked down woodenly before bringing it to her lips, which had suddenly gone dry. Then she continued. "I'd just received a full academic scholarship to attend the University of Virginia, and I was working to save up enough money to enjoy my first year at the university without getting a part-time job." She blinked back tears and sniffed loudly as if she could make the pain go away by toughening up. "I wanted to focus on my studies because I had never really traveled beyond Alaska before and I was concerned that the stress of a new school and a collegiate life would be too much for me to handle while studying and trying to work. The last thing I wanted to do was fail out my first year of college and be forced to come home with my tail between my legs."

Sam knew that she was babbling, presenting facts that didn't really relate to the case, but she couldn't help herself. This story was just so hard for her to tell all at once.

She took another deep breath, lifted her chin, and closed her eyes, trying to gain the courage to continue. But when she closed her eyes, all she could do was see *his* face—the face of the monster that had attacked her that summer evening. "I worked long hours at the diner, but I didn't care because it was all going in the bank for school. I was excited and looking forward to a new life." She opened her tear-filled eyes and looked up at Nick in front of her. "Then, late in the day after working a twelve-hour shift, I was accosted by a man in the alley as I walked home. I'd seen him before. I had even waited on him a couple of times. He tried to talk to me.

But something about him gave me the creeps, so I ignored him and continued to walk home with my head down as if I hadn't heard him. It wasn't long before I realized that he was still following me, and I got scared. I mean *really* scared—to the point that I couldn't even think. The next thing I knew, he grabbed me from behind. That's when the instincts kicked in. I'd been training since I was young at the Taekwondo studio near my home and decided then that I wasn't going down without a fight. So, I punched and kicked him until he let go. But he wasn't deterred by my fighting back. He lunged at me again. He was...relentless.

Sam's entire body began to shake violently. Taking another deep breath, she put the glass on the table before spilling it. Nick poured her more water, but Sam just looked at it for a moment. "Thank you," she whispered.

"It's all right, Sam," Nick said quietly. "Just tell me what happened next."

Sam, who was normally so calm and cool during stressful situations, felt herself begin to crack as she recalled that fateful evening ten years ago. She turned away, focusing her eyes through the closed glass door on an officer who was sitting at his desk in the next room. She needed something ordinary and mundane to focus on. It helped tether her to the here and now.

As Sam began to talk again, she steadied herself by thinking, *this didn't happen to me; it all happened to someone else, and I am merely relating the facts.* "He seemed to become enraged at this point. I think it was because I fought back and hurt him. So, when he came at me a third time, I gave him everything I had. He almost seemed shocked that I was not giving up. That's when I landed a good kick to his side and heard something pop. I must have broken one or two of his ribs because he stood there staring at me for a moment with this ghastly, perplexed look on his stupid face. That's when I lunged at him and raked my fingernails down the entire left side of his face. He jumped back and screamed so loud that I thought, *now someone will come running to find out what is happening.* But nobody came."

"You must have been terrified," Nick said with such sympathy that Sam brought her eyes back around and they locked with his.

"I was petrified. But then my legs stopped shaking and I ran as fast as I could to the main street, ducked into the nearest store, and called my parents. They came and got me and took me to the police station."

"Did they scrape your nails for DNA?"

"Yes," she replied softly. "I was there for hours, answering questions. It felt as if they were interrogating me. As if I'd done something wrong. It was awful, humiliating, and degrading."

"What happened next?" Nick asked, taking the seat beside her and looking intently into her eyes.

Sam looked down at his hand now covering hers and more tears came to her eyes, spilling out and running down her cheeks. Wiping tears away with her other hand, she was grateful for the lifeline he presented with his simple act of kindness. "The police attempted to track the guy down but were unsuccessful. They never found him. I had terrible nightmares every night, waking in the middle of the night, screaming in terror, convinced that he was coming back for me. It got so bad that I had to be sedated so that I could get a few hours of sleep each night. Then, my mother and father packed up a few things. They left most of our possessions because it was just too expensive to move them. We traveled across the country so that I could attend college and my family could stay close to support me. It took me four years to sleep most of the night with the lights off."

Putting her hands up to her tear-stained face, Sam shook her head before wiping the tears away with a quick swipe. Then, as if she could simply dispel the memory of that terrible time in her life by sheer willpower, she stood up and walked over to the glass wall that looked out onto the police precinct floor. "I find it hard to believe that after all these years everything would come full circle, only to have me standing here possibly hunting the madman who once hunted me."

Then, shaking her head, Sam growled under her breath, hit the wall with her fist, and turned to face Nick. While she was turning, she noticed that several heads from the adjoining room had turned to see what had caused the wall to reverberate. Ignoring their glances, she continued, "It couldn't be the same man. It would be too much of a coincidence. The probability would be ridiculous. Absurd, even!"

"I think you should recuse yourself," Nick said, coming to stand next to her. "You are too close to this case."

"No!" she exclaimed gruffly, then softened a bit. "No."

"I'm right, and you know it, Sam." Nick placed a hand on her arm. "This case is too important. I can't allow you to continue, given your history with the suspect."

"Let me stop you right there," Sam quickly fired back. "We don't know for certain that I am connected to this particular case, and just because I experienced something similar to the victims doesn't mean that I can't be objective."

"It's obvious," Nick said. "At least, it is to me."

"Well now, who can't be objective?" Sam scoffed. "You think I can't be objective because I had a similar experience in my youth? Because I ran into a man that was very similar to the UNSUB? Do I appear to be some weak, helpless wallflower, unable to hold my own against a predator?" She glared at him and dared him to say yes.

Finally, Nick spoke, "Sam, you're not thinking clearly. It's just—"

"It's just *what*, Special Agent McLeroy? That I'm too vulnerable? Weak? Delicate? You tell me. What am I?" Sam shouted.

Putting his hands up as a sign of surrender, Nick answered, "I don't want to fight with you." He placed a hand on her shoulders, something he'd recently learned at Quantico during conflict resolution training. "You're none of those things, Special Agent Stevens. It's just that you are too close to this thing and I'm worried that you will get yourself killed."

Brushing Nick's hand aside, Sam lifted her chin and backed away from him. "This is my case and I will say when I've had enough. I'm not stepping away from this, and you don't have the right or authority to insist that I do!"

"All right, all right." Nick took a step back. "It's your case. What do you want to do next?"

"For starters, why don't you stop looking at me like I'm an alien who just stepped off my UFO?" Sam pulled her shoulders back and took a few steps over to the whiteboards. "We need a plan. We also need to take this guy alive—preferably before he kills again."

"Why do we need to take him alive?"

"Because he knows where all the bodies are buried and we have families that need closure. They need to learn what happened to their loved ones." Then, turning to face the whiteboards, she added, "I would like to apologize for my moment of weakness—"

Nick cut her off. "If anyone has the right to be upset, it would be you, Sam."

"I appreciate that, Agent McLeroy, and I can assure you that it won't happen again." Tipping her chin up slightly, she continued, "I'm not prone to fits of tears. Besides, I'm the best chance we have of catching this maniac."

"Why is that?"

"Because now we know what he wants."

"And what might that be, Agent Stevens?" Nick questioned, matching her professional tone.

"Me! He's been killing someone that looks like me," she said, pointing at each one of the photos on the board, "over and over and over again for ten years."

Nick jumped up from his chair and shook his head. "You're not suggesting that we use you as bait, are you? Because that would be insane."

"What could go wrong?" Sam said, looking up at him. "I will have the entire Juneau police force behind me. Besides, with partners like you and Murphy to back me up, honestly, what could go wrong?"

"We need to discuss this further," Nick said, then swore under his breath when Sam rolled her eyes at him. "A hundred things can go wrong. Do you realize that you are putting yourself in a hell of a spot?"

Turning away from the expanse of windows when she saw a young officer return with their lunch, Sam took a seat facing away from the door.

"Not when you have my back," she whispered. "You do have my back, right, Special Agent McLeroy?"

"Of course I have your back!" he retorted, insulted by the question. "What kind of a stupid question is that?"

"Good. Then we will make a plan and catch this UNSUB before he kills any more women. And, most importantly, you will keep my secret because you have my back."

"Sam?" he quietly said, realizing he wasn't going to win this argument. "When you are ready to unpack that emotional suitcase you've been lugging around for all these years, you'll let me know, right?"

"You will be the first to know," she answered as the young officer knocked and then opened the door to hand Nick their lunch.

That night, Sam slept with the lights on. Long forgotten terrors revisited her whenever she thought of turning out the lights. She had a good poker face, but she couldn't bluff herself. Sam was scared, maybe even petrified, if she was being honest with herself.

This man had taken everything from her, starting with her family and sense of security. Because of him, Sam knew that monsters really existed, and they thrived in the cover of darkness, even if they did make their presence known in the light of day.

Nick softly knocked on her door. The clock on the nightstand read 11:45 p.m., and Sam tried to make her voice sound normal. "Come in," she called.

"Can't sleep?" he asked, opening the door. Murphy came over and licked her outstretched hand.

"No. I'm fine. Just doing a little light reading," she lied.

"Really?" Nick looked around for a book. "What are you reading?"

"What?"

"You said you were reading. So, what are you reading?"

Quickly picking up her phone, Sam pulled up the first thing she could find. "'Can Repetitive Negative Thinking Speed Up Cognitive Decline?' by Christopher Bergland. It's a truly riveting article. I couldn't put it down."

With a half-smile that told Sam he wasn't buying it, Nick sat down in a chair near her bed. "Do you want to talk about it?"

"The article?"

He shook his head. "The reason you have all the lights on in your room and the bathroom."

"Oh, that's just an oversight. I forgot to turn them off—"

"Cut the crap, Sam." His tone was serious now. "I know that we stirred up a hornet's nest today. Did you really think I didn't notice your hand shaking today or observe how quiet you were tonight? I'm not a complete Neanderthal, by the way!"

Murphy sat on the carpet between Sam and Nick with his eyes turned toward her now. Sam put her hand out and he got up and came just close enough for her to scratch his ears. Swallowing her pride, Sam slowly brought her eyes up to meet Nick's intense look. "I am fine," she said. "How many times do I have to say it? I can even say it in three other languages."

"Then I will simply turn out the lights on my way to bed," he said, taking several steps toward the bathroom.

"No!"

Turning back to face her, Nick stood in the middle of the room and crossed his arms. "I don't care how many languages you can say it in, Sam. You are not fine."

Putting her head down, Sam knew that she had to come clean. "You're right, Nick, I'm not fine. We stirred up a hornet's nest today with all the memories."

"So, why not admit it? You can pull out of this case at any time. Who could—"

"No!" she yelled, louder than she meant to before softening her tone. "No, Nick, I can't. I need to end this. Here. Now. Or I will never be whole again."

Nick came to sit on the bed near her. "I can see that this is tearing you apart, Sam. Let me help you. I can take some of this burden from you."

"You can't, Nick. No one can. I told you that we are all broken in our own way. Well, this is my broken." Tears filled her eyes as she attempted to keep them from spilling over. "It is my burden to carry. And mine alone. My broken pieces to put back together."

"You aren't alone. I'm here." Nick placed a gentle hand over hers.

Murphy nuzzled his nose between them, making Sam smile through her sadness. "Are you saying you have my back, too, boy?" Murphy let out a low bark in response. "Who's a good boy?" Sam said. "Who's a good boy?"

CHAPTER TEN

Not Our Guy

ARRIVING BACK AT THE PRECINCT the next day, Sam and Nick were met with several news vans, cameras and lights, and a barricade. The local media had caught wind of a possible serial killer in the area and at least three news stations, along with two newspaper reporters, were now lined up behind the cordoned off area, anxious to get a statement from anyone who would stop to talk with them. Microphones were shoved towards Sam and Nick's faces as they attempted to cross the barricade, the reporters stretching their arms over the railing in an attempt to get an exclusive comment or sound bite for their respective news outlets.

"Can you tell us why the FBI is here?" one reporter asked.

"What can you tell us about the missing girl? Is there more than one?" someone else shouted.

"No comment," Nick said, pushing the microphones out of his face.

"Agents, can you give us—?"

"He told you, no comment," Sam insisted, shoving another microphone out of her face. Then, leaning over so that only Nick could hear her, she uttered, "It's a madhouse—like a feeding frenzy at the crocodile exhibit. And they have obviously caught wind of something more than we have released to them."

Nick and Sam were met by Officer Stanwood, who escorted them into the building. "We've located your Joe Smith, a.k.a., Joseph Hughes," he said triumphantly.

"Great," Nick said, clapping Officer Stanwood on the back. "Where is he? And when can we interrogate him?"

"We've been questioning him for four hours now. Turns out he owes his old lady a lot of child support. He's been hiding out down here—doing odd jobs and trying to fly under the radar. But you can have a crack at him if you'd like. He's in Interrogation Room 4." He pointed the way down the hall.

"After you, partner," Nick gestured to Sam. "Who knows, we may have just gotten lucky."

"I just need to get a look at him," she said, as a look of consternation crossed her face. "Chances are, he's not the one. Our UNSUB isn't going to be that easy to catch or have a family to support. Of this, I'm certain."

"Why do you say that?" Nick asked, a crestfallen look taking the smile off his face as disappointment filled his voice.

"Because, if we had the right man," she replied blandly, "I guarantee he wouldn't be hiding anything at this point. These killings are like a drug to him. He would be proud of what he has done and he would be feeling completely justified. There will be no hiding behind denials. He would want the world to know what he has done."

Pausing to catch her breath, Sam slowly leaned in towards the one-way window to peer at the man on the other side, then quickly turned away, declaring, "That's not our guy."

Nick himself took a look inside. The suspect had a full sleeve of colorful tattoos on his left arm and flames on his neck. There was even something across both hands. "How can you be so certain after a two-second glance?"

"He's just an ordinary man who skipped out on his wife and kids, Nick. Look at his posture," Sam said, pausing to explain. "Does he look like a highly intelligent person? No self-respecting psychopath is going to tattoo himself up like that. It attracts too much attention. While doing their killing, or whatever deviant behavior they do, they have the need to blend in, even to the point of becoming invisible. Does that man look as if he wants to be invisible?"

Nick looked again at the heavily inked-up man in the interrogation room. With a shake of his head, Nick straightened up and looked at Sam. "No."

"Besides, he's too small and scrawny and he doesn't have scars on his left cheek," Sam pointed out. Then, realizing she'd said too much, she back-tracked. "With the possibility that he's the guy I dealt with, there's a good chance that our guy will have prominent scars running down the left side of his face where I clawed him years ago. I believe I mentioned that to you before." She walked away.

Chasing after Sam, Nick stopped her by putting a gentle hand on her shoulder. "Wait. What? No, you didn't actually say that you'd marked him, but thinking about it, it would make sense that he could have some scars." He lowered his voice. "I'm confused. I thought you said it couldn't be the same person. Now you are saying that we are dealing with the same man you ran into years ago."

"Potentially."

"So, how can you be certain that he would have gnarly scars on his face, after all this time?"

"I clawed his face hard enough to leave...what did you call it? Oh, yes, gnarly scars. I'm certain of that much," she insisted, shrugging off his hand. "So, I guess you do need me since I'm the only *potential* victim to have seen this guy and lived to tell my tale."

Nick ran a shaky hand through his hair, blowing out his breath slowly. Then he went to find Officer Stanwood to inform him that they had the wrong guy and to turn Mr. Hughes over to the authorities in Fairbanks, where he was from.

Once he had finished his business, Nick found Sam sitting in the conference room, staring at the whiteboards.

"We need to hold a press conference here in Juneau and draw The Magician Killer out into the open," she said, bringing her eyes up to meet Nick's. "That way we can control the narrative."

"That's a terrible idea," Nick stated. "Hell, why don't we just send him an engraved invitation to join us in the hotel room while you're at it? I'll pour the guy a drink and ask him why he does what he does. It will be a regular—"

"Where is all this sarcasm coming from, Nick?"

"I believe that's called deflection," he interjected as he reached down and released Murphy from his leash. The dog immediately curled up under the table at Sam's feet, which made her smile.

She was getting used to Murphy being around. The night before he had come looking for her and sat outside of her bathroom door, waiting for her to come out. His presence was beginning to make her feel safe.

Nick walked over to a whiteboard and slapped it hard. "This could be you, Stevens! If we splash your face all over the news, we are essentially inviting trouble to come knocking on our door. Even if he isn't the same guy as your attacker, you look like his victims." His voice grew more adamant.

"Melodramatic much?"

"I'm being serious here, Sam."

"So am I, and I think you're wrong," she said softly, but with conviction. "We need to take this to him!"

"Invite him to pull up a seat at the table?"

"If we bring him back here, we control the situation. We set a trap for him and not the other way around. I'm also hoping that we can get to him before he kills again, and that's important to me."

They locked eyes for a long moment. Neither one of them wanted to be the first to break the spell.

"I could never forgive myself if something happened to you, Samantha Stevens."

Sam shook her head. "Don't call me that."

Nick hesitated. "That is your name, isn't it?"

"Once upon a time, yes. But not anymore," she said, her voice sounding odd.

"Why? Why change your name?" Nick asked, hoping she would further open up to him. "It really is a beautiful name. Help me understand."

"Because, he called me by my name the day he cornered me in the alley," Sam blurted out. "He actually called me Samantha as if he knew me. He used my name, Nick! It wasn't a random crime; it was personal. And ever since that day, the sound of my full name sends goosebumps up my spine." She turned away from Nick to hide the pain the memory caused her. "Maybe after he's caught...? I don't know." She turned to face him again. "Maybe someday I will be able to stand hearing it roll off someone's tongue again. But not now."

Nick laid a comforting hand upon her arm. "I'm sorry, Sam. I didn't know."

Chief Mercer entered the room. "Am I interrupting?"

Sam stepped away from Nick and shuffled some paperwork.

"Of course not, Chief. What can we help you with?" Nick said.

"Excellent. Have you decided what our next move will be?" His eyes traveled between the two agents.

"Yes," Sam said. "We're going to hold a press conference and draw him back out into the open and directly to us."

"Have you lost your mind?" Nick protested.

"Why would we want to bring that psycho back here?" the chief quickly jumped in.

Sam placed her hands on her hips and looked between the two men. "Because, as I was just explaining to Special Agent McLeroy here, we want to control the situation, not the other way around."

Then, turning to address the chief directly, she continued, "You will want to put extra men on the phones that day. I'm certain that we will be flooded with calls from everyone and their mother, reporting that they've seen our killer. We'll need to filter out the loonies from any legitimate tipsters. I'll provide a list of questions that your officers and volunteers will ask each caller." Looking down at her phone to see the time, she added, "I'm scheduled to sit down with the sketch artist in five minutes. I'll do my best to remember what the UNSUB looked like ten years ago—"

"Wait," Chief Mercer interrupted. "What did you just say?"

"I am sitting down with a sketch artist," Sam repeated.

"Yes, that part. Why would you sit down with a sketch artist? What have you not told me?"

Sam winced, realizing that she had slipped up. "Sir, I can explain—" she began to say when the chief cut in again.

"Well, I think you sure the hell owe me one big explanation as to when you had dealings with this fellow!" he bellowed.

Sam walked over to the door and smiled at the officers, looking at them as she shut the door. "Sir, I need you to stay calm—"

"This is me calm! And that's 'Chief' to you, little missy."

"Chief Mercer, if you will stop interrupting me, I can explain," Sam said, stepping closer to the chief.

"I'm still waiting for you to start talking, Stevens."

"I was nineteen, living in Anchorage with my parents while working to put myself through college, when I was attacked by a man on my way home one day," her voice started to shake. "I fought the man off by sheer luck," Sam said. Then Nick cut in.

"I wouldn't call it sheer luck, Agent Stevens," Nick said, turning to face the chief as he gave Sam a moment to pull herself together. "We believe, *potentially*, that the same man Agent Stevens fought off ten years ago, in an alley on her way home, may actually be our current UNSUB, sir. We also believe that Agent Stevens might have been his first victim if she hadn't put up such a heroic fight. For now, we are treating this working theory as a possibility, not a probability."

"And why the hell didn't anyone bring this matter up to me earlier?"

Sam put her hand up. "That would have been my call, sir. The possibility just became apparent to us yesterday and we didn't have time to brief you on the matter until today. I insisted that Nick keep the matter between us until we had the opportunity to inform you, sir. We aren't even certain. But, it could be him. It's just a hunch, sir. I'm sorry. We should have found the time to say something earlier today."

Putting his hands on his hips, the chief blurted, "You think?"

"Agent McLeroy wanted to tell you, but I insisted, sir."

"I think I need to speak with your superior—" he began to say, when Sam cut in.

"That would be a very bad idea, sir," Sam insisted.

"And why is that, Agent Stevens?"

"Because, sir, murder is bad for tourism, and the longer he's out there running free, the worse this situation will get. I am your best hope of catching this guy."

"Oh, and how do you figure that, Special Agent Stevens?" Mercer said, skepticism oozing from his voice.

"Because, as far as we know, I *could* be the only victim who has seen him and lived."

"Potentially the only victim," Nick interjected.

Then, blurting out before Mercer could interrupt her again, she continued. "I know this guy inside and out, sir.

I get him and what he's after. I live, eat, and breathe this case. I've gotten into his head. Anyone else coming onto this case would just be playing catchup."

Taking a deep breath as he pondered what Sam had just said, Mercer stared through the glass wall, with his back to the two agents, at his men working on the main floor of the police station. "Why are you bothering with a sketch artist before you find out if the man from your incident and the man from this case are one and the same?"

"If it isn't the same man, we will know quickly, because what serial killer wants someone else taking credit for his work. He will find a way to tell us we are on the wrong track," Sam smiled knowingly. "And if it is the same guy, we will have a picture of him circulating, which will throw him into a tailspin and some kind of action."

"And you think sending this guy into a tailspin will be a good thing?"

"It will be something," Sam replied"

"Say that I go along with this little scheme of yours, Agent Stevens, and it all goes sideways. What then?"

"You blame it all on me and my career is basically over, sir. But if it all goes right, you will be the hero," she replied, talking fast, just like a used car salesman trying to make a sale. "So, what do you say, sir? Do you want to hear the rest of my plan?"

"Why do I think that this is all going to blow up in my face, Special Agent Sam Stevens?"

"But it won't, sir." Sam said, looking the chief directly in the eyes. "And this is what we are going to do. I will sit down with a sketch artist, who will age the picture and add some 'gnarly scars,' as my partner put it, on his left cheek where I marked him. His picture will then be splashed all over the news, in every diner, restaurant, hotel, and motel lobby from here to Canada. That should flush him out."

"Or enrage the holy crap out of him," Nick said. "He's going to come after someone with a vengeance, Sam. It could be new victims. Or it could even be you."

She saw the concerned look in his eyes. "We don't even know that he's the guy that attacked me. But if he is, I'm not a helpless nineteen-year-old girl anymore, Agent McLeroy. I'm a fully trained, gun-toting agent of the FBI and considered by most to be a lethal weapon. If he's the same guy, I dare him to come after me. I outsmarted him once; I'll do it again."

Nick wasn't fooled by her fearless bravado. He knew the truth. Sam was scared out of her mind. He'd seen the lights left on in her room all night from under her door. He intended to protect her from this madman if it was the last thing he ever did.

"We will hold this news conference in two days," Sam announced. I will prepare a script for each of you. The most important thing to keep in mind is that we need to inform and educate the public about this man and let them know just how dangerous he is. I have to warn you both: the moment we out him, plastering his picture from here to the Canadian Border, he won't have any place to hide, and he might become even more dangerous."

"So, we will, in essence, be weaponizing this man?" Nick blanched.

"Gentlemen, this isn't an exact science. There's always a possibility that he will become crazed, like a cornered animal, and strike out at anyone who comes near him. And, there is also the distinct possibility that he could go into hiding and wait for his opportunity to strike back," she said matter-of-factly. "Either way, it will be better for us to force his hand rather than wait for him to take his next victim. Otherwise, he could potentially disappear for another year. And that will not be good for anyone," she assured them both.

"And, if it is the guy I met in the alley, I'm betting that once he looks at me, nothing will matter more to him than to finish what he started ten years ago. And even if he isn't the same guy, Nick pointed out that my features are similar to those of the missing women, so that could spark a reaction."

"Are you certain about this, Sam—I mean Special Agent Stevens?" Nick asked. His penetrating gaze scrutinized Sam for any weaknesses. "It seems like a very risky move if you ask me."

"Leaving him out on the street would be the riskier move, Agent McLeroy. In the worst-case scenario, he comes here and we miss the opportunity to catch him because we didn't prepare properly. Best case scenario, we catch this psychopath and lock him away until hell freezes over so he can't hurt anyone else."

"You're the expert in this matter, Special Agent Stevens," Chief Mercer grudgingly admitted. "I'm going to give you the benefit of the doubt and follow your lead."

"Thank you, sir. You won't regret this," Sam assured him.

"I'd better not, Agent Stevens, or it will be your hide that I hang out to dry!"

"Yes, sir. I completely understand," Sam said, giving Nick a look that said that she was sorry for letting it slip about her relationship with the killer in front of the chief.

"Special Agent McLeroy and I won't let you down, sir."

Dinner with the Mercers

AS SAM AND NICK were packing their things up for the evening, Chief Mercer walked into the conference room. "My wife insisted that the two of you need to come over tonight for dinner. So, this is me asking you to come over for a home-cooked meal."

Looking over at Sam, Nick took the lead. "Thank you, Chief—"

"Ted, please. Call me Ted. And I must apologize for coming down so hard on you both earlier."

"You have nothing to apologize for, sir," Sam said, looking at him over her computer. "I am the one who should really apologize to you for leaving you out of the loop. That is on me, Chief."

"We would be delighted to join you and your wife," Nick said. "Neither of us has had a home-cooked meal in over a week."

"Text us the address and we will be there," Sam added. "Please allow us to bring the wine. It's the least we can do."

"Certainly, but I like red, and my wife only drinks white."

"Then we will get one of each," Nick said.

"Excellent. Let's say, six-thirty. See you two then. I mean, the three of you. Murphy is welcome to come too."

"He appreciates that, Chief." Nick smiled.

Mrs. Mercer was a delightful hostess. She stood about five-foot-five and was a little soft in the middle. Her shoulder-length bleached blond hair was teased up at the top and contained enough hairspray to keep it from moving in a wind storm. Her blue eyes twinkled as if she always had a great joke she wanted to tell.

She greeted the special agents effusively, "Welcome to our humble home."

"Allow me to present one red and one white bottle of wine," Nick said. "The red is from us," he motioned to Sam. "And the white wine is from Murphy."

"I never realized that dogs had such good taste in wines. Murphy, my boy, you picked out one of my favorites," Mary Mercer gushed, petting the top of Murphy's head. "Come in, come in." She ushered them through the door.

Over a delicious meal of pot roast, mashed potatoes with gravy, and green beans, Mary delighted them with her stories of life with the chief, whom she always referred to as "The Chief." Afterward, she served her famous chocolate cake with cream cheese and powdered sugar filling topped with chocolate buttercream frosting. Stomachs full, the two agents graciously thanked their hosts for the excellent meal and entertainment and made their way back to the hotel for the night.

Nick and Sam were grateful the chief hadn't pulled them aside after the meal to discuss the case. An evening with a home cooked meal and Mary's pleasant chattering was just the antidote they needed to clear their heads and start the next day with fresh eyes on the case.

They made small talk all the way back to the hotel. Upon reaching their suite, they said their goodnights and went to their own rooms.

Sam took a long, hot shower, hoping to untie the knots that had formed in her shoulders. Putting on a pair of shorts and a T-shirt, she crawled into bed and tried to relax with a good book, but despite the evening's refreshing distraction, her mind continued to race. She finally dozed off with the lights on, only to be awakened suddenly when she felt a pair of hands shaking her awake.

She instinctively lashed out, punching the other person in the chest as she screamed.

"Whoa, now!" Nick yelled, blocking any further attacks upon his person while rubbing the spot where she'd punched him.

As Sam's eyes cleared and she realized what she had done, she was mortified.

Murphy began to bark loudly. Nick reached his hand down to quiet the dog. "Everything is okay, boy. Calm down, Murphy. Sit!" he sternly ordered.

"What *the hell* are you doing?" Sam said, still clutching at her chest as her heart beat rapidly in her rib cage. "I could have killed you."

"Your light was on and you were thrashing and crying out in your sleep," he explained, shocked at her violent reaction. "I was also trying to prevent the people in the next room from calling the police and reporting a murder."

Still visibly shaken, Sam's eyes began to focus as she absorbed Nick's words. "I'm sorry, Nick. I didn't mean to snap at you like that."

Murphy jumped up onto her bed and stuck his wet nose in her face, giving her a sniff. Sam scratched Murphy's head and nuzzled him before looking up to see Nick studying her intently.

"You have to stop looking at me like that or I will start to think that you care," she said flippantly.

"Of course I care," Nick answered. "You're my partner. I have your back and you have mine. And Murphy has everyone's back." He hoped the joke would help lighten the mood. "So, why don't you tell me what is *really* going on with you?"

"What do you mean?"

"It's written all over your face." Nick pointed at her. "You may be this bigwig of a psychologist-slash-profiler, but I can see everything you're feeling just by looking at you."

Sam attempted to deflect his words by looking away and focusing her attention on the dog, but Nick wouldn't let her get away with it. Sitting on the edge of the bed, he ordered Murphy to get off the bed and lay down.

Murphy immediately obeyed, walking sullenly to the corner before plopping down, resting his head on his front legs, and eyeing the two of them.

"Come on, Sam, level with me. I saw the lights on last night. And tonight you cried out in your sleep—not to mention, you left the lights on again. You're scared, aren't you?" he pressed. "You can tell me the truth; I won't report you. I know you act as if this whole thing doesn't faze you, but admit it, you're rattled by the possibility of this guy coming back into your life."

Nick didn't miss the fact that Sam's knuckles were blanched white from clenching her fists.

Her eyes misted over and it took every ounce of willpower Sam had not to cry. "All right, you got me. I'm terrified," she snorted. "Is that what you wanted to hear?"

"Well, now we are getting somewhere," Nick said, jumping to his feet. "Finally, the truth."

"Don't sound so pleased with yourself," she said, her voice tinged with bitterness.

"That's it, get angry," Nick encouraged. "We can work with anger. Scared doesn't do either one of us any good."

Pulling a pillow from off the bed, Sam threw it at him, smacking him in the chest. "Why don't you leave the psycho-analysis to the professionals," she ridiculed. "You're an ass."

"I've been called worse," he assured her calmly, sitting back down on the bed and setting the pillow aside. "I'm just trying to help…"

"Well, stop it, because you're doing a lousy job."

Scooting closer, Nick picked up her hand and held on when she tried to yank it back. "All I want to do is help, Sam. And to do that, you have to be truthful and forthcoming with me. You have to tell me what is going on."

Sam sighed. "You want honesty?"

"It would be a start."

"I've hardly slept since we found the remains of our victim. And yes, let's be honest. If it's the same guy, that could have been me in some shallow, unmarked grave ten years ago."

"How can I help?" Nick asked, his voice thickening with emotion.

They were both silent for a long moment before Sam finally shrugged her shoulders. "I don't know, Nick. That's just it—I don't know what will make this all better except to catch this guy and put him away so that I can put this all behind me."

"I was thinking about right now," Nick said, his tone serious. "What can I do for you right now to make you feel better, Sam?"

Looking up with uncertainty, Sam quietly asked, "Could you and Murphy watch over me while I sleep?"

"We will do you one better," Nick snapped his fingers, causing Murphy's ears to perk up. "Come, boy."

Murphy jumped up onto the queen-sized bed, and Nick directed him to the corner. "Down, boy."

Then Nick walked over to the bathroom, pulling the door part of the way closed, allowing a small amount of light to infiltrate the room before turning off the main bedroom light.

"What are you doing?" she questioned.

"I'll just be a moment," Nick answered, then left the room to turn out the lights in the rest of the rooms and retrieve his service revolver, placing it on the nightstand opposite from her.

"Murphy and I will be right here with you the entire night to make sure that no one comes for you," he assured her, then added, "But strictly as your partners, nothing more. You don't happen to have your gun handy?"

Reaching into the nightstand next to her, Sam pulled the loaded gun from the drawer and showed it to him. "I keep it here."

Taking the service weapon from her, Nick placed it into the drawer on his side. "That will keep us both safe," he said with a smile before she could object. "This way, neither of us will have to explain why your gun went off accidentally."

Nick laid next to her, on top of the blankets, and crossed his legs at the ankle and then his arms over his chest. "Of course, if you need anything more from me you will be sure to let me know, won't you?" he grinned, wagging his eyebrows up and down like Groucho Marx in a bad Three Stooges movie.

She playfully punched his arm and shook her head, sliding down into the blankets as she curled up on her side, next to him.

Closing her eyes, Sam took several deep, slow breaths and was soon asleep. Exhaustion had taken its toll. Nick couldn't help but notice that she had dark smudges underneath her eyes. She looked so helpless, reminding him of a small child as she lay there sleeping. But, of course, he knew better than that. Sam was a highly trained, competent woman. He'd never met anyone as strong or self-reliant as Special Agent Samantha Stevens. Everything about her impressed him. In fact, he had lied to her when they first met. He had read her dossier and knew things about her that she didn't know he knew—like the fact that she was from Alaska and moved away suddenly when she was nineteen. But perhaps it was for the best that she was in the dark about his knowledge of her. Her stellar reputation in her field was the whole reason he'd requested her help on this case in the first place.

Nick had been alerted by several law enforcement agencies to the fact that women were going missing in the Interior, Southcentral, and Southeast regions of Alaska. When he began to dig around, he discovered a pattern—a very alarming pattern. But never in his wildest imagination would he have ever guessed that it was actually as large as it was turning out to be.

Nick watched over Sam for some time before his own eyes grew heavy. He had every confidence in Murphy's abilities and knew that he would alert him to any danger if it came through the door, or a window for that matter, so he allowed himself to relax and doze off for a few minutes.

CHAPTER TWELVE

Strange Bed Fellows

S AM STIRRED, ENJOYING THE SENSATION of a warm body lying next to her back. She cracked one eye open and could see sunlight coming through the drawn curtains. Suddenly, a wet nose nuzzled her neck and she turned to discover Murphy was the source of the warm body laying up against her.

Nick must have gotten up earlier and left Murphy to watch over me, she thought with a wry smile as Murphy now licked her face.

"Well, if it isn't our resident Sleeping Beauty," Nick teased as he poked his head into her room before entering with two cups of hot coffee in his hands. "Don't worry, I didn't put any of that powder creamer in yours. I dutifully ran downstairs to get some real cream from the restaurant."

Taking the cup from him with a grateful smile, Sam brought it up to her nose. The freshly brewed coffee aroma was enough to wake her up. "You two are the best partners a girl could ask for," Sam grinned. "One of you keeps me company in bed, while the other fetches me hot, fresh coffee with real cream in it. What did I ever do to deserve all of this?"

"To be fair, I would have gladly traded places with Murphy. But this guy doesn't have any thumbs," Nick said, giving her a wink. "Oh, who am I kidding? Murphy, you're on coffee duty tomorrow while I sleep in."

"What time is it?" Sam asked, looking around for the alarm clock that usually sat on the nightstand next to her bed.

Nick looked sheepishly at Sam before answering. "I unplugged it because you were really beat last night and I thought you could use a little extra shut-eye."

Picking up her phone, Sam turned it over and saw the time. "Nine-fifteen!" she gasped. "Are you kidding me? We're late!"

"Late to what?" Nick asked, unperturbed by her reaction.

Sam thought to herself for a moment and realized that he was right. They didn't have an appointment, and she *did* feel better having slept in this morning.

Nick's cell phone rang in his back pocket and he pulled it out to see who it was. His eyes got wider as he quickly pushed the button to answer it. "Special Agent McLeroy. Yes, sir. Right away, sir. We were finishing up here and we will be there in..." He looked directly at Sam and mouthed, "How long to get ready?"

She flashed him ten fingers and immediately jumped out of bed with her cup of coffee in hand, shutting the bathroom door before he'd even finished giving his answer to the person on the other end of the phone.

The local coroner had completed the forensic work on the bones found at the crime scene and was anxious to deliver his findings. They were all to convene at the Juneau police station's conference room.

Dr. Stephen Archer, the coroner, was a short man with jet-black hair, brown eyes, and a friendly demeanor. He'd established a reputation as a top-notch coroner for the city of Seattle for ten years when he decided his talents and personality would be of better service in a less busy city. Juneau was proving to be less sleepy than anticipated.

As Sam, Nick, and Murphy entered the room, Dr. Archer turned to greet them and stopped short when Murphy stepped in front of the two agents. "Is he going to eat me?" Dr. Archer said, half-jokingly.

"Murphy, heel," Nick ordered, waiting as Murphy sniffed the doctor and decided that he was a good guy.

Nick extended his hand first. "I've heard about the infamous Dr. Steven Archer, and here you are. It's a real pleasure to meet you, sir."

"I could say the same about you, Special Agent Nicholas McLeroy," Archer replied, giving Nick a firm handshake before greeting Sam. "And this must be Special Agent Sam Stevens, the one that I've heard so much about."

"Please, call me Sam," she insisted with a nod.

Chief Mercer walked in as introductions were being made. "Good, everyone has introduced themselves. Let's get right to it. Doc, will you do the honors?"

Dr. Archer waited until everyone had taken a spot around the conference table before he began to talk about his findings. "First of all, one of the DNA samples found at the scene was that of our last victim, Amy Mathews. There was, however, another set of bones found in the makeshift grave," he said, laying out photos on the conference table.

"There were two victims buried in the same spot?" Nick and Sam uttered simultaneously.

"Yes, indeed there were. The second set of bones belonged to our seventh victim, according to the timeline you have here on the whiteboards. Tess Ashton, abducted June 1, 2017."

The two agents allowed the new information to sink in. Doctor Archer went on to explain his findings as they both pulled out notepads.

"We could tell by the teeth and other marks on the bone fragments that they were made by a canine—most likely a wolf, and possibly afterward, even a few scavengers, like buzzards. As you can see from the photos, we don't have complete skeletal parts for either victim. Which means that the remains of most of the two female victims were carried off and consumed elsewhere."

Sam felt herself involuntarily shiver, vomit rising in her throat. She swallowed hard and continued to take notes. It was just as she had envisioned at the hunting blind.

"We believe that our victims were staked out and left for the predators because when we excavated the site, we found eight wooden stakes buried. We also found pieces of shredded material that, I believe, but cannot say with certainty without further testing, were most likely undergarments. I hypothesize our victims were left tied to the stakes in their undergarments. It is likely these victims were alive when they were attacked. This would explain the types of marks left on the bones."

Sam shivered again at the thought of such a terrifying experience. Finally finding her voice, she said, "That would fit with the profile of our perpetrator. He needs to be in control. And what better way to control his victims than to strip them of all of their dignity? We are dealing with a true psychopath. It's not that he doesn't have the ability to feel empathy. It's simply the fact that he doesn't care about anyone else's feelings but his own."

"I'm sorry. Can you repeat that?" Chief Mercer asked. "Because, from what I'm hearing from you as well as the good doctor here, these two things don't go together. How is this madman able to have any kind of empathy if he is able to do what he does to these women?"

"Most murders, we simply look at the motive, means, and opportunity, right?" Sam said. Then she continued when everyone nodded their heads. "Then we also like to find the reason behind why our killer murdered someone in the way that he did. But in this case, the motive, means, and opportunity are not necessarily relative in this situation. Or any situation we are dealing with at the moment. When you are dealing with a true psychopathic murderer, you must deal with the human propensity and human impulses. Does that make sense?"

"None of it makes sense, Special Agent Stevens," Chief Mercer said.

Sam could see the confusion and frustration in everyone's eyes, so she tried to further explain the mindset of a true psychopath. "Let me try this another way. You get into an elevator and face the opposite direction as everyone else is facing; basically, you are looking at the back wall. What does everyone on the elevator do?" she asked, then continued without waiting for anyone to answer. "They freak out, right? Because it is unnatural or uncommon. We all strive for some commonality. But with a true psychopath, there is no commonality. One thing impacts upon the other like dominoes falling. What we are dealing with is what we call 'Lust Murder.' Our perpetrator could have a problem performing sexually unless he witnesses a violent act upon another person. His need drives him to create these situations that put this person, the one he has been fantasizing about, into one of these dire, dangerous, and or deadly situations. This, in turn, brings him ecstasy, or release, sexually. And that is a simplified definition of a Lust Murder.

"It's also another reason why the name "The Magician Killer" fits him. In a way, he creates an illusion when he kills his victims because he doesn't have to actually touch them during the killing, since the animals do the actual act. He can just watch it unfold."

Everyone in the room remained silent for a full thirty seconds while they digested this new information, satisfied they understood what they were up against.

When they arrived back at the station, Sam turned the day's reports over to Nick to handle for a change since Dr. Archer had given them a lot of valuable Intel to record and file. Sam got to work writing out everything that could possibly be asked of them during the press conference and what they were to answer. Every word was concise and scripted. Each aspect of the information that would be covered was meant to draw their killer out into the open.

Capital punishment had been abolished in 1957, when the State of Alaska was preparing for statehood, making it the first state on the West Coast to outlaw executions for hei-nous crimes. In the back of Sam's mind, she wondered if, giv-en the chance, she would pull the trigger and end the killer's life. Did she have that kind of rage growing inside of her to do that?

CHAPTER THIRTEEN

Sparring Partners

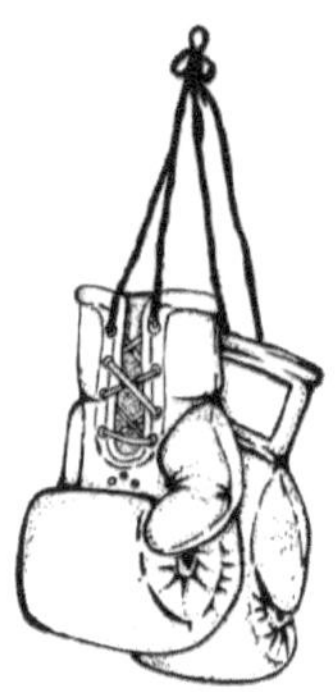

SAM FELT ON EDGE ALL EVENING, and Nick could sense it, too. He decided what she needed was a good old sparring match. It would take the edge off for both of them.

Meeting in the hotel gym, Nick secured two pairs of boxing gloves and headgear and presented them to Sam when she walked in.

"You honestly want to spar with me after our last go around?" Sam taunted, giving him a lopsided grin. "Don't think that I'm going to take it easy on you just because we are becoming friends."

Lifting an eyebrow, Nick smiled back. "I wouldn't dream of asking you to lower your standards and cut me a break. Let the trash-talking begin."

"Did I mention that the guys in my training class stopped challenging me because I would always kick their butts?" she bragged while putting on her headgear.

"You do realize that none of those guys was me," he fired back, fastening the strap of his headgear.

"Sure," she sarcastically fired right back at him.

Tugging his gloves on, Nick pulled the tie tighter with his teeth. "Well, I must warn you that I was awarded the Golden Gloves for boxing when I was at Quantico," he said. "Three times in a row."

"Oh, really?" Sam laughed. "Well then, I guess it was a good thing that we didn't attend Quantico at the same time because I would have ruined that winning streak of yours with my *four*-time Golden Gloves award, plus two-time kickboxing trophy."

Wondering if she, too, was exaggerating like he was, or telling the truth, Nick ramped up the trash talk. "Wow, you were only awarded the kickboxing award two times in a row. What are you, some kind of slacker? What happened, someone take the title away from you after only two times?"

Sam smiled even broader as she knocked her gloves together and began bouncing around and stretching to loosen up. "Nah, you dork. No one would get in the ring with me after that."

Questioning what he had gotten into, Nick finished tying his gloves and began stretching his legs. "Is it too late to ask you nicely if you could take it easy on me?"

Sam began to laugh out loud as an evil glint came into her eyes. "You're kidding, right?"

"No, really. I'm serious," Nick quickly backpedaled. "You're beginning to make me doubt myself. Legit. I think I might even be a bit scared of you."

"You should be."

Murphy was relaxing in the corner, with his head resting upon his front paws, a disinterested look on his face.

They came together, knocking gloves as they sized one another up, throwing a few light jabs and dancing around each other. Suddenly, Sam threw a kick, nailing Nick in the side, hard.

"Come on, McLeroy, I thought you said you were good," Sam taunted, throwing another punch to his head, which he blocked while stumbling back a step or two.

"I was just trash-talking. I wasn't serious, Stevens."

"I wasn't trash-talking, McLeroy," Sam assured him. "And I was deadly serious."

Nick threw two punches in rapid succession, catching Sam in the arm and in the side. She smiled a sadistic grin and he felt his insides twist up.

Sam turned and landed a roundhouse kick and then swept his feet, knocking Nick to the mat unexpectedly before pinning him down.

When Sam stood up and offered her hand, Nick chuckled, "So, that's how it's going to be then," he responded, getting slowly to his feet.

"You should be able to spring to your feet, McLeroy," she said. "You aren't getting soft on me, are you?" Sam motioned for him to make the first move, then simply smiled, showing her teeth this time.

"You realize that this means war," Nick jeered.

"You say war, I say sparring," she teased. "Now, are you going to fight me or talk me to death?"

"Oh, it's on, like Donkey Kong," he announced with a smug grin. "And sister, I hope you're ready for the unleashing."

"Don't do that," Sam said, bouncing around him on her toes.

"Do what? Tell you what's coming?"

"No. Make me laugh."

"That's what makes you laugh?" Nick sputtered, bringing his hands up to protect his face as he threw another punch that she easily blocked.

Throwing a punch that landed against his jaw hard, Sam danced behind Nick and then kicked him in the legs, causing him to stumble.

"You know what?" she challenged. "You were right."

"Oh? About what?" he asked, slowly getting up using one knee.

"This is exactly what I needed tonight."

Raising his hands up again, Nick threw another punch, which she again easily blocked. Then she immediately threw a punch to his head and danced out of his reach just as he threw another, missing her.

"I'm so happy that I could make you feel good about yourself," he said blandly.

"You will tell me when you've had enough, right?" She grinned smugly, striking him in the side again with another kick that he didn't see coming. "I wouldn't want to damage your delicate sensibilities."

Shaking it off, Nick was beginning to regret his decision to spar with Sam. He'd read in her file that she was a badass, but he didn't realize how badass she truly was.

"Two-time kickboxing champion?" he questioned as he leaned over, putting his hand on his left side to catch his breath. He needed to stall her a minute and give himself time to recover from that last kick.

"Double black belt," she added, gloating just a bit. "I've broken a cinderblock or two with my bare hands."

"You don't say?"

Sam merely grinned as she danced back in toward him to strike again. The sparring went on for another fifteen minutes before Nick cried Uncle, and tapped out. Then he feigned extreme hunger as his excuse. The truth was, Nick McLeroy wasn't used to having his backside handed to him by a woman. And not just any woman, but his beautiful, tall, ultra-athletic partner.

After dinner, they went upstairs to prepare for the press conference. Nick brought back a bottle of wine he had bought and opened in the restaurant downstairs. Pouring two glasses, they now sat down and began looking at their notes. They were on their second glass of wine, going over the script for the third time, when Nick put down the script and looked at her strangely.

"Are you certain about this, Sam?" Nick asked. It was the fourth time he'd asked her that question that day. "I truly think we could be poking the hornet's nest with this guy."

"That's kind of the point." She scooted closer to him on the couch. "We have to invoke an emotional response from him or we aren't going to get him back here. And if we don't get him back here, he's going to kill again, then disappear for another year. I can't have that on my conscience. Can you?"

"I get it. And I'm trying to understand this from your point of view. But I just don't understand the part where you put yourself out there as bait," he said, sounding almost angry at her.

Sam desperately needed him to be on board with this. After all, it was her life on the line, not his. And she needed him to be all in. How could she explain it to him any plainer than she already had? Placing her hand on his, she tried to reassure him. "Nick, I know what I'm doing—"

"But do you?" he challenged. "Do you really?" He ran a frustrated hand through his hair, making it stand on end as Sam inched her way even closer to him.

Nick laid his arm across her shoulders. They were drawing so close now, and Sam had a moment's hesitation about letting him in. She knew that it was unprofessional to mix business with pleasure. But there was something about the way he looked at her that just made her want to melt. After all, she was a big girl and recognized that look in his eyes. It was the same look most men got when they were around her too long. Nick was about to kiss her, and for a moment, she actually wanted him to. But Sam wavered, knowing that they were about to cross that line—the one that was difficult to come back from. He leaned in closer.

"Nick, this is a bad idea."

An inch from her face, he whispered, "I know, but I just don't care."

Clutching at her silky strands of hair, Nick branded her mouth to his own, searing her to her core. Time and place ceased to exist as she reciprocated his need, pressing her mouth against his almost frantically.

Sam splayed her hands against his chest, then wrapped her arms around his back as she pulled him against her. She marveled to herself for a moment as her fingertips dug into the muscular flesh of his back. It had been a long time since she had let anyone get this close. Her need and desire felt so raw at that very moment that it hurt. She could feel his heart racing and wondered if he could also feel her racing heart as it threatened to beat a hole through her ribs.

Then Nick growled. It was a very carnal sound, which only served to inflame Sam even more as he slid his hands under her hips to pull her closer.

Sam tipped her head back, giving him free rein as his lips left a hot, passionate trail down her neck, across her collarbone, to the ample swells of her breasts. This time it was Sam who let out a harsh, primal cry as he touched her.

Nick's mouth captured hers once again as his lips laid siege to hers, their tongues performing an intricate dance while his hands roamed freely over her silky soft skin. He lifted her shirt over her head, then pulled his off as well, depositing them carelessly on the floor, their eyes never breaking contact.

Wrapping a large, strong hand behind Sam's neck, Nick pulled her to him, kissing her soundly. He was attempting to gauge her reaction as her desire matched his own.

"Do you want this?" he asked as he pressed a kiss on the side of her neck, trying to regain some sense of control before things went too far.

"Yes," she sighed. "Desperately."

Nick stood up, drinking all of her in before reaching out a hand to pull her to her feet. "I was hoping you'd say that," he replied, leading her to his room and shutting the door.

Murphy sat down next to the closed door and waited patiently for it to be opened to him again. Little did he know that he would be waiting all night.

CHAPTER FOURTEEN
News Conference

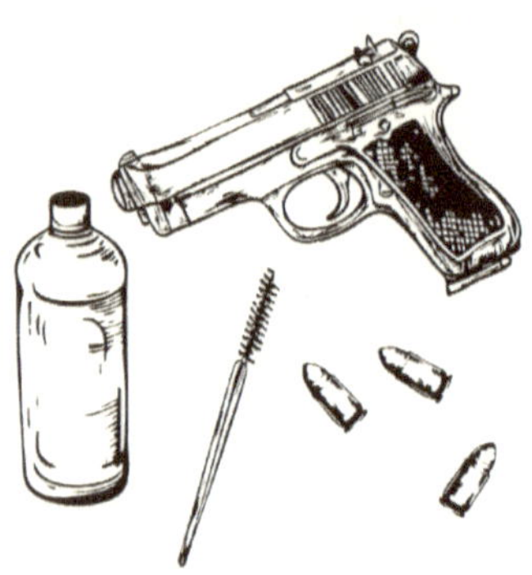

ONCE AGAIN, SAM FELT A WARM BODY next to hers as she cracked open an eyelid, and recollection hit her. The memories from the night before played over and over in her mind in Technicolor.

Inwardly, she cringed. Panic set in as thoughts tumbled through her mind:

How was this going to affect their working relationship? How does one backpedal something like this? And do I truly want to? If anyone from the bureau finds out about the two of us, my career will be over.

Sam Stevens, you really did it this time, she berated herself as she attempted to slip out of bed without waking him.

"Where do you think you're going?" His sultry, groggy voice pierced through her foggy mind and stopped Sam dead in her tracks.

With a forced laugh, Sam tried to act casual as she rolled back over. "I was going to check to see what time it was, and I didn't want to wake you," she lied, flashing him a brilliant smile.

"You weren't feeling awkward this morning about last night, were you?" he asked, lifting one eyebrow.

Letting out a loud sigh, Sam pushed stray pieces of hair out of her eyes. "No!" she insisted, then back-tracked, immediately changing her answer to a resounding, "Yes!"

"Thank God," Nick exhaled. "I thought it was just me."

"What do you mean, thank God? We're two consenting adults." She scrutinized him while sitting up in bed, pulling the sheet up to her chest. "We can work with this."

"Sure. Of course," he said, sounding less than certain of her words while pulling himself up to a sitting position, resting his head next to hers against the headboard. The memory of the night before and the three times they'd made love was making him grow hard again. Putting his hand down to hide the evidence, he forced those thoughts from his mind.

"This doesn't have to be awkward. And it certainly doesn't need to change anything between us," Sam pointed out. "As long as you don't start acting completely possessive and weird when we are around others. Right?"

"No. That would be completely unprofessional."

"And I will still carry my own weight," she said, looking directly into his eyes to make her point understood.

"Of course. Why would anything need to change?" Nick replied, swinging his feet off the bed and pulling on his shorts before turning around. "I'll run Murphy outside. He's probably sitting at the door crossing his legs by now. And I'll get us a couple of coffees downstairs."

"That sounds amazing. And Nick?"

"Yes?" he replied from the door, turning to give her a brilliant smile.

"Last night was amazing," she smiled back. "Maybe when this case is wrapped up, we could do it again."

"I think that could be arranged." He winked before turning and opening the door. "I will only be a few minutes."

"Take your time, Nick. I could use a shower. We wouldn't want people talking about my new scent and how much it smells like yours, now would we?"

"That would be completely unprofessional, Special Agent Stevens."

"That's what I was thinking, Special Agent McLeroy."

Sam lay there listening for the door to close behind Nick and Murphy before jumping out of bed. She gathered up her clothing, strewn about the floor, before running to her own room and kicking the door shut behind her. "You are such an idiot," she ranted outloud before sitting on her bed to gather her thoughts. "What were you thinking compromising this investigation like that?"

Walking over to the closet, Sam retrieved a pair of black slacks and a white blouse. The press conference would begin at nine-thirty, and she had to be on her game, not distracted by a handsome, blue-eyed FBI agent named Nicholas McLeroy.

After showering, Sam noticed Nick had set fresh coffee for her on her nightstand. That simple act of kindness made her smile as she rethought her stance on office romance and how it could mess up a perfectly good working relationship and her career. She was, after all, attracted to Nick. The only real problem was that they found themselves smack dab in the middle of a career-making case, and Sam had let her primal desires fog her mind. *Rookie move and not how I operate,* she thought. *And so out of character for me.*

Shaking off her regrets, Sam decided what was done was done. They would move forward from here, and she would remain vigilant and focused.

Sam took her Glock 22 apart in the living room as she waited for Nick to finish getting ready. Spraying a cotton rag with Hoppe's solvent, she attached it to the cleaning rod, forcing it into the barrel of her gun. Pulling it out, the rag was gray with carbon powder. She repeated this process three more times, put the gun back together, and reloaded it.

The simple act of pulling something apart and then putting it back together gave Sam a sense of order and control.

When Nick came out of his room fifteen minutes later, freshly shaven and smelling of soap and aftershave, Sam nearly pulled her gun apart again. The two of them discussed work matters on their ride to the police station and avoided direct eye contact. Neither of them was particularly hungry, so they skipped breakfast.

When they arrived, seven news vans and six newspaper reporters were lined up on the streets, all vying for attention. The reporters shoved microphones and tape recorders into Sam's face as she attempted to get around the barrier and into the police station.

"Can you give us any quotes?" someone yelled out.

"What can you tell us about the serial killer?" someone else called out.

Holding the reporters back, two police officers came rushing over to help Sam and Nick get in through the doors. "Back it up, folks. You will get all the information shortly."

Sam was in charge of running the press conference. She started going over the order of things with Nick and Chief Mercer and reviewing the scripts she had written for them. She wanted to make sure that everyone was on the same page and that there would be no last-minute surprises. If someone got into a bind, they were to turn it over to Sam, and she would field the reporter's questions.

"Are you certain you want us to use your full name when introducing you, Sam?" Nick asked for the second time that day.

"Yes," she answered, exasperated by the repeated question. "I want him to remember me. But more than that, I want him to know that I'm coming for him. Not only will it shake him up, it will likely send him into a tailspin."

Chief Mercer and Nick both gave Sam a somber nod, supporting her decision to coax the serial killer out into the open even though neither of them fully agreed with her.

"Have all of the potential victims' families been notified ahead of the news conference, sir?" Sam asked the chief without looking up from her script.

"I was told that they had all been reached by phone as of last night at seven o'clock."

Giving the chief a nod, Sam acknowledged, "That's perfect. Then we are all set to go." Taking one final look at the papers with the details of the press conference, she stood up and closed the folder with a snap.

Lieutenant O'Rourke, A burly redheaded man, walked into the room and handed Nick a package. "This just arrived for you, sir."

"What is that?" Sam asked, looking at the small envelope in Nick's hand, marked overnight mail.

"Just something I ordered from my home office yesterday. Thought it might come in handy at some point," he said, being evasive. "I will share with you later. Now is not the time." She decided to drop it. There was too much going on and she didn't have time to probe into the matter further—picking one's battles and all.

"Are the two of you ready?" Chief Mercer asked, sounding a bit like the coach of a little league team just before the big game. Sam half-expected him to call them into a circle so they could throw their hands up into the air and yell, "Go, team!" But instead, they all walked somberly from the room and began to exit the building toward the horde of reporters and news agencies.

The loud, excited chatter of reporters quickened, and a few questions were thrown out as the doors opened and the agents and Chief Mercer stepped outside.

Chief Mercer approached the podium with the mayor standing behind him to his left side. In front of him were multiple microphones in a row. The chief loudly cleared his throat, silencing the low rumble of voices.

"I'm Chief Mercer of the Juneau Police Department, and I would ask that you hold all questions until the end." He paused for dramatic effect before continuing. "The Mayor and I have called this formal press conference to inform the public of a very serious situation that has recently come to light." The speaker whined with some feedback and Chief Mercer pulled back while a sound technician stepped up to make some adjustments to the main speaker.

Mercer's expression now hardened, with a crease forming along his mouth and forehead. "It has come to our attention that there are a number of women who have gone missing from the Interior, Southcentral, and Southeast regions of Alaska." Murmurs from the crowd momentarily halted him from saying anything more until it quieted again. He loudly cleared his throat. "We have established that this situation has occurred over a ten-year period. We have a total of seventeen women that we have linked together in this timeline. And the reason no one has connected their disappearances before is because these cases have been spread out over ten years and in many different locations throughout the State."

Several reporters attempted to interrupt Chief Mercer at this point, and he raised his hand to stop them. "As I said in the beginning, please hold all of your questions until the very end." Then he continued, following the carefully crafted speech that Sam had prepared for him, before turning it over to Nick.

Lucy Jones entered the café, sporting a new bright pink streak in her otherwise wavy brown locks. She was just returning from a quick smoke break at Sweet Tooth Café in Skagway when somebody yelled out, "Turn it up!"

Deidre was working behind the counter and reached over to pick up the remote to turn up the mounted television's volume.

There had been a lot of anticipation from the patrons regarding the Juneau press conference, so now everyone in the place was riveted to the television set. Announcers had been airing teasers on the morning news outlets and all the morning shows. The room fell quiet as the handsome FBI agent, Special Agent Nicholas McLeroy, was introduced. When he had finished speaking, he introduced his partner, Special Agent Samantha Stevens, her name running across the bottom of the screen in large bold letters.

Stepping to the podium, wearing her black FBI windbreaker, Sam placed her cards down before she looked up and began to speak. "*Good morning. I would like to begin by reiterating what Chief Mercer and my partner, Special Agent Nicholas McLeroy, have already addressed. This is an ongoing investigation, and there are certain details we will not be able to discuss because of the nature of this investigation. I am here to give you the available details as we know them so far. The FBI is working in conjunction with the police department and Forest Rangers throughout Alaska. The names and faces of each of our suspected victims will appear on your screen, beginning with the most recent incident. We are working in this order because we need the public to be aware of the* magnitude and scope of this investigation. I also want people to see these victims and remember their faces. These young women have concerned families. They are someone's daughter, granddaughter, sister, and best friend. You need to know that each one of them matters. And although we believe their lives may have been cut short by a man who has little regard for human life, we will work tirelessly until we have justice for each and every one of them. Some of them come from small towns, others from large cities. I want you to look closely at their features. If you know anyone who fits the profile of one of these young women, or if you are someone who looks like these young women, I urge you to either stay home or travel in groups of three or more. Don't go out alone until we have apprehended this man. I cannot stress enough the need for caution. We are dealing with someone who is meticulous in his planning. He studies his victims for weeks before striking. He has no empathy and does not feel remorse or guilt for his crimes. He will inflict pain upon his victims and feel nothing but euphoria."

"He is most likely awkward around others—women in particular. Our perpetrator will have trouble forming attachments to people. He will appear normal and ordinary. He will attempt to blend into his environment seamlessly and won't stand out because the last thing he wants to do is bring unwarranted attention or scrutiny to himself."

Sam held up two sketches for the cameras. "We have two different compositions of our alleged perpetrator. The first one *shows him with three large scars running down the left side of his face. He will be careful to hide the marks by wearing large sunglasses and maybe a hat that he never takes off. He will avoid eye contact and position himself so that only the right side of his face shows."*

"We have posted a phone number on your screen. *If you see this man, please make no attempt to approach him or try to detain him yourself. He is extremely dangerous and will not hesitate to strike out if he feels trapped or cornered. The tip line will be open twenty-four hours a day until he is caught. We are offering a fifty-thousand-dollar reward to the person or persons responsible for bringing this man to justice,"* Sam announced. "Again, let me reiterate this part for the public's safety. Please, do not attempt to apprehend this person on your own. I will now use this time to take a few questions from the media." She pointed to a reporter.

"Cole Hanlon, Anchorage Daily News. *What is his motivation? What makes him attack these particular women?"*

"That is an excellent question, Mr. Hanlon, and the short answer is, we don't know what motivates him to strike out at these particular women," Sam replied. *"I will be sure to ask him when he's apprehended."* She pointed to another reporter in the front row.

"Joyce Fredricks, from the Juneau Empire. Are these attacks sexual in nature?"

"Thank you, Joyce. While it appears that he does not actually rape his victims, we do believe that the crimes against these

women are psychosexual in nature. What I mean is that he is most likely impotent and unable to perform any real sexual act with an actual flesh-and-blood woman. But he gets off on the violence that he perpetrates against his victims. In other terms, it brings him sexual pleasure."

Everyone in the diner was glued to the television set and did not see the subdued man sitting in the back corner booth. Not one person pulled their eyes away from the news long enough to notice the man stand up, place a twenty-dollar bill on the red-and-white-checkered tablecloth, and quietly leave the café. Everyone was so engrossed in what Special Agent Samantha Stevens was saying that they didn't turn around when the little bell sounded at the front door as he exited.

But Lucy's coworkers in the café all turned to look at her, shock registering across their concerned faces.

"Lucy, dear, those girls all look so much like you," Deidre gasped, reaching out to touch Lucy's arm.

Slowly, Lucy turned to look at the back corner booth for the man she had served breakfast to that morning—the strange man who had come to the diner nearly every other day for the past four weeks now. She began to hyperventilate, feeling weak in the knees as she pointed at the empty booth, unable to speak.

The motherly figure of their small but tight-knit group grabbed Lucy's arm, forcing her to take a seat at the counter. "What is it, darling?" Josie cried. "You have to breathe, sweet girl, or you will simply faint away."

"The man...the man who always...always sits there," Lucy stuttered, pointing a shaky finger toward the back corner booth.

"What man, Lucy?" Deidre asked, looking toward the booth Lucy was pointing at. "There's no one there."

"The hat and glasses man," she sputtered. "He's been here nearly every other day. He never takes his hat and glasses off, and he never looks directly at me." Both Deidre and Josie gasped.

"That harmless man? You think he could be the... the man they're looking for?" Deidre said incredulously.

Lucy looked back at the television and wordlessly nodded her head as tears leaked from her eyes. "Yes. It was him. I know it was him."

Josie put her arms around Lucy and hustled her into the back office where they could call the number on the television screen.

A Dead Head

"**T**HANK YOU ALL FOR YOUR TIME," Sam concluded, then stepped away from the podium. Reporters continued to clamor and shout questions, but Sam ignored them. She was finished speaking. The trap had been set.

"That went well," Nick said as two officers held open the precinct's doors for them.

"So, what's next?" Chief Mercer asked.

"We wait," Sam said, offering the chief a reassuring smile. "The calls will start coming in soon."

As if on cue, two of the precinct phones began to ring almost immediately, and then a third.

"See, I told you it wouldn't take long," Sam said, watching the phone lines light up in the next room. "Aren't you glad you listened to me about hiring extra volunteers?"

"The important thing to remember here, Chief Mercer, is we have to keep people manning the phones twenty-four-seven," Nick added. "We can't afford to miss someone with a legitimate sighting."

Lieutenant Conrad stepped into the conference room. "I think we have a live one," he said excitedly.

"What makes you so sure, Lieutenant?" Nick asked.

"The tip comes from a young woman in Skagway," answered Lieutenant Conrad, reviewing a sheet of paper. "It sounds credible. She says the same man has been hanging around her work for about four weeks. He always wears a hat and sunglasses, even when he is inside, and she is certain he is the guy we are looking for."

Sam gave Nick a high five. "Now *that* is how it gets done! When do we leave?"

"We can be there in a couple of hours," Nick said.

After slipping out of the precinct's back door to evade the media storm, it only took them a few minutes to reach the float plane. Nick climbed into the pilot seat and immediately turned to Sam with an inquiring look.

Cutting him off by holding up her hand, Sam insisted, "Nick, we are good. Really. I just want to focus on this case. When this is all over, we can investigate what this"—she made a sweeping gesture with her hand, back and forth between them—"could or could not be."

Nodding his head, Nick smiled at her. "How do you know I wasn't going to ask you what you wanted for lunch?"

"You had that *'holy crap, I need to discuss my feelings'* look in your eyes. Please, tell me I'm wrong."

Nick opened his mouth and immediately closed it again before starting the engine. Then he handed her the headset. "Here, put these on."

Nick climbed into the back to attach Murphy's harness to his seat, then climbed back to the front and buckled in.

"I will take your silence as a yes, then?" she said, putting the headset on and feeling rather self-satisfied.

"Did I tell you how beautiful you looked this morning and that you absolutely nailed that press conference?" Nick replied, swiftly changing the subject.

"Thank you. You weren't half bad yourself in front of the cameras. In fact, the camera loves you. Ever think about changing careers and becoming a movie star?" she teased. "I really think the girls would go crazy for you." Then, looking out the window, she muttered under her breath, "If you're into that sort of thing."

Nick grinned as he maneuvered the plane away from the docks and into position for takeoff. "Hang on Murphy," he called over his shoulder to his other partner.

Sam braced herself for takeoff. As if conducting a press conference wasn't stressful enough, she now had to fly in a small plane. Her fear of flying was bad enough in a smooth jumbo jet.

"Say, do you want to learn to fly?" Nick offered, turning to Sam and gesturing to the controls in front of her.

"No! Absolutely not!" Sam replied.

"It'll be fun," he assured her. "Besides, if something happened to me, you would need to know how to fly this thing. It has been said that the best way to get past your fear is to go straight through it."

Sam looked out the window and watched the churning water blown by the plane's propellers. "I assure you, I do not wish to learn to fly!"

Just give it a try—" Nick persisted, not getting the hint.

"Nicholas Emory McLeroy," she warned.

"Hey," Nick objected, "only my mother gets to call me by my full name. And while we are on that subject, how *did* you know my middle name?"

Looking sheepishly at him, Sam shrugged. "I may or may not have had a peek at your file."

"So, which is it?" Nick asked. "Did you or did you not have a peek at my file, as you so indecisively put it?"

"Fine. I glanced over your file before we met," Sam confessed. "There. Are you happy?"

With a smile of satisfaction, he nodded his head. "I *knew* it." Then without missing a beat, Nick reached over and placed Sam's hands on the steering handles. "So, when I tell you to, pull back on the handles," Nick said. "I'll be here the entire time guiding you."

"Are you crazy?" she fired back. "What if I crash us?"

"I will guide you and I swear, nothing will happen. You must try it at least once in your life," Nick said with a boyish smile. "We are getting up to speed—"

"I'm not doing this!" Sam insisted, hesitating before letting go of the controls.

"Now!" he shouted. "Pull back now."

Sam let out a low growl, but then quickly put her hands back on the controls and pulled back, lifting the plane out of the water and into the air. "I did it! I did it!" she yelled over the roar of the engine. "I really did it."

Nick smiled broadly and took back the controls as he banked left to put them in the right direction. "You did great," he praised. "To be honest, I didn't think you had it in you."

"Tell me what to do next," Sam insisted, suddenly excited by the power of flying the plane herself.

"Okay. Rest your hands on the controls again and let me talk you through it. But whatever you do, don't make any sudden moves or the three of us will end up in the water."

"That would *not* be good." She looked out the window and craned her neck down.

"No, that definitely would not be good."

The short forty-five-minute plane ride was over in the blink of an eye. Sam radioed ahead, arranging for the Skagway Police Department to meet them at the landing strip.

Lucy Jones was still very shaken up by the incident. Ever since she'd called the tip hotline, she was unable to stop sobbing. She was a tear-soaked mess, blubbering about her boyfriend being out to sea on a fishing boat. Deidre refused to leave her friend alone, even for a moment.

"Miss Jones, we would like to ask you a few questions about the man you say has been stalking you for several weeks, if that is all right with you," Sam said softly, hoping to not send the poor girl into another crying frenzy.

Blowing her nose into a now well-used tissue, Lucy clutched her friend Deidre's hand. "Sure. I want you to catch this monster before he comes after me. I don't think I will sleep a wink again until he's caught."

The cozy two room cottage was modestly decorated and painted a crisp white inside and out. Shabby sheik repurposed wicker furniture smattered the living room, making it warm and intimate. A fluffy, soft blue throw hung over the back of a wicker rocking chair, while gray and blue pillows dotted the chairs and loveseat.

"What can you tell us about the man you believe to be our suspect?" Sam probed gently. "Did you happen to notice what type of vehicle he drove? Have you ever seen him without his hat or glasses?"

"This one time, maybe a week and a half ago, I saw him get into a white truck when I just happened to be looking out the front window. It had a camper on the back," Lucy said, looking up at the ceiling, trying to recall all the details.

"Do you remember anything else about the truck or camper?" Sam pressed.

Once again, Lucy looked up as she tried to remember. "It was so busy," she said.

"Try closing your eyes, Miss Jones, and take several deep breaths for me. It will help calm you, making it easier to remember more," Sam continued, wanting more than anything to help the young woman find those memories.

"Please, call me Lucy."

"All right, Lucy. But first, I need everyone to please clear the room, except for my partners," Sam insisted, giving Deidre a look that indicated that she meant for her to leave as well.

"I will just step outside with the officers, Lucy."

"But you won't leave?" Lucy said, her voice sounding very small.

"No, my dear Lucy, I will not leave you, sugar," Deidre assured her with a stiff smile while shaking her head. She looked directly at Sam, then back at Lucy. "I would never do that to you."

Once everyone had left, Sam turned to Lucy and concentrated on controlling the tone of her voice, trying to soothe Lucy's frazzled nerves.

"I need you to close your eyes and I want you to listen and focus on my voice, and only my voice, Lucy. We will do this together. First, we are going to take a deep breath in and then hold it until I count to three. Ready?" Sam waited for Lucy to nod her head in agreement before proceeding. "Good. Now, breathe in through your mouth...one, two, three," she counted slowly. "And breathe out through your nose. Again." Once Lucy appeared calmer, Sam continued. "Now, Lucy, I want you to take me back to the day that you first saw the man leaving the café. Describe to me what was happening around you."

"It was the end of a very busy morning," Lucy replied.

"What time was it?"

"Ten thirty, I think. Yes, ten thirty. My back was hurting me, so I stepped to the window to see what it looked like outside. I was in desperate need of a smoke break and was stretching my sore back for just a minute when I noticed the man outside. I remember thinking how strange it was that he was looking up and down the street before walking over and getting into his truck. I think it was a Ford, or maybe it was a Chevy." Her voice warbled. "I'm not so good with the different models."

"You are doing great, Lucy." Sam noticed that Lucy was getting agitated again. "Now take another deep breath and let it out slowly like before. You are doing quite well. So, it was a white truck with a camper shell. Do you recall if there were any distinguishing marks or scratches on the truck or camper? Maybe there was a dent someplace, or maybe a stripe?"

Concentrating, Lucy squinted her eyes. "It was an older model truck because the paint was faded a bit...and there was a sticker in the back window of the camper."

Sam leaned in. "What kind of sticker, Lucy?"

Lucy sat quietly for a few seconds as she thought about it. "Grateful Dead. It was a Grateful Dead sticker on the back window." Lucy sounded proud of herself for remembering that detail.

"Very good, Lucy. Now, can you describe the sticker to me?"

"It's the one that is red, white, and blue, with the skull in the middle and a lightning bolt down the middle of the skull," she said, looking directly at Sam. "I thought it odd at the time."

"Why is that?" Sam inquired, looking over at Nick, who was taking down the notes.

"Because I would not have pegged him for a Dead Head," Lucy replied, very matter-of-factly. "I figured that he listened to James Taylor or The Bee Gees—the kind of mellow music they play in the diner."

"Lucy, you have been incredibly helpful," Sam said. "You gave us a lot of information that we can use. You are a very brave young woman. I want to thank you, and if you can think of anything more, don't hesitate to contact me." Pulling a card from her pocket, she continued, "You can call me any time. That is my personal number."

Nick, Murphy, and Sam left Lucy's house, confident that she would be well protected. There was a police detail assigned to her residence around the clock, and Deidre promised to remain by her side the remainder of the day. Lucy's coworkers from the little café had all decided that they would take turns staying in groups with Lucy until her boyfriend returned from his fishing trip. They said it would be like an ongoing slumber party.

Nick called Chief Mercer to give him the update regarding their new lead so that he could put out a statewide BOLO (Be on the Lookout) for an older model white pickup truck with a camper shell and a Grateful Dead sticker in the back window.

That night, back in Juneau, Sam turned off the nightstand light on her side of the bed but left the other side on, as well as the light in the bathroom with the door partly closed, then drifted off to sleep. In the living room, Nick had set up camp on the couch so that he could be near if she needed him.

Flipping on the television, he fell asleep almost as soon as his head hit the pillow.

Just before two in the morning, Sam began to thrash about. She awoke with a jolt. Sitting straight up in bed, she grabbed at her chest. She felt damp all over as sweat soaked through her shorts and T-shirt.

Seconds later, Nick came through the doorway, his gun drawn. Sam realized that she must have called out in her sleep. The light wooden door banged loudly against the wall and bounced back as he stopped it with his foot. Nick looked startled, trying to ascertain what had happened, while Murphy wasted no time jumping onto the bed and sticking his cold, wet nose into Sam's face.

"I'm sorry, Nick," Sam apologized, feeling embarrassed for waking them yet again in the middle of the night.

"What happened?" he asked, stepping further into the room.

Lowering his eyes, Nick noticed that the bed looked more comfortable than the couch he'd been curled up on. He walked over, sat on the edge, and saw the sweat on her damp forehead. Then he propped up a pillow and positioned himself next to her, leaning back against the headboard. "We are just glad that it was a nightmare and not the real thing," he said, carefully placing his gun on the nightstand before crossing his legs and then his arms over his chest. "We've got your back, partner," he added as he closed his eyes.

Sam gave him a grateful look before settling down and throwing an arm over Murphy, who had positioned himself between her and Nick. "You two are the best partners a girl could ask for."

"I come in with my gun drawn, ready to kill for you, but Murphy's the hero here?" Taking a deep breath to slow down his own racing heart, Nick reached to turn off the nightstand light. "Goodnight, Sam."

"Thank you." She sighed softly, her eyes already closed when she reached out a hand, resting it on his thigh. "I don't know what I would do without you."

The next morning, Sam awoke before Nick, her arm now around Murphy's side. She silently climbed out of bed, careful not to wake Nick, and went to the bathroom. The memory of her earlier nightmare still haunted her. It was always the same terrible dream—instead of fighting back ten years ago, she was too paralyzed with fear and taken by that awful man. His hands gripped her neck, choking her to death. Everything had felt so real; the memory of it chilled her to the bone, even in the light of day.

Sam was scared. She freely admitted that fact to herself. And yet, how could she do her job effectively and be expected to catch a serial killer if she felt petrified?

Splashing cold water on her face, she stepped into the shower to wash the dried sweat from her skin. She leaned her head against the cool tiles and let the hot water roll over her back and neck.

Thirty minutes later, Sam stepped out of the bathroom with a towel wrapped around her. Nick and Murphy were no longer asleep in her bed and she poked her head outside her bedroom door to listen for them.

"Nick?" she called, but there was no answer. His bedroom door stood wide open, and the room was empty. An involuntary shiver traveled up her spine. "Keep it together," she told herself out loud.

After getting dressed in black jeans, a white button-down shirt, and boots, she dried her hair and put it up in a high ponytail. When Sam was fastening her gun and holster to her right hip, Nick and Murphy appeared in her doorway with two cups of coffee and breakfast.

"About last night..." Nick began. "Do you want to share anything with me?"

Looking away, Sam forced a pleasant smile to her lips before turning to face Nick. "No, not really."

"Don't you think that your nightmares are a manifestation of something bigger and that you should talk to someone about them?"

"I'm fine, Nick. This guy just has me spooked. I'm seeing shadows in the dark where there aren't any. That's all. Nothing more, nothing less."

"If you say so. But if it were me, I'd swallow my pride and talk to someone before it gets out of hand."

"But I'm not you and you don't know what you're talking about. Besides, I've talked to plenty of shrinks. The only thing that will help me at this point is catching this guy. I will talk with someone just as soon as this case is wrapped up, I promise." But in Sam's mind, she wasn't so sure she would ever be fine again. And if the bigwigs back home knew that the shrink needed a shrink, they would laugh her out of the Bureau.

Forty-five minutes later they walked into a hub of commotion inside the precinct.

Nick leaned over the desk of Sergeant Neil and asked, "What's going on, Officer?"

"They found an abandoned older white Ford pickup truck with a body in it. It was torched," Sergeant Neil informed them as his desk phone rang. "They're waiting for the vehicle to cool off enough to remove the body."

"Where did they find the burned-out truck?" Sam asked before he could answer the call, her mind racing.

"In a wooded park area just outside of Seward. It looked like it had a camper shell on it. Now, if you'll excuse me."

Sam was already headed for Chief Mercer's office when Nick and Murphy caught up to her. "Where are you going in such a big hurry?"

"It's not him," Sam blurted out.

"Who?" Nick asked as Sam gave a cursory tap on the chief's door before they entered.

Sitting behind his desk with the phone pressed to his ear, the chief waved them in. "Thank you so much, and let me know as soon as there are any updates," he said to the person on the other end before hanging up. "Did you hear the good news?" His broad smile signaled his pleasure.

"It's not him." Sam's insistent tone left no room for argument as the chief's smile left his face.

"What do you mean, it's not him? How can you know this before forensics—?"

"I'm telling you, it's not him," Sam said.

"Then who the hell is that poor bastard who's been roasted in the vehicle?" Chief Mercer shouted, getting to his feet and leaning forward on his desk.

"I can't say for sure," Sam quickly answered, "but one thing I can tell you with certainty—our killer didn't commit suicide."

"Now, how can you know that for sure, Agent Stevens?" Chief Mercer came around the desk to stand toe-to-toe with Sam. "Maybe he felt the long arm of the law closing in on him."

"Not likely," she replied, as if it were a foregone conclusion. "Our killer is a narcissist. He values his own life too much. Let's check to see if there are any police officers or park rangers that haven't reported in yet. Or maybe some unfortunate tourist, in the wrong place at the wrong time." Then, with a shake of her head, she continued, "I know just as sure as I am standing here in front of you, Chief Mercer, *that* isn't our killer in the burned-out truck. It is someone else, and our killer is still on the run."

Chief Mercer raked a shaky hand through his hair, leaving it looking disheveled and messy. He took a deep breath, allowing his bulk to land in the nearest chair with a disgruntled sigh. "How certain are you about this, Agent Stevens?"

"I would bet my life on it, Chief," she said as she held his gaze.

Mercer placed his head into his hands and shook it. The stress of the manhunt was wearing on him. "I'm not as young as I used to be."

"Did you get any sleep last night, Chief?" Nick asked with concern.

Mercer merely shook his head no.

"Why don't you go home, kiss your wife, take a shower, and have a quick nap," Nick suggested. "You look like hell."

"We'll put out an all-points alert to be on the lookout for our suspect," Sam added. "In the meantime, we will check in with the other agencies to see if anyone has gone MIA. We will also put out an alert to be on the lookout for any tourists who missed a check-in or didn't return their rental car. Chances are, he is trying to throw us off his trail to buy more time."

"Stevens, McLeroy, you had better be right about this one. I'm getting very tired of the runaround," the chief said, slowly getting to his feet.

"We understand, sir," Sam answered. "He's on the run, and hopefully he makes a mistake—"

"Is that before or after he drops another body into our laps?"

"Fingers crossed, before, sir."

"And Stevens?"

"Yes, sir?"

"When I return from kissing my wife, I want some good news."

"We will do our best, sir." Sam looked at the chief with all seriousness. "But as you know, this is a manhunt, and everything is very fluid."

"Good news, Stevens," the chief called over his shoulder while waving farewell.

"Yes, sir. Good news," Sam called after him, turning to her partner with a sigh. "That man doesn't have the stomach for this sort of thing."

"I'm not sure if I do, either," Nick said.

CHAPTER SIXTEEN

This Is Not an Exact Science

A TENSE FIVE HOURS PASSED without any new information. They were no closer to identifying the body in the burnt-out truck when Chief Mercer returned at noon.

Their first break of the day came that afternoon as Nick and Sam were sitting at the conference room table spit balling ideas. A report came across the wire regarding a Seward Forest Ranger's work vehicle being discovered abandoned at Ocean View Park in Anchorage.

"We need to find out if there are any stolen vehicles reported in the immediate vicinity," Nick insisted.

Sam stood and walked over to the map. "He's adapting and changing." She scratched her head in concentration and then picked up a pushpin and stuck it in the map in Anchorage.

She was marking every place they believed The Magician Killer to have been.

"But he's moving away from Juneau," Chief Mercer pointed out. "I thought you said that he would come back this way."

"When dealing with a dissociative personality, there is no exact science, Chief Mercer," Sam interjected. "But we told you already that when he gets cornered, he could strike out. Unfortunately, some young stranger was the closest thing in range. For now, we can only wait and see what he does next," Sam said, throwing her hands in the air. "He may simply be playing us, leading us around by the nose ring, so to speak, and away from his true target."

"Which is?" Mercer asked.

"Me." She turned to look directly at him. "It's obvious, by the victims that he's chosen, that he has been killing 'me' over and over again for the last ten years. You can bet he won't lose his focus so easily."

"What in the holy name of our Lord are you talking about, Agent Stevens, and why are we allowing you to stick your neck out this way? You are going to end up dead, and it will be on my conscience," Mercer bellowed.

Quickly closing the door to the conference room so they could have privacy, Nick came to Sam's defense. "Sir, if you would allow her to explain without losing your temper—"

"If someone doesn't start talking, and I mean fast, you are going to see more than my temper being lost," Mercer said, looking between the two agents.

"Sir, I can explain," Sam said as she looked at the chief nervously. "When I was nineteen, I was attacked by a man on my way home from work."

"Yes, you told me all of that."

"And we also told you that the man I fought off was potentially our current unsub," Sam added.

The chief raised his voice. "Yes, you said it was a possibility, but not a probability."

"Sir, before, it was just speculation, but the killer hasn't corrected us."

"So?"

"So, that means we are no longer speculating," Nick interjected.

"Since at this point the killer hasn't corrected us regarding the picture, it means we are on the right trail. So, we must be dealing with the same man who attacked me. And," she said holding up a finger to make a point, "it now seems possible that because I thwarted his efforts in such a devastating way, he began acting out, killing women. Or, in this instance, me, over and over again. And he won't stop these killings until he gets what he wants or we catch him."

"Yes, but I want you to get to the part where you didn't tell me that all this time he has been killing you over and over again," the chief demanded impatiently while clearing his throat. "That's a pretty big possibility you seem to have conveniently left out in order to convince me to let you continue on this case.

"Yes, about that, sir, it is just now becoming clear that this could be his motivation," Sam clarified. "As I said, at the time it was just speculation. I wasn't exactly sure about any connection and I was worried that you would throw me off the case if the connection was confirmed."

"What makes you think I won't throw you off the case now?" Mercer said, taking a threatening step toward Sam.

"Because, sir, that would be a mistake," she insisted, taking a step closer to the chief so that now they were standing toe to toe. "And I am going to tell you why."

"Well, get on with it," the chief insisted, scowling at Sam and crossing his arms over his broad chest. "And be quick about it."

"Our UNSUB, The Magician Killer, wants only one thing, and that is to kill me, the only one that got away as far as we know."

Seeing that she was getting through to the chief, Sam stepped back a few steps and licked her lips before she continued. "When we had the news conference, we showed the killer that I was here. Basically, I was telling him to come and get me, and ever since then, he has been acting out. Hence, the change in his behavior. But this isn't necessarily a bad thing. It means he is thinking about how he is going to get to me. He's making a plan, and we have to wait."

"How can you act so calm about all of this, Sam—?" Nick caught his slip up and quickly corrected himself by clearing his throat, "*Special Agent Stevens.*"

Then, getting to his feet, he came around the table to stand next to Sam.

"Who said anything about me being calm, Special Agent McLeroy," she answered with a crisp tone before glancing over at the chief. Hastily, Sam quietly directed her words to Nick, talking out of the side of her mouth. "Inside, I'm a shaky bowl of Jell-O dessert, if you must know."

"Then say that," Nick harshly whispered. "I can't help you if you don't talk to me."

Stepping to one side to be hidden entirely from Chief Mercer's view, Sam glared at him and quietly said, "Are we really doing this now?" She craned her head in the direction of the chief, who sat on the other side of the table.

Nick gave a slight shake of his head and responded between clenched teeth. "But know this. We *will* talk about it. Later." Nick glanced over his shoulder at the chief and forced a smile as he stepped aside.

"I apologize, Chief Mercer," Sam said. "We just needed to confer a moment."

"No apologies necessary, Special Agent Stevens." The chief waved her off as he slowly got to his feet. "I get it. I had a partner once upon a time, many years ago. But that doesn't negate the fact that I have serious reservations about this case moving forward with you on it."

"And no one understands that better than me, sir. Yet the fact still remains: I still have the best chance of catching this guy!"

"I believe I have asked this before, but I will ask again. Do your superiors know about you being involved so intimately with this case?" the chief questioned.

"Well, not exactly," Nick answered.

"What my partner is trying to say, sir, is we didn't even know ourselves that I was a part of this case until we were in the middle of it. In fact, it's only the most recent updates that seem to point my way. So, to answer you transparently, if headquarters knew, I would be removed, then reprimanded, and we would most likely lose this guy. And the only problem with that is," she paused for dramatic effect, "he would go on killing. This would, in turn, cause you bad publicity, panic in the streets, loss of revenue, and more headaches..." she trailed off.

Holding up his hand to indicate that he got the picture, the chief said, "All right, all right, I get it. You take care of my rodent problem, and I will keep your secret."

"Exactly," Sam sighed, then swallowed hard.

"I've said it before, but it bears mentioning again. There had better not be any blowback on me," the chief muttered.

"No, sir," Nick replied. "We will make sure of it."

With a forced smile and a nod, Sam turned away from them both as the chief walked from the room. This case and the long hours were beginning to take their toll on everyone involved.

Nick took a deep breath and let it out slowly. "I have an errand to run. But I will be back here within an hour. Don't go anywhere without me. I'm leaving Murphy with you."

"Where are you going, Nick?" she asked, trying, yet failing, to make her voice sound casual.

"It's personal," he answered evasively. "I won't be long."

"All right." She sighed, turning back to the whiteboards and studying the map as if she could somehow predict where the killer would strike next.

The relief she felt that Chief Mercer finally knew her secrets was almost overwhelming, so she plopped down in the chair nearest her computer and, with nothing else to do, began to write up the day's reports.

An hour and twenty minutes later, Nick returned, walking into the conference room to find Sam staring at her computer and the day's report.

"I'm starving and you're twenty minutes late!"

"I thought we agreed yesterday that I was going to type up the next report," he teased, attempting to lighten the mood. Then he noticed the intent look on her face as he set a cup of coffee in front of her. "One tall latte, just the way you like it. One sugar and just a sprinkle of cinnamon."

"Thanks, you are a life saver," she replied, hitting send and closing her laptop before looking up at him. "And we did agree that it was your turn to do the report, Agent McLeroy," Sam said, with a wry grin. "But when you did not return, and I was left sitting here twiddling my thumbs, I decided to put said thumbs to better use. Besides, I didn't want to sit here half the night watching you peck out the day's reports with two fingers. It truly is quite painful to watch."

"Oh, is that so?"

"I call them as I see them."

Nick put both hands over his heart as if he were mortally wounded, then groaned, "I think that one actually hurt. I'd have you know that these fingers were fast enough to get me through school, Agent Speedy Gonzalez." Then, getting serious, he apologized, "Look, I'm sorry that my errand took longer than expected. But on a good note, I completed my task, and I am now free for the rest of the evening." Nick smiled broadly, showing off his magnificent white teeth.

Picking up the cup of coffee in front of her, Sam took a sip while giving Nick an analytical look over the rim. "So, do you care to share with the rest of the class what you were doing?"

"Not at this time," he answered, looking away. "Murphy, time to eat and stretch your legs."

Giving Nick a presumptive *humph* from deep in her throat, Sam gathered up her things and grabbed the coffee Nick had presented to her as a peace offering. "A cup of coffee will only buy you so much goodwill, Nicholas McLeroy."

Nick smiled. "I also thought that we could stretch our legs and walk back to the hotel," he informed her, attaching Murphy's leash to his harness. "Unless you're too tired."

"I could use a good walk as well. I also could run circles around you both," Sam said, her tone leaving no doubt that she was challenging him.

"Challenge accepted." Gesturing towards Sam's backpack," he continued. "I'd be happy to carry that for you even though I know you are more than capable. I'm feeling a little guilty since you did all the heavy lifting with the reports today."

"So gallant of you. But just know that that doesn't get you off the hook for doing the reports tomorrow."

"Of course not," Nick responded as he took the backpack off her shoulder and slipped it onto his back while they walked through the precinct.

Poking their heads into Chief Mercer's office on the way out, they let him know that they would be available for all updates, no matter what time it was.

Nick held the front door open for Sam. As they walked briskly back to the hotel, Nick kept glancing her way.

"Stop doing that," Sam said tersely, stopping in the middle of the sidewalk. "You're acting weird."

"I'm concerned, Sam."

"About me?" she gasped. "Save your breath, Nick. I've been taking care of myself long before you came along."

"See there, *that* is what worries me. You act as if you have to do everything yourself."

"Because I do. The only person I can completely trust or count on is myself. It's always been that way and probably will always be."

Reaching out to take her arm, Nick gently forced her to look at him. "But it doesn't have to be like that, Sam. I'm here for you." He then pointed down at Murphy. "We are both here for you. You don't have to be an island unto yourself. Some people care what happens to you."

Biting the corner of her bottom lip, Sam tried to look away, but he tenderly touched her face and pulled her back around to face him. He could see the emotions warring inside of her. "Trust me, Sam. I'm truly on your side. And I think that this is a dangerous game you are playing, using yourself as bait."

"Don't you think I know that, Nick? I'm scared all of the time."

Still holding on to her arm, Nick tilted his head to one side. "Finally, you admit it." He let out the breath he'd been holding. "I'm scared too. I'm scared for you. I'm scared that I won't be able to protect you." He dropped his hand in frustration. "Hell, I'm scared that I won't be there when he comes for you and that I will be too late to save you."

"This isn't on you," she said. "This is my mess."

"But you're wrong," he said, unable to conceal the anguish in his voice. "We made this decision together. So, technically, this is on both of us if you get yourself killed."

"No, Nick, I made this decision and talked you into it."

"Regardless of whose decision it was, we both agreed to the plan," he corrected. "I want to be there for you, but you have to let me in."

Tears sprang to her eyes. "All right, Nick."

"All right, Nick, what?" he asked, his voice softening. "Does that mean that you will tell me what's going on? Or is this just lip service, and, in the end, you will attempt to go it alone, regardless of what I say?"

Shaking her head, Sam gave him a half smile. "You think you know me so well, don't you," she challenged, as she took a second to continue speaking because of the lump in her throat. She licked her lips then said, "It means I will keep you in the loop." She reached down and scratched Murphy behind the ear. "You too, mister."

Looking up at Nick, she cleared her throat. "Now, can we continue back to our home away from home? I'm starving."

Nick nodded. "Of course, but on our way back I want to stop off at this new place I spotted today. I'm getting bored with the same thing for dinner every night. It's beginning to wear on me," he added. "How about you? Are you up for a little adventure?"

"Definitely!"

CHAPTER SEVENTEEN

The Amulet

NICK AND MURPHY HAD TAKEN UP residence in Sam's bedroom each night since they seemed to end up there anyway because of her night terrors. Waking from a restless sleep, Sam sat straight up in bed and shook Nick. "I know what he's doing," she cried out, startling Nick awake.

Nick looked around, sitting up and immediately reaching for his gun on the nightstand. "Who's doing what?"

"Put that away," she said, flipping on the nightstand light and nearly blinding Nick in the process. She continued, "I think I know what he's doing."

"What the hell are you talking about?" he asked sleepily, looking over at his phone to see what time it was while putting his gun back on top of his nightstand. "It's five-fif-teen in the morning, Sam—"

"I figured out what he's doing," she repeated, sitting in bed cross-legged.

Murphy jumped up from his resting spot in the corner of the room and came over to the bed to see what was going on.

"Did you even go to sleep last night?" Nick asked before yawning loudly.

"Yes, of course, I slept." She thought for a minute and then recanted. "Well, maybe I slept last night. This is usually when I get my best work done. Now get yourself up and ready. We have to see if I'm right," Sam demanded, jumping out of bed and grabbing fresh clothes as she headed for the bathroom. She turned back around when she reached the bathroom door. "Well? Why aren't you moving?"

He sat up, throwing his legs over the side of the bed. "Sam? Seriously?" Nick called out to her in his groggy voice, holding his head in his hands. "Can't this wait another hour or two?" he pleaded. But Sam had already shut the door and turned on the shower. "You could have at least invited me to shower with you to save time," he mumbled.

Thirty minutes later they were headed out the door and over to the police station. There, Sam grabbed the first of-ficer she saw on duty. "What's your name, officer?" she en-quired of the strikingly handsome young Native American in his early twenties.

"Officer Brooks, ma'am," he replied quickly. "Steven Brooks."

"Well, Officer Steven Brooks, I need a report of any activity regarding our case ASAP," she said as politely as she could before continuing to the conference room.

Closing the conference room door behind them, Nick let Murphy off his leash. "When are you going to tell me exactly what is rattling around in that head of yours?"

A minute later, Officer Brooks flashed the report in his hand as he knocked on the glass door, then opened it and handed the pages to Sam. "Will there be anything further, ma'am?"

"No," she said, then changed her mind as he turned to leave. "Just a minute, Officer Brooks. I do have one request. Don't call me 'ma'am.' It makes me feel old. Agent Stevens or Sam will do."

"Yes, ma'am...I mean, thank you, Agent Stevens. I will endeavor to remember that." And with a respectful nod, he left.

Waiting impatiently since there was only one report between them, Nick asked, "Well? Share with the class?"

Looking up at Nick with a smile, Sam turned the page as she walked over to the board. "Look who didn't get enough sleep last night and is a bit grumpy this morning," she teased while she began sticking pins in the map at Fairbanks and Delta Junction.

"You wake me up at the butt crack of dawn, keep me in the dark about what is going on, and then wonder why I am crabby."

"I will be sure to tuck you in extra early tonight so that you can catch up on your beauty sleep."

Flopping into a chair, Nick sighed loudly. "Does that come with a bedtime story and a back rub? Because frankly, I would really like to get more than three hours of uninterrupted sleep for a change."

"I'm sorry, Nick. When I close my eyes, I see—"

"What do you see, Sam?"

"This case has awakened some unexpected demons from my past. And they don't seem to sleep very much. It's to the point that I don't even want to close my eyes."

Feeling like a cad for complaining, Nick came over to stand next to her, taking Sam's hand in his. "I'm sorry, Sam."

"I'm not interrupting anything, am I? I heard you were in early," Chief Mercer said, stepping into the room.

Sam flushed slightly, stepping away from Nick and flashing a smile. "No, sir. And thank you for joining us." She watched Nick take a seat. "I think I know what our suspect is up to. The Magician Killer, I mean."

"So, spill it," Mercer insisted, sitting next to Nick across the table from the whiteboards.

Turning to the map, Sam pointed out the place where the suspect's white pickup truck was found torched with a body in it just outside of Seward. Then she pointed to the push-pin where the ranger's work truck was found in Anchorage. Finally, she indicated the push-pins she had just added where their suspect had been possibly sighted at Delta Junction and Fairbanks.

"In the past ten years, our UNSUB has managed to remain under the radar. Yet, in the last two days, he has meticulously led us on a merry chase as if he were leaving us a trail of breadcrumbs to follow. Why do you think that is, Agent McLeroy?" she asked.

"He's rattled," Nick answered.

"He's gotten sloppy," Mercer chimed in.

Shaking her head, Sam slapped the board. "No, I don't think so. He's meticulous about everything he does and plans each move to the last detail."

"So, what is he doing?" Nick asked. "Why is he so public now?"

"Maybe to your eyes he seems like he's rattled," Sam replied. "But everything he is doing is deliberate and well planned out. He is leading us where he wants us to go. And excuse my saying so, but it's like a magic show. The illusionist directs your eyes to where he wants you to look while he manipulates the act and pulls a rabbit out of the hat."

Scratching his head, Chief Mercer asked, "So, where is he leading us?"

"Away from here," Sam answered quite simply, as if it should have been obvious to everyone in the room.

"Ah! Now I see what's happening. He's distracting us," Mercer answered.

"Exactly! The more he distracts us, the more we chase our tails, and the less we are looking into him. If he can keep us busy enough, following up on all of the obvious moves he's making, we will have less time to investigate what he isn't showing us."

"So, what are you suggesting?" Nick asked.

"We put out the word that no officer, sheriff, highway patrolman, or forest ranger be allowed to patrol the streets on his or her own. Everyone will double up," Sam insisted. "And that is not simply a suggestion, sir. It is a must. He will be looking for vulnerabilities, and we cannot give him any."

"Done," Mercer said. "What else?"

"This may hurt tourism for a while, but we also need to remind the public that we have a manhunt going on here and they need to be vigilant and aware of their surroundings at all times. Hotel, motel, and Airbnb managers need to make sure they immediately report any late or missing people and be on the lookout for any strange occurrences."

"I will reach out to the newspaper wires and news outlets and inform them. Anything else?"

Lieutenant O'Rourke tapped on the glass, causing everyone to look in his direction before he opened the door. "Sir, *Anchorage Daily News* received a letter from our guy and they have apparently printed it." He presented the chief with a copy of the newswire.

Chief Mercer took the paper and read it silently to himself.

"It seems he likes the moniker 'The Magician Killer' because he signed the letter as such. He goes on to say that he objects to us saying that he is sexually motivated. Claims that he has never sexually assaulted any girls and that he's not a pedophile."

"This is good. He's correcting the narrative," Sam mused out loud, sitting down in the chair across the table from Nick and Chief Mercer. "Being thought of as someone who is crazy is a weakness in his eyes. The mere thought of his name being associated with being a predator is intolerable to him. Public image is everything to our killer and he won't allow his good name to be tarnished or sullied with such terms. We can work with this." She brought her eyes up to look at the two men. "He was quick to right the wrong when the media got that incorrect, in his eyes."

"But why take the time and possibly expose himself by contacting the newspaper?" Nick asked, sitting up a little straighter in his chair.

"Is he simply getting off on the media publicity or the killings?" Chief Mercer added.

"It could be both," Sam stated. "When he kidnaps the girls, it's foreplay—the actual killings are the sexual acts. The media coverage is his reputation. It's all psychosexual in nature. He's an organized sexual predator with psychotic propensities. And, he thinks he's too smart to get caught."

"So, what do we do next? " Chief Mercer asked.

"Communicating with the media and controlling the narrative is about control to him. It's all a fantasy...and he is the puppet master." Sam surmised. "So...*we take away his control.*"

Both men looked at her.

Sam smiled wickedly. "We inform the media that our Magician Killer is really just some Joe Blow who likes to kill. By taking back the narrative, we take away his control. It will make him crazy. Well, crazier," she mused out loud while her mind was busy forming a plan.

Mercer sat back in his chair. "It's that simple?"

Sam nodded. "It's that simple. He has this bigger-than-life persona—stories he tells himself to make the killings palatable. But really, he's just some guy who likes to kill innocent women. He's created this person in his mind, someone who wronged him, and most likely, he's personified that person as me."

"Won't this simply enrage him and send him on a killing spree?" Nick pointed out. "Do we really want to load that gun and point it at the public?"

"Maybe, but on the other hand, we might just throw him off his game enough to cause him to slip up."

Shaking his head, the chief got to his feet and looked down at them both. "I can't say that I have much experience with these types of cases. So, I will do the only thing I know how to do, and that is leave the case and figuring out in the hands of the two of you. I will go along with it, but I don't have to like it."

Looking up at the chief with sympathy, Sam nodded. "I understand, sir."

"Well, I will leave the two of you to craft the perfect rebuttal for The Magician Killer. Let me know when it's ready and I will call Joyce Fredricks over at the *Juneau Empire*. She will make sure that it makes it into tonight's news feed. I'm sure that all of the other affiliates will pick it up as well. This crap is big news around here."

"Thank you, sir," Nick said as Mercer left the room.

Then Nick looked at Sam and said, "Well, I'll leave you to it."

"Whoa! Hold up there," Sam exclaimed. "Where do you think you're going, Special Agent McLeroy?"

"I just figured that you would need a little peace and quiet to craft the perfect rebuttal," he said with a smile.

"*We*," she indicated by gesturing between them, "will be crafting the perfect rebuttal together. That means you and me."

"You want my help?"

"Of course I want your help. I read your file. You are the master at crafting press releases."

"Oh, that," he said sheepishly.

"You get started, and I'll put on the coffee. It's going to be a long day."

"Sam, before I forget, I have something for you." Nick pulled a box from his pocket. "When I was younger, I, too, had nightmares. That's when my grandmother gave me a bracelet, an Obsidian Orgone stone, and the Tree of Life talisman inside a shiny amulet." He showed her his multi-stranded leather bracelet and medallion as he handed her a box. "Open it up."

Inside the box was an Obsidian Orgone necklace with a Tree of Life amulet hanging from a leather strap. "It's beautiful, Nick. But why did you get this for me?"

Taking it out of the box, he stepped behind her and fastened the clasp. "It stands for your past and future and helps you face your inner demons. It also shields you from the negativity of the outside world. I just thought it would bring you luck and maybe some strength. But only if you never take it off. That is the key," he said, turning her to face him. "Understand?"

Nodding her head, Sam lifted the amulet in her hand and took a closer look. "That means a lot to me. I promise to keep it on, except in the shower, of course."

"Of course," he smiled broadly.

The two of them worked on the press release for several hours to ensure that the wording was exactly right before handing it over to Chief Mercer.

Lunch was brought in as they poured over new incident reports and missing person reports, and finally, retraced the killer's steps to be sure that they didn't miss anything.

As night fell, they grabbed any new missing person reports before heading out for the evening. They would pick up dinner to take back with them and finish the day's reports from the comfort of their hotel room.

CHAPTER EIGHTEEN

The Killer Strikes Again

H E FELT THE HAIR ON THE BACK of his neck prickle. He was angry, there was no denying that. Things were getting out of his control.

This last ranger had caught him by surprise while sleeping in the front seat of his pickup truck in the middle of a wooded area. He had intended to just take a short nap, so he didn't even bother to use the camper space in the back.

At first, he thought he would be able to talk his way out of the entire thing by spinning some ridiculous story about his wife kicking him out of the house. But then the young ranger had to ask for his identification. When he said that he'd forgotten to take it with him on his way out the door, the young ranger insisted that he step out of his vehicle.

That had been the beginning of the end for Ranger Cody Martin. He caught the young man by surprise, knocking him to the ground with his vehicle door as he exited the truck. Then the two of them struggled, tussling about on the ground for a minute or two before he managed to hit Ranger Martin in the head with a rock, knocking him unconscious.

How fortunate for me, he thought to himself. *He really is a nice-looking young man—the outdoorsy, rugged type. How could he have been so naive, letting me get the drop on him like that?* He mentally chastised the young officer as he dragged him into the white Ford, maneuvering the young ranger into the driver's seat and cuffing him to the steering wheel, all the while plotting how he could turn this change of events to his advantage.

Going through the man's personal belongings, he pulled out a picture of a pretty young woman from his wallet, just as Ranger Cody Martin came to.

The ranger began to struggle, suddenly aware of his situation as he tried to free his hands. The killer was pleased to no end by the wild-eyed look on his face.

"What the hell are you doing?" Ranger Martin yelled, trying to sound intimidating before he looked closer at the man who had taken him prisoner. "You're *him*, aren't you?" he cried, immediately regretting that he hadn't run the plates or called the vehicle in before approaching it. *How could he have been so stupid?* He suddenly felt truly afraid for the first time in his life. "Hey, man..." he began to say, licking his suddenly dry, parched lips. Then he realized that the man sitting next to him held a picture of his girlfriend.

"She's pretty," the killer said, shoving the picture into the ranger's face.

"I won't report this incident. I swear it," the ranger pleaded. "You drive away and I won't tell anyone I saw you. Just don't kill me. I'm supposed to get married in two weeks. Please, man."

A wicked smile crossed the killer's face when he smelled that familiar acrid stench of fear. It caused an air of excitement to course through his blood. Suddenly, he felt that tingle that he'd only felt from his female victims. Could it be true? Yes! He felt the excitement building, and he wanted to explore that response further, but he told himself he would take his time with this one. Slow and painful. That would do the trick.

"We are going to play a little game. You tell me what I want to know and I won't hurt you. But if you don't tell me what I want to know," he warned, pulling out a large hunting knife from his glove box, "I will have to punish you."

"Wait, wait, wait!" the ranger screamed. "We don't have to resort to this. I'll tell you whatever you want to know."

"Very good," he crooned, as his mirth and pleasure only increased with his victim's growing fear. "What's her name?" he asked, shoving the picture closer to the ranger's face.

Licking his lips, Cody knew her name was on the back of the picture so that he couldn't lie. "Julie. Her name is Julie."

With a nod, the killer acted impressed, but really, he was winding up to ask the really tough questions. The kind of questions no man in his right mind would answer about the woman he loved.

"What's she like in bed?" He narrowed his eyes as if he were analyzing everything about the man, from his breathing to the sweat running down the side of his face.

Gripping the steering wheel with both hands, Cody could feel the blood drain from his face and tears pool at the back of his eyes. "Why do you want to know about that?" he asked.

"Wrong answer," the man yelled, immediately slicing his victim's upper arm and laughing when Ranger Martin screamed out in pain.

"Wait!" Cody screamed as he tried to get his fear under control.

"I really like this game," the killer said. "Don't you really like this game, Ranger Martin?"

Turning in his seat as much as he could with his hands bound to the steering wheel, Cody was having a hard time breathing. He knew he was hyperventilating, but he couldn't stop the fear from taking over.

"Oh," the killer said, faking sympathy but unable to hide his sarcasm. "Maybe we should try a simpler question. What do you say?"

"Yes, yes, that would be better," Cody agreed.

"You said you and Julie are getting married in a couple of weeks?"

"Yes, yes," Cody nervously answered, nodding his head to hide the fact that his entire body was shaking.

"Does she live with you?" he asked coolly, pulling out the Ranger's wallet and looking at his driver's license.

All the life's blood drained from Cody's face as he realized that this madman had his address and knew where he lived.

"Could I call her to say goodbye?" Cody pleaded. "Please, man. I need to hear her voice one last time."

"I'm not an unreasonable man," the killer said. Once again, a wicked smile played across his full lips. "Sure. Why not? But first, tell me where the keys to your truck are."

With questioning eyes, Cody hesitantly pointed with his chin to indicate his right pant pocket. Reaching into the pocket, the killer sensed the ranger's raw fear and, with it, his own familiar pleasurable tingling response. Prolonging the sensations and the building excitement, his fingers searched for the keys and slid them out ever so slowly.

"Should we make that phone call now?" he said, smiling slyly before making eye contact with the ranger.

Cody nodded his head. It was too late to save his own life, but at least he could make sure that Julie, the love of his life, was safe.

"What is the code to get in?"

"It's a fingerprint. If you will bring the phone closer," the ranger said, raising the pointer finger of his right hand.

Using the man's finger, the killer opened the screen and pushed the phone icon. A picture of Cody and Julie popped up as the background picture. "Oh, what a lovely couple," he purred. "It's such a shame." He found Julie's name atop the Favorites and pushed the dial button.

Then, pushing the speaker on, he held the phone close to Cody's mouth and scooted next to the ranger so that he could also hear everything being said.

"Cody?" Julie answered. "What are you doing calling me in the middle of your shift? Is everything all right? Are you hurt?" she asked, sounding concerned.

"No, baby," Cody replied. "I just needed to hear your voice." His own voice warbled a bit and he had to take a deep breath to calm himself.

"Oh, Cody, honey, that is just so sweet. But something is wrong. I can hear it in your voice, baby."

"No, I'm fine, honey," Cody quickly lied. "Are you still at your mom's?" He tried to keep the emotion from his tone as he sucked in the air sharply, trying desperately not to cry.

"Oh, Cody. Are you missing me?" she sighed. "I was missing you too. I can come over later if—"

"No!" Cody said, sounding harsher than he intended.

"Cody, what's wrong?" Julie asked again, her voice cracking with emotion.

"Nothing, baby. I need you to promise me that you'll stay put at your momma's and not come over," Cody insisted, his tone more forceful than usual. "Promise me, honey."

"Well, all right. I promise, Cody."

Cody could no longer keep his emotions under control. His voice cracked as he blurted out, "I love you so much, Julie. You have been the only woman for me." A sob escaped his lips as the killer skillfully pulled the sharp hunting knife across the ranger's throat, cutting just deep enough to ensure a slow, agonizing death.

A sharp gasp of pain was the last thing Julie ever heard.

"Cody?" Julie cried. "Cody, answer me, baby." Then the killer ended the call.

"Oh, naughty, naughty," the man taunted, pulling the phone away from Cody's mouth. "You did not play the game right, Ranger Cody Martin. Such a shame, too."

CHAPTER NINETEEN

Emotions Running High

SAM STOOD OUTSIDE the conference room to make a call to the local police station at Fort Yukon and asked to speak with the police chief.

"Yes, sir. I'm Special Agent Sam Stevens of the FBI. I need you to put a protection detail on the Griffin home." She paused and listened before continuing, cutting off the police chief. "Yes, I want twenty-four-seven..." Her tone sounded slightly irritable to her own ears. "Until the Magician Killer is caught. That's how long. I realize we are not certain that this murder is tied to the Magician Killer as of yet, but we need to err on the side of caution..." She took a deep breath and counted to three in her mind before she spoke again. "No, sir... well, I'm going to have to insist. I have spoken with the girlfriend and she was on the line with Ranger Cody when he was killed. She is scared and heartbroken. I believe we owe it to Ranger Cody Martin to protect her. Thank you. You have a very nice day as well."

Letting out a disgruntled breath, Sam stepped back into the room and walked over to the whiteboards, adding the newest victim, Ranger Cody Martin, to their ever-growing roster. Shaking her head, she was beginning to doubt herself. Maybe she wasn't as smart as she thought she was. Trying to throw the killer off his game was a risky move at best, and it had resulted in another death—precisely what she had hoped to prevent. It seemed the only person who was off his or her game was her.

Chief Mercer walked in, placing crime scene pictures down in front of Sam and spreading them out. "These just came in from Fort Yukon."

The macabre photos visibly shook Sam, causing her to wince and turn away. The body still handcuffed to the steering wheel of the vehicle upset her the most.

"By the position of the mouth, it looks as if he may have been alive when the truck was set ablaze," she quietly said to Nick. "Forensics said he fought so hard to escape that he broke his left arm trying to get out."

Placing her twitching hand behind her back, Sam blew out a weary breath before addressing the two men. "Up until now all evidence has indicated that he's deliberate and his actions are well thought out. Now, because of his actions over the last two days, it's obvious the killer's escalating. We would typically call this acting out. He is likely angry because we outed him on national television."

Nick gave Sam the strangest look, and she wondered if he had seen her hand shaking moments before as she hung the ranger's photo.

"Then, was that truly the best move for us to have made?" Chief Mercer asked. "The press conference and all." The chief leaned back in his chair, crossing his arms over his chest.

"Now, hold on a moment," Nick said, jumping to Sam's defense. "There was no way of knowing this would be the outcome."

"I thought the two of you were supposed to be some kind of experts at this stuff," Mercer fired back, his tone critical as he sat forward in his seat now, pointing a finger at Sam specifically.

Murphy jumped to attention by Nick's side, feeling the immediate rising tension in the room. Nick placed a hand on the dog's head and signaled him to stand down.

"Again, Chief Mercer, there is no way to absolutely predict how someone will react to outside pressures—especially a madman like our killer," she repeated. "And we did say that he could react by acting out."

"Well then, I suggest the two of you figure this mess out, and quickly. Because a good man is lying in the morgue who gave his life because of what we did." He scooted his chair back with a loud scraping noise and quickly got to his feet.

"Honestly, I don't know how much more of this I can stand," he grumbled as he left the room.

As the ghastly crime scene photos invaded Sam's mind, the room suddenly felt stifling. She felt as if she were suffocating, unable to breathe, as if someone had sucked all the air from around her. The chief was right. Ranger Martin's death had been senseless, and Sam couldn't help feeling that somehow it was all her fault.

Sam could no longer hide the fact that her hand was trembling. In addition, she heard ringing in her ears. She knew it was only a matter of time before... "Put a pin in the map at Fort Yukon, would you please?" she said, using every ounce of self-control to calmly set the papers down on the conference room table as she headed for the door. She desperately needed to get out of that room and breathe some fresh air before she embarrassed herself by throwing up.

Using a measured voice to hide her emotions, Sam told the others, "I need some air. I'm just going to take a walk," as she left the room.

"Sam!" Nick called to her as she rushed out of the room.

Nick quickly attached Murphy's leash to his harness and then pursued his distraught partner.

Sam was already out the precinct door and partway down the block as he rushed to push open the door.

"Sam, wait!" Nick shouted, but Sam kept walking quickly, as if someone was hot on her trail.

Sam had no idea where she was headed. All she knew was that she had to get out of that conference room and away from this madness for a moment or she would go insane.

By the time Nick and Murphy managed to catch up with her, she had put several blocks between her and the station. Tears shimmered in her eyes.

"You are having a panic attack, Sam. You need to breathe," he insisted, trying to catch his breath after frantically chasing her down.

Sam acted as if she hadn't heard him, so Nick gently pushed her up against a building and shielded her from the view of any passersby. "Sam! Didn't you hear me calling you? Why didn't you stop?" He gave her a slight shake, and her prior clouded eyes looked directly at him.

"Let go of me," she demanded, yanking her arm out of his grasp.

"I'm sorry, Sam. I was just worried about you. Where are you going?" he asked, gripping her arm tighter as she attempted to shake him off. "What are you doing?"

"You are hurting me, Nick. Let go of me!"

Letting go and suddenly feeling bad for manhandling her, Nick took a breath and ran a hand through his hair. "I'm sorry, Sam. Please forgive me. I was just worried. What happened back there?"

"I don't know!" Sam sobbed. "I don't know. It's all such a..." She searched for the right word.

"Mess," Nick said sympathetically, finishing her sentence.

She nodded. "I would have used a stronger word, but yes."

Sam leaned her backside against the wall as she bent forward at the waist and placed her hands on her knees, trying to catch her breath. Nick pulled her up against him, and she stiffened for a moment before melding into him.

"This can't be my life," she sighed. "This can't be all that becomes of it."

"It's all going to work out." He held her close. "You're just tired. You have been going at this without much sleep for days."

"I never cry," she said as tears fell on his shoulder. "Never! And that's all I've wanted to do for days," she hiccupped, unable to catch a good breath of air. "I'm losing control, Nick. I'm losing control," she whispered into his shoulder.

Spotting a nearby bench, Nick pulled Sam over to it. "Take a seat," he said. "Hold your arms over your head and take a deep breath." When she sat there glaring at him from the side, he reached down to help lift her hands into the air. "Really, it helps. I swear to you. My little sister used to have panic attacks all the time. You will thank me later," he assured her.

Feeling completely foolish, Sam continued to hold her arms in the air, following his instructions, breathing in through her mouth and out through her nose. She knew this to be an expert way of handling an overanxious person, but she had never had anyone do it to her.

"That's it, Sam. You've got this."

She did this several more times until she was no longer hyperventilating. Sam nodded her head. "You were right; I feel better. Can we forget this ever happened?"

"No way. I intend to hold this over your head for the rest of your life," he joked. "Let's get you cleaned up, Stevens. And I'll buy you a drink."

Sam followed Nick into the nearest bar and headed straight for the washroom to scrub her face clean of tears and mascara streaks.

"I ordered you a red wine and a tequila shot," he said when she rejoined him at the end of the bar. Licking the back of his hand before shaking a bit of salt on it, Nick cleared his throat. "Here's to catching the Magician Killer before he catches us," he said, then downed his shot of tequila before licking the salt off and biting into a wedge of lime.

Sam followed his lead, emitting a satisfying groan when she was done. "Another round," she called out to the barkeep.

"Whoa now, slow down there, partner. We still have to maintain a semblance of professionalism. What happens if we suddenly get called back to work?"

"A liquid dinner never hurt anyone," she shot back, giving Nick a large smile. "Just one more, and then I will drink my red wine like a good girl. I might even manage to eat a hamburger and some fries before we go back to the hotel suite because I am definitely done for the day," she added defiantly, picking up the new shot of tequila and downing it.

"Why do you think he did it?" he asked, catching Sam by surprise.

"What?"

"I said, why do you think he did it? You know, kill that young ranger?"

Turning to face Nick, Sam took a moment to gather her thoughts before speaking. A sad look crossed her furrowed brows. "We think of motive in a rational perspective: passion, greed, fear, jealousy, revenge, and money. But when you are dealing with a mental defect like our killer, he doesn't have rational motives. What drives him is different than what drives a normal human being. It is difficult to pinpoint his profound contempt for human life."

Sam wrinkled up her nose as if something distasteful had soured her stomach. "He appears to be meticulous in his calculation and with every move he makes, and yet, this one seems different. It is possible that this murder occurred because he was surprised by the ranger and didn't have time to plan his actions. After all, this was the first male that we know of. It seems like he's evolving as the situation changes.

"There are a lot of moving parts here. It's almost as if, well...if someone tugged at the right loose thread, the entire woven tapestry would come apart."

Nick pondered her words. "It sounds to me as if you are suggesting that we tug at a loose thread."

"Maybe. But we must be careful about which loose thread we decide to pull at," Sam mused as lines etched across her face. She pondered over the death of Ranger Martin and what tugging at a thread had already cost him and his young bride-to-be. Sam could not take that decision back, no matter how much she wanted to.

They slipped into a booth, ordered, and ate dinner, feeding Murphy scraps under the table. For just a few welcome minutes, Sam forgot that they were FBI agents stalking a mass murderer who had been killing women for a decade. She even forgot about the horrific details in the most recent crime scene report.

Nick got the bill and they both stood up to leave when Sam's phone rang. She saw the caller ID and her entire countenance changed.

"Special Agent Stevens," she answered. "Yes, sir—No, sir." Her voice remained measured and even in tone. "I was about to—Sir, I can explain." She paused, listening for a full thirty seconds before answering again. "No, sir, but I—Yes, of course. No, of course not, sir—I don't understand—No, sir. That will not be necessary."

There was another long pause, and then she exploded, "Jameson Scott! That hack? Why would you send him?" She suddenly lowered her voice to a quiet whisper as her face flushed red with fury. "I understand. Yes, sir, it has become national news. But I am certain—No, sir, I am not being insubordinate—Loud and clear, sir," she finally said before hanging up the phone without a proper goodbye.

"By the look on your face and the tone of that conversation, I would wager to say that things didn't go so well," Nick said, trying to lighten the mood he was reading from her face.

With a deep sigh, Sam leaned back as if she were about to pitch her phone across the room. That's when Nick rescued it from her hand. "I'll hold onto that for you. You'll thank me later."

"Are you positive about that?"

After another deep sigh, Sam lowered her hand. "As you may have guessed, that was Supervising Special Agent Tom Hagen. I've been given two days. That's when the 'heavy hitter' shows up."

"This Jameson Scott fellow?"

"He's another profiler from the D.C. office. We've worked together before. It seems the Bureau feels that Mr. Jameson has more experience in the field of profiling and with the media and that perhaps the situation would be better suited for someone else."

Sensing his partner's disgust, Nick asked, "So, is he really a hack?"

Sam looked puzzled, then genuinely embarrassed when she realized she had blurted all that out in her rant. "No," she admitted, with a shake of her head. "He's not a hack. He's actually very good at what he does. He trained me. I guess that's what makes this so hard to swallow." She turned away from Nick.

Nick reached out and took her hand. He wanted to comfort her, but Sam was in no mood to be comforted by anyone.

"It's my fault, really," she said somberly, pulling her hand away from Nick's. "I let myself get distracted."

Her words were like a door slamming shut in Nick's face, and he didn't know how to respond. He let his empty hand drop to his side as they stood up and left the bar in silence.

CHAPTER TWENTY

A Voice from the Past

"HERE WE ARE," Nick said, pulling up to the hotel and parking the Jeep. "I will run Murphy out for a few minutes so he can do his business. Meet you upstairs?"

"Nick, is everything all right? You've barely said two words to me on the way back."

"Everything's fine. I'm fine."

Sam could tell that Nick was holding back but was unsure of how she could get him to open up. "Okay. I'm going to get a hot shower before turning in for the night."

"I won't be long."

"Take your time. I won't be going anywhere. After all, I need to have everything ready to hand off to Jameson in two days."

Riding up the elevator, Sam felt uneasy. The hairs on her neck stood on end as she got off and headed down the hallway to their room. She tried to shake it off, convincing herself that she was being paranoid.

Opening the room door, Sam closed it quickly behind her. Normally, she would walk to her room, remove her gun, and set it down on the nightstand. But tonight, she decided to sweep the rooms. Then, she would continue to wear her gun on her hip until Nick came back with Murphy.

She drew her service revolver and began sweeping the rooms, starting with Nick's room since it was the farthest room from the door. When she had swept her room as well, she holstered her weapon and then collapsed onto the couch. Turning on the evening news, Sam never took her eye off the front door. Thirty minutes passed before Nick walked through the door with Murphy and she finally exhaled a sigh of relief.

Nick could tell something was wrong the moment he saw her face. "I thought you were going to take a shower. Is something wrong?"

"Nope. I wanted to catch up on some news tonight," she lied. "Do you want me to keep it on for you?"

"No. I've heard enough bad news today and I already know all that I need to know about The Magician Killer. I'm going to feed Murphy and get a shower myself."

"But you're going to wait until I get out of the shower before you take yours, right? Right?" Sam repeated.

"What's eating at you, Sam?" he said, standing in the kitchenette area as he prepared Murphy's food and grabbed two bottles of water from the small fridge, grateful that they had stocked up on water a few days before. "You know I'm here for you. So, spit it out. What has you so rattled?"

"I don't know, Nick. It's just a feeling," she confessed. "I'm jumping at shadows and acting like a newbie. I'll be fine. I'm just being ridiculous."

Nick left a bowl of food on the floor in front of Murphy and then sat next to Sam on the couch, handing her one of the water bottles. "Go take your shower. I'll be here, guarding the door until you're done."

Her hand brushed his. "You are the best partner anyone could ask for."

"I know."

After her shower, Sam traded places with Nick, waiting until he came out before they turned in for the night.

Thirty minutes passed, and Sam still couldn't fall asleep. Rolling over, she whispered, "Nick?"

"Hmm?" he mumbled half-awake.

"I can't sleep."

Half-heartedly reaching out his hand, Nick began to massage her back. "No one is getting past me. You really do need to get some sleep, Sam. You're running on empty."

"I know. You're right, but I can't sleep." She sighed and stifled a yawn. "I see his face every time I close my eyes."

"Murphy and I will stand guard."

"Now, who is being ridiculous? You can barely keep your own eyes open."

"I don't have to, and neither do you. He will stand guard," he said, pointing at Murphy. "Any strange sound or smell, Murphy will be all over it before you blink. He won't let the boogeyman get you."

Sam smiled in the dark, snuggling closer to Nick and closing her eyes. But Nick's assurances couldn't keep her from awakening with a start two more times before dawn's light broke the skyline.

Waking to find Nick staring down at her, Sam yawned and sat up, wiping the sleep from her eyes.

"What time is it?" Sam asked.

"It's still early," he replied. "How are you feeling this morning?"

"Like someone should have gotten the number of the truck that ran me over."

"You look like hell."

"Well, aren't you just the sweetest."

"Someone has to keep you humble," Nick said. "It would be a crying shame if I admitted that you look absolutely stunning for a woman who barely slept last night."

Sam turned to climb out of bed. "No wonder you're single," she said as Nick gently grasped her arm, halting her escape.

"Wait," he said as she faced him. "You do look stunning. I was just joking."

Sam laughed. "I know."

Nick looked into her eyes for a full breath before letting go of her arm. "Sam?"

"Hold that thought, Nick." She shook her head. "We—"

"I know. But it is nice to think about it."

She smiled sweetly and nodded in agreement. "But your timing is, well, bad. Dare I say, awful? The worst—"

"All right, all right. I think I get the picture," he grumbled, sitting up and throwing his legs over the other side of the bed. "On that note, I'd better take Murphy out for a potty break," he said, getting up and walking toward the door without looking back. "I won't be long."

"Nick?" she called out, stopping him mid-step as he reached for the door, then slowly turned around. "Me, too."

Nick left the room smiling.

While Nick was outside with Murphy, Sam brushed her teeth, washed her face, and put her hair up in a ponytail. She heard the front door open and then close again. "That didn't take you long," she called out.

But when Nick didn't answer, she stepped to her bedroom door, looked around, and then called, "Nick? Murphy? Here, boy." When she didn't get a response, she backed up into her room and retrieved her service revolver and cocked it. Then, cautiously, she stepped out of her room and began doing a full sweep of the suite, keeping her back to the wall so no one could come up behind her. She opened all the closets, checked under beds, and peered behind Nick's shower curtain. That is when she realized that Nick's sliding door was wide open. She carefully stepped over to it, peered down at the ground below, and then shut and locked it. Could someone have climbed over the railing and into the next-door room?

Sam shuddered as if someone had just walked over her grave. It was an eerie feeling.

"Sam?" Nick poked his head into the bedroom, startling her. On instinct, she brought her gun up, leveling it directly at his chest, before quickly lowering it.

"What the hell, Sam?" he yelled while jumping back.

"I heard the front door open and then close and thought it was you. But when I didn't receive an answer, I got jumpy and swept the rooms. I was in here when you surprised me."

"It was probably someone from the cleaning crew checking to see if we were gone yet," he said. "They probably backed out of the room when they heard your voice."

"Did you see a cleaning cart in the hallway?" she questioned, as her eyes continued to scan the room for anything out of place.

Murphy came into the room with his nose in the air. Nick reached down and scratched the dog's ears as he thought about her question. "Well, no."

Walking out into the living room, Sam noticed that her laptop had been moved and that a few papers were scattered on the floor. "Did you touch my computer this morning before you went out?"

"No. I just got Murphy's leash and the room key and went outside," Nick insisted. "I never went near the coffee table."

"Nick," she gasped, "someone was here!"

"Did you sweep the entire place?" Nick's eyes quickly darted around the room.

"Yes," she said. Her voice was barely a whisper as she sat down hard on the couch. "You left your sliding door open, by the way."

"I never opened that door. It would be too easy for someone to slip inside."

Sam felt a shiver crawl up her spine. The two of them just looked at one another.

"We need to put everything away from now on. There cannot be anything left out when we leave or go to sleep," Nick said.

"What do you think the person was after?"

"It could have been a newspaper reporter looking for a lead," he speculated. "Whoever it was, we can't give them anything."

"You don't think it was...*him*, do you?" Sam asked with wide eyes.

Sitting next to her, Nick placed a comforting hand on her arm. "I don't think it could be him, but just to be safe, maybe we should put a couple of plain clothes on the entrances."

Shaking her head, Sam said, "You're right, of course. I'm just being paranoid. Besides, Mercer already has his men working overtime."

But before leaving for the precinct, Sam put the do not disturb sign on the door. Then she hid a small piece of folded paper between the door jam and the door, near the middle hinge, as she closed the door so they would know if anyone had entered their room while they were out. "Old spy trick I learned from a master spy," she told him. But the idea had really come from an old James Bond movie.

"Hello, Stevens," a voice called out to Sam from the precinct conference room's doorway.

Sam felt herself immediately bristle as the hairs on the back of her neck stood on end. Pursing her lips together and squeezing her eyes shut, she paused for a second, taking a deep breath and blowing it out through her mouth. Then Sam forced a pleasant smile to her lips that was so stiff she worried that her face would crack. Slowly, she turned to face her mentor, Jameson Scott, standing beside Chief Mercer.

"Look who I found wandering the halls here. He says you and he go way back," the chief said.

"Oh, we go way back, alright," Sam replied, trying to keep her voice even.

With salt and pepper hair that was once a rich brown, Jameson was a handsome, well-dressed man in his mid-forties. He was in very good shape, causing him to look even taller than his six-foot-two-inch height. His blue eyes had lost some of their spark but none of the sharpness that made him an excellent profiler in the first place.

"Hello, Special Agent Scott. Fancy seeing you here. And so soon." Sam's voice took on a cool but brittle tone, causing the temperature in the room to drop by ten degrees. "I was told that you would be arriving tomorrow."

"When I received the call about this case, I decided to cut my vacation short and fly in today," he said.

His condescending tone always cut Sam to the quick, and today was no exception. "What you meant to say is, you called your buddy in the DC office the moment this case hit the national news circuit and told him that you wanted in," Sam retorted.

Special Agent Scott smiled even broader, as if they were longtime friends. "Come, come, Agent Stevens—"

"Please, *Special Agent* Stevens, if you would be so kind, Special Agent Scott," she corrected with a saccharine sweetness. "And I would thank you to remember that in the future."

The tension in the room was palpable. Nick quickly took his place next to his partner, hoping to dispel any bad blood that had been obviously brewing between the two agents.

"Special Agent Stevens, my apologies," Jameson said, offering an indulgent smile. "I would never want to step on your toes—"

"It isn't my toes I have to watch out for around you," Sam offered, flashing her own fake smile even wider.

"I hear you have a new nickname," Jameson said.

Nick stood behind Sam and frantically tried to wave Jameson off from his current line of thought, but it was too late. The words had already left Jameson's mouth, causing Nick to cringe and bury his face in one hand as he sighed.

"The Robot. It fits you."

Sam's face immediately reddened with anger.

"Why don't we give you two the room," Chief Mercer interrupted, getting up from his chair and tapping Nick on the shoulder.

"Personally, I think—" Nick began to say when Sam motioned with her head for him to get out. "On second thought, that's an excellent idea, Chief Mercer," he agreed, following the chief out of the room and shutting the door behind him.

"Did I say something wrong?" Jameson asked the moment they were alone.

"Oh, you...you..." Sam stammered, searching for just the right word to use while her anger mounted. "You have said so many things wrong over the years, Jameson. And that right there was a fine example of you sticking your foot in it again. I honestly didn't think it was possible for anyone to continue to speak with both feet in their mouth, but, once again, you have proven me wrong." Sam fumed as she began to close the blinds to shut out the view of their disagreement from the people who had already started looking their way.

"Never, and I emphasize the word never for a good reason, so please, pay close attention because I don't intend to repeat this. NEVER call me 'The Robot' again!"

"All right, all right, I won't. But, Sam—"

"Special Agent Stevens!" she growled under her breath. "You gave up the right to call me by my first name a *long* time ago, Special Agent Scott."

"Can we bury that hatchet, so to speak—?"

"I would love to—right into your big, dumb, thick skull. And while I appreciate the fact that you have traveled all this way to get in on a case that I—we," she corrected, "have well in hand—"

"I don't want to argue with you, Sam—Special Agent Stevens," he quickly corrected when Sam narrowed her eyes menacingly. "I'm here now—"

"I can see that. The only thing I keep asking myself is why?"

"Your supervisor thought that you could use some help," he insisted.

"You were my mentor years ago. And as such, I would really like to give you the benefit of the doubt. But the fact is, I know you too well. You are—"

"Charming? Good at my job?"

Sam let out a disgusted sound. "Ugh! Does your ego have no boundaries, Agent Scott? Honestly, I would have thought that you would have matured by your age."

"Come on, Sam—"

"Don't you 'come on, Sam' me!" she fired back, waving her arms in the air. "You are a spotlight grabber, always grandstanding everything for the attention and adoration of it all. You are a self-absorbed, arrogant, ambulance-chasing narcissist."

"Now, that's not fair, Sam," Jameson protested. "We made a good partnership once."

"That was a long time ago, Jameson," she said. "Before you—"

"Before I what?" His voice purred as he attempted to calm her down. "I'm a guy. We are all, by nature, flawed. You can't blame me for trying."

"Oh, so you admit what you did was wrong? And who says I can't blame you for being a complete douchebag?"

Jameson shrugged his shoulders. "Come on, Sam. At best, I was a cliché."

"You were my supervisor. My mentor. I looked up to you," she added with contempt. "You were supposed to protect me!"

"I was a jerk. I freely admit it."

"I would say you were a lot more than a simple jerk."

"Fine, I was an ass-hat, a real idiot. Some might even call me the scum of the earth." He faced her with palms out. "Believe me, Sam. I've called myself all of that and more."

"It took me a long time to get past it all, Jameson," Sam railed, then punched him in his right arm, hard.

"Okay, I deserved that," he said, grabbing his arm and rubbing it before looking around to see if anyone was looking through the part of the window Sam had neglected to close. His face turned red with embarrassment when he noticed someone quickly turn away.

"You certainly did have that coming. And if I'm being honest, you deserve a lot more than a gentle punch in the arm."

"That was gentle?"

"We can take this to the sparring ring if you'd prefer. I can still kick your ass in the ring without being accused of insubordination. Besides, no witnesses, no evidence. Isn't that what you taught me?" she said bitterly.

"I was wrong, Sam. Is that what you need to hear from me?"

"It isn't so much what I need to hear but what you needed to say to me years ago, Jameson. You had a wife and kids. Hell, I was just a kid myself."

"I'm sorry, Sam. Really, I am. If it makes you feel better, I'm no longer married."

"Ha!" Sam scoffed. "Now, why doesn't that surprise me? And your being married was never the point!" Lifting her chin a degree higher, Sam narrowed her eyes. "If you ever try anything...well, let's just say you truly will be sorry next time."

Throwing his hands up in the air, he signaled surrender. "Truce?" He put a tentative hand out as a peace offering.

Sam glared at the offending hand a moment, then looked him in the eyes, refusing to take his hand. "This is my case, and I'll be damned if I'm leaving it to the likes of you."

"Then it's a good thing that you don't have to. I told them I needed your help. So, I can comfortably say that you won't be going anywhere."

"Is this some kind of joke?" Sam asked, eyeing him suspiciously. "Since when did you ever need help from another agent?"

Throwing his hands up in the air again, Jameson blew out the breath he'd been holding. "I forgot how tough you were, Stevens." With his right hand, he crossed his heart. "I swear to you, Sam, I'm not lying. You have my word."

"Your word isn't worth that much to me anymore."

"Duly noted."

"And, Jameson—"

"Yes, Sam, I mean Special Agent Stevens?"

"If you ever touch me again, it will be the last thing those hands ever touch," Sam threatened. "You get me? Because I won't hesitate to take them off at the elbow. And keep in mind, you owe your career to me since I was too young and naïve to report your actions."

"Yes, ma'am. I have made a note to self in my mental notebook. Never touch Special Agent Sam Stevens again upon penalty of death, and I owe you one."

"It's good that we understand one another, Special Agent Jameson Scott."

Keeping Up Appearances

"THESE ARE THE LATEST PHOTOS of The Magician Killer's victims," Nick said, rolling a whiteboard out from the corner of the conference room and moving it closer to Jameson as he took a seat in one of the chairs. "As you can see from the timeline, he is escalating."

"He is now playing with us," Sam added. "No trace has ever been found or left behind until these last two victims. Yet, now he is being obvious—drawing us in with the grandeur of it all."

"How do we know he hasn't simply gotten sloppy because he feels seen and cornered?" Jameson proposed.

"Because I have a gut feeling. He is playing with us," Sam insisted. "Everything he does is deliberate."

"But his motive?" Jameson asked, looking up from the photos. "Do we know what's driving him?"

Sam and Nick looked at each other. Did they tell Jameson the truth and take the chance that Sam would be removed from the case?

"We haven't discovered a motive yet," Sam lied as she turned away from Nick. "As you know, when dealing with a psychopath—"

"What was that?" Jameson said, pointing his finger between Sam and Nick.

"What was what?" Sam asked innocently, keeping her tone light.

"That look you just gave one another."

Plausible deniability wasn't for the faint of heart, Sam thought to herself. "I have absolutely no idea what you are referring to," she countered.

"We are partners. Working on this case has connected us on an intuitive level," Nick said. "Oftentimes, we don't even need words."

Sam took a seat in a side chair and Murphy jumped up and laid down next to her, resting his head at her feet while leaning against her.

"Since when did you start liking dogs?" Jameson asked. Then, before she could answer, he looked up and boldly asked, "Are you two—?"

"No," Nick and Sam answered simultaneously.

"Absolutely not," Sam added, looking over at Nick. "It is

strictly business with us. I don't believe in distractions. Isn't that right Agent McLeroy?"

"Absolutely, Agent Stevens. All business, all the time."

"My mistake," Jameson apologized, not letting on that he didn't believe a single word coming out of either one of their mouths. He had been a profiler for a very long time and could read the signs. They were trying to pull one over on him. But he decided to keep it to himself, for now. "Of course," he simply said. "My mistake. Again. I believe that I have all the information I need for now regarding this case." He got to his feet and looked down at his watch. Gathering some paper-work from the table, he placed it back into a folder. "Do you mind if I take these? I need some late-night reading material back at the hotel."

"No problem," Sam answered nonchalantly. "We can print out more copies. I intended for you to have a copy of every-thing we have anyway."

Tipping his head in gratitude, Jameson walked to the door, then turned around. "It's good to see you again, Agent Stevens." It was going to take an act of God to get her to believe in him again. But he was willing to do whatever it took to earn her trust.

Upon arriving back at the hotel, Sam stopped Nick from opening the door so she could examine the folded-up paper she had placed in the door jam. Then, nodding her head, she gave Nick the go ahead to unlock the door.

Once again, Sam had a very restless night. She and Nick had decided that it was just too risky for them to continue to sleep in the same bed together with Jameson Scott staying in the same lodgings—even if he was on a different floor. Nonetheless, as she cried out from another nightmare, Murphy was the first one through the bedroom door, with a blurry-eyed Nick just behind him. Then he lifted the covers and crawled into her bed, pulling her into his arms.

"I know we said we would stay in separate rooms, but I really can't sleep knowing you are struggling with this alone."

"I'm sorry, Nick," she cried, feeling guilty for keeping him from his needed sleep. "You must think me the worst partner in the world."

"Not at all." He patted her arm. "You are a *great* partner. I can't think of anyone else I'd rather wake me up in the middle of the night."

"Do you want to talk for a few minutes?" Sam said.

"Will you share what happened between you and Jameson Scott today?"

Pursing her lips together, Sam let out a deep sigh, revealing nothing more, yet she scooted closer.

"I didn't think so," he murmured.

Honey, I'm Back

THE NEXT MORNING, Nick fed Murphy as Sam climbed into the shower, waiting for her to get out before he jumped in. He knew that it made her feel safer when one of them kept an eye on the front door. When Nick finished, Sam was sitting in the living room with her computer open on her lap.

"Hey, I thought I'd run Murphy outside for a few minutes to do his business," Nick said. "Do you want to come?"

"I think I'll pass," she said, focused on her screen.

Nick leaned down, reached into the mini-fridge, and pulled out two bottles of water. Opening one, he offered it to her. "Stay hydrated," he said, setting it on the table beside her. Then he leaned down and kissed her on the cheek without a second thought, as if they'd been together for years, before joining Murphy who was waiting at the door.

"I won't be long," he said, wondering to himself why he had just done that.

Looking up, Sam smiled and reached for her bottle of water. "I'll be done by the time you get back," Sam assured him, as if Nick kissing her goodbye before walking out the door was an everyday occurrence.

Who was she kidding? That small act of normalcy thrilled her to her core. Plus, she was a little dehydrated. He did know how to read her, she admitted.

After Nick shut the door, Sam took a long drink of her water, then continued her work on the computer.

Several minutes had passed when she noticed that she was seeing double. *Monitor display eye strain*, she rationalized. Rubbing her eyes, Sam closed the laptop and set it aside.

Standing up and taking one step towards the kitchenette, she lost her balance and nearly fell back onto the couch. That's when the room tilted and the door to the hotel room opened. Sam felt a moment of relief. Nick had returned. But relief quickly turned to dread when a strange man in a baseball cap stood before her.

"You have the wrong room," Sam said, squinting her eyes to see him better.

"Oh, I have the right room," he said, smiling broadly at her.

Sam noticed the gloves right away, and then the gun. That's when her stomach felt like she was on a roller coaster car that just dropped thirty feet in two seconds. Her body flushed with heat and she swallowed hard to keep the contents of her stomach in.

After her initial shock, Sam felt as if she were moving in slow motion when the man took a cautious step closer. That's when she recognized him—the very same man who had haunted her nightmares was standing directly in front of her.

"You!"

His confident smirk told Sam that he knew something she didn't. "Feeling woozy? That would be the effect of the drug I laced your water with."

His voice sounded far away to Sam, even though he only stood a few feet from her. Slowly, she picked up the partially-empty bottle, staring at it, dumbfounded. "Why?" she managed to say. "When?"

He stepped further into the room and the kitchenette area. Opening the mini-fridge door, he removed the remaining bottles of water and dumped them down the sink, then placed the bottles into a small bag he pulled out of his jacket.

"It's important that we clean up after ourselves," he smirked.

The man from her nightmares stood before her, destroying evidence, and she couldn't do anything about it. "This...isn't...real." Her words were becoming heavy and slurred. Just standing took so much effort. If she didn't have so much adrenaline rushing through her veins just then she might have fallen over and relished the sleep.

"Oh, but I can assure you that this reunion is very real," he said, dumping the last bottle of water down the sink. Then he ran water behind it to wash the evidence away. "And I have waited a very long time for this moment. I've even dreamt of it many times."

"As is evident by the many women you have killed over the years," she said as she looked at the bottle of water still in her hand.

Sam ceremoniously poured the contents onto the couch and carpet. Then, taking a clumsy step backward, she shoved the table's lamp to the floor, shattering it.

"Now, why did you go and do that?" he scolded.

Taking another step backward as the man slowly approached, Sam looked for any way to stall him until Nick returned with Murphy. How long had it been since they left? Time seemed to have slowed to a crawl, but she knew it had probably only been a few minutes.

"There's no place for you to run," he said, savoring each moment.

In her increasingly foggy mind, Sam wondered why he was taking his time. He was playing with her like a cat does a mouse. "Maybe, but there will be evidence of a struggle," she insisted. "Besides, my partner will be back...any minute..." she began to say as she stumbled and dropped to her knees, now lacking the strength to get back up. Tears of frustration burned at the back of her eyes.

"No, he won't," the man chuckled almost gleefully. "There's no hero coming to your rescue. Or did you forget that I laced *all* of the bottles of water? Your partner is currently face down on the front lawn with his faithful companion by his side. But don't worry. I'm certain that someone has called him an ambulance by now."

Sam felt her mouth go dry. The sound of blood pumping through her body pounded between her ears. *There wouldn't be anyone coming to save her. This was how it was all going to end. There would be no escaping him this time. He was making sure of that.*

She felt a hysterical laugh on her lips and wondered why she had done that. "So, you've evolved?"

"I've had plenty of time and practice," he said smugly, then stopped and simply stared at her. "There's that look—that look one gets when they suddenly realize that they're not the smartest person in thc room."

Legs slack, she fell forward onto the low-pile carpet of the hotel room, feeling the fibers against her cheek. Blurry sneakers filled her shrinking field of vision, and then all went black.

CHAPTER TWENTY-THREE

You Can't Keep a Good Man Down

J AMESON SCOTT STEPPED FROM HIS ROOM into the hotel lobby to see what all the fuss was about. His room was on the first floor so he heard everything, and right now he was a bit jealous of Stevens and McLeroy being on the third floor, insulated from all of this commotion of the comings and goings of people.

As he walked outside, he recognized Nick lying there in the grass and Murphy by his side, hindering the rescue workers' efforts by keeping them at bay.

"Hier, boy," Jameson called out in German. Murphy immediately obeyed.

Coming to stand obediently in front of Jameson, Murphy looked up at the man before looking back at his longtime handler, Nick, as if he were about to return to his partner's side. That's when Jameson took hold of his leash and restrained him.

"Fuss" Jameson said, giving the command to heel. Murphy glued himself to his side.

Two paramedics immediately stepped toward Nick. "We are really lucky you were here," one of the paramedics said to Jameson. "How did you do that?"

"Military dog training and a little rudimentary German," Jameson said.

Murphy whined and whimpered as he tugged at his leash. Jameson held on tightly to the end, even choked up on the leather leash, shortening it until Murphy could do nothing but sit and watch.

Both paramedics then began working on Nick. One young man took vitals while a young woman attempted to get a response from Nick by grinding her knuckles into his sternum.

"Sir, can you tell us your name?"

Jameson stepped forward. "I know this man," he said, whipping out his ID and flashing it to the paramedics. "He's an FBI agent as well. His name is Special Agent Nicholas McLeroy. Is it a heart attack?" It seemed strange that someone so young and fit could suddenly keel over, but he still had to ask.

"We aren't able to make that diagnosis, sir. We will know more when we transport him to the hospital and a doctor runs a few tests," the young man said.

The two EMTs lifted Nick onto a gurney and rolled it toward the ambulance as Jameson followed closely behind. He was about to climb into the ambulance when the young female paramedic turned around, putting up a hand to stop him. "We cannot transport an animal in our bus," she informed him.

Jameson bristled. "This is no ordinary animal, ma'am. This is a highly decorated officer of the law," he fired back, pointing to the stars of honor on Murphy's harness.

"All the same, sir," she snapped, "we cannot allow you on this bus with your dog, highly decorated or not."

Looking around, Jameson suddenly realized that Sam was missing from the scene. Did she not know? Was she still in the suite upstairs?

Pulling out his phone as the ambulance sped off, he dialed Sam's number, but it went straight to voicemail.

Taking Murphy by his leash, Jameson went in search of her. Riding up the elevator to the third floor, Murphy immediately began sniffing around the elevator. "What is it, boy?"

When the elevator doors opened, Murphy barked twice, then put his nose to the floor, pulling at his leash until they reached Nick and Sam's door. Whining, Murphy scratched wildly.

Jameson firmly knocked, and when he didn't get an answer, he called out, "Sam! Sam, are you in there?" Silence was his only reply.

Down the hallway, he spied a cleaning cart parked outside an open room and barged inside. The housekeeper, clearly startled, looked up from the tub she was wiping dry.

"You cannot be in here, sir," she protested.

"It's an emergency," he blurted out, shoving his FBI ID into her face. "I have a downed agent, and another one is missing. I need to get into their room." Next, he hurried the flustered woman to her feet and walked her down the hallway to the room in question.

"But, sir, it is against the rules to allow anyone other than the guest into a room," the housekeeper objected, floundering for the key card in her pocket.

Grabbing the card from her, Jameson shoved it into the slot. "What part of 'I have a missing agent' do you not understand?" he bellowed, nearly kicking the door open. He held tightly to Murphy's leash as the dog strained to get inside. Then he put a hand out to stop the woman from entering the room behind him. "I must insist that you stay put."

"But, sir..." she protested.

"I said, stay put!" Jameson yelled, handing the woman Murphy's leash before removing his revolver. He had that bad feeling inside that told him something was very wrong. Eyes wide, the housekeeper instantly complied.

"Sam?" he called out, taking a few steps inside. He noticed the broken lamp immediately. "Sam, you here?" Then, quickly checking the other rooms and finding nothing, he came back to the front door.

Taking a deep breath, he turned to the distraught housekeeper and took Murphy off her hands. "Alert the hotel manager that I need to see him pronto. And no one is to enter this room! Oh, and block off the hallway where your cart is. No one is to go past that cart to clean any more rooms. This entire floor is now a crime scene." Next, he pulled his cell phone from his pocket and dialed Chief Mercer to order a forensic team to be dispatched to the hotel room ASAP and to send someone to the hospital for Special Agent Nicholas McLeroy. "Special Agent Stevens is missing. And Officer Murphy is acting strange. I don't know what in the hell is going on, Chief Mercer, but I need a team out here *now!*"

After he finished up with the forensic team, Jameson and Murphy made their way to the hospital. They stopped at the front desk and enquired about the man who was brought in unconscious. Jameson was directed to the second floor. Stepping off the elevator with Murphy pulling on his leash, he spotted two officers standing guard outside a hospital room.

Poking his head into the room, he found Chief Mercer standing at the foot of McLeroy's bed, speaking with the doctor.

"What's the diagnosis?" Jameson inquired.

Looking rather serious, the doctor said, "I'm sorry. Are you a family member?" Then, in the same breath, the doctor said, "We do not allow animals in the hospital."

The corners of Jameson's lips turned up and he held the label of his jacket out for the doctor to examine. "Why, as a matter of fact, I am. We are both members of the FBI family, and I want to know what happened to my brother here."

Chief Mercer put a hand on the doctor's shoulder. "Dr. Carter, meet Special Agent Jameson Scott and Officer Murphy. He's working on this case with us, and this fine officer is Agent McLeroy's partner. I think it appropriate they hear what you just told me."

"Agent McLeroy's blood test shows a high level of Benzodiazepine—"

"Excuse me, doctor. I don't mean to interrupt, but can you refresh my memory about how Benzodiazepine affects the body?" Jameson asked.

"It's a member of the tranquilizer family," Dr. Carter said. "It looks like he ingested a large amount of it. Does he have a history of recreational drug use?"

"Hell no! Special Agent McLeroy does not have a history of recreational drug use."

Tearing open an alcohol wipe, the doctor cleaned an area of McLeroy's upper arm before administering a dose of Flumazenil to reverse the effects of the ingested drug.

"How long will it take to work?" Chief Mercer asked as he and Special Agent Scott waited for McLeroy to stir.

"It won't take long," the doctor replied. Just then, McLeroy's eyes fluttered open.

Nick jerked straight up in bed, gripping the sides of the railings, his eyes wildly darting around the room. "What... what the hell is going on?" he said, pulling at the tube of oxygen sitting under his nose. "And why is my mouth so dry?" He looked down and saw the IV in his arm.

The doctor placed a hand on Nick's shoulder, then gently pushed him back down against the bed and replaced the oxygen tube.

Jameson reached for the water cup and held it to Nick's lips, supporting the back of his neck. "Here you go, bud. Just take little sips. Can someone set this bed up for Agent McLeroy?" Jameson asked impatiently, as he looked directly at the doctor.

"Of course, just a minute," Dr. Carter said, quickly adjusting the bed into the sitting position. "You may be a little dizzy at first. It shouldn't last long."

"No kidding," Nick replied as his eyes rolled around his eye sockets. "What happened?"

Murphy stood up and rested his front paws on the bed railing as Nick reached over and patted his head. "Sitz, boy," he commanded, and watched as Murphy immediately sat next to the bed.

"We were hoping you could tell us," Chief Mercer said. "What is the last thing you remember?"

Putting his head into his hands, Nick let out a loud sigh, then quickly looked around the room. "I was taking Murphy outside. We stepped off the elevator—" He paused, then shook his head. "I threw away the water bottle after drinking half of it because it tasted strange. Bitter. Then, after warming up a bit for my walk, I stepped outside and felt dizzy—"

"Do you know where Special Agent Stevens could be?" Jameson asked impatiently.

"Sam...I mean, Special Agent Stevens, is missing?" Nick cried out, shaking his head to clear any residual fogginess as he began to climb out of bed. "We have to find her!"

"I'm sorry but you're in no shape to walk out of here," Dr. Carter said.

"Get out of my way!" Nick reached down and ripped the IV from his arm, not caring that it hurt like hell or that he was trailing blood. He climbed around the bed's railing, putting his bare feet down on the cold tiled floor. "My partner is out there and—"

The doctor immediately grabbed Nick's arm, took a sterile bandage off the tray, and pulled a roll of self-adhesive bandage wrap from his pocket, wrapping the wound. "I would advise against leaving, sir."

"Maybe the doctor is right, McLeroy," Jameson intervened, blocking Nick's escape.

"Get the hell out of my way, Jameson, before I knock you out," Nick threatened.

Jameson backed up, putting his hands into the air as a sign of surrender. "If you want to fall on your ass, who am I to stop you?"

The doctor took several steps back as well.

"Where are my clothes?" Nick shouted with frustration when the room began to tilt sideways. Grabbing the bed railing, he sat back down on the bed. "That maniac has Stevens."

Nick stood up again, feeling less dizzy this time, and pushed past Jameson. "Get me some clothes!" he bellowed, not caring that people had gathered outside his room, staring at him. He grabbed Chief Mercer's arm and looked straight into his eyes. "Please. That's my partner out there, and I made a promise to watch her back and keep her safe."

"Get him the forms to sign himself out," Chief Mercer said, looking at the perplexed doctor watching from a safe distance. "It won't do any good keeping him here. He'll just find a way to leave the moment we turn our backs."

A grateful sigh escaped Nick's lips. "Thank you, sir."

"Think nothing of it, Special Agent McLeroy. But if you keel over and die on me, this is on your head, not mine."

CHAPTER TWENTY-FOUR

Sam's Grave

SAM WAS SEMICONSCIOUS, feeling herself awaken slowly. Her mouth was dry and she felt cold all over.

Her limbs felt heavy, even rubbery. A rhythmic but familiar scraping noise rattled around in her head. She couldn't remember why it was familiar, just that it was something she'd heard before. Something smelled rank and made her nose hurt.

Cracking her eyes open just a bit, the light was too bright. She immediately shut her eyes again to escape the pain.

"Just another minute, Mama," Sam softly murmured to herself as her mind momentarily took her back to a more innocent time when she was ten. Her mother had come in to wake her for school. "I promise I'll get up, Mama. Just five more minutes, please," Sam pleaded, rolling over onto her side. That's when she noticed something was very wrong. She heard the rattle of chains. And something was wrapped around her ankle.

Time had no meaning to her. Minutes could have been hours as far as she was concerned. Finally, she was able to open her eyes without the piercing pain. Looking out through small slits at first, she peered down toward her feet and saw a large, heavy chain attached to her left ankle. One foot was shackled.

Looking to the other side of her, she heard the earth being shoveled and saw dirt flying up into the air.

Someone was digging a hole.

He was digging her grave. Her final resting place.

It all came flooding back—the drugged water, the hotel suite, the killer saying Nick was outside, face down on the lawn.

The Magician Killer was back to claim her; this time, he meant to make it permanent.

She squeezed her eyes shut, feeling something rise in her throat. It was either a laugh or a scream—she couldn't tell which yet. *Don't go getting hysterical on me now, Stevens*, she told herself. *Keep your cool.*

Sitting up quickly, Sam cradled her head in her hands as a wave of nauseating dizziness washed over her. When the stars stopped dancing around her brain, she looked around cautiously. She was in a clearing, surrounded by trees. A large circle had been etched into the dirt around her, roughly six feet from where she sat. It had been deliberately drawn to indicate her range of motion with the chain attached to her ankle.

Well, you really put your foot in it this time, Stevens.

Looking down at herself, Sam realized why she was so cold. She wore only her black sports bra and matching briefs. All her nightmares had come true. She pulled frantically at the chain to test its sturdiness, but the stake didn't budge at all. It had been pounded securely into the hardened earth.

She must have made too much noise rattling the chain because the sound of shoveling paused. Sam's blood ran cold.

Round and round, the same thought raced about Sam's mind: *It's him, The Magician Killer.* The man from her nightmares had come to life, and he was digging her grave. *This is how it is all going to end.*

The sour taste of bile bubbled up in Sam's throat.

A shovel was tossed out of the pit, and then the figure from her nightmares emerged, looking over at her with a smug, crooked smile on his lips.

"Good, you're awake," he said, pulling a short, makeshift ladder from the hole. "I was worried that you would miss all of the fun." He picked up the shovel and approached her, stopping short when he realized he'd accidentally stepped over the demarcation line in the dirt. "Oops. Don't want to step into the viper's den." He gingerly stepped back before walking outside the line he'd drawn until he stood some six feet away from the hole he'd just dug, admiring his handi-work. The new leather necklace that Nick had just given her hung proudly around his neck for her to see along with a chain holding the gold ring he'd brutally pulled off of her left hand ten years earlier. Both were hanging there like trophies on display.

Sam's tongue felt thick and dry as she licked her parched lips. "Why?" she asked. The simple word painfully squeaked out, sounding strange to her ears.

"You have to be a bit more specific," he taunted. "Why am I standing back behind this line? Why am I digging this hole?" He pointed the shovel at her. "Or, why am I doing this to you?"

Sam nodded. "Yes, to all of it." She got up onto her knees before slowly standing upright.

"Because I know the level of your tenacity," he stated bluntly. "That is why I stand behind this line." He smiled at her smugly. "Why I dig the hole...well, we both know why I'm doing that." His lips twisted strangely into something resembling a grimace. "As for why I am doing this to you... Well, Sammy, old girl, that is easy. Because I've dreamt of this moment for ten years now." His dead eyes pinned her to the ground.

Sam saw intense anger and hatred in his eyes. It fright-ened her, and she was transported back to the day she first met him in the alley when she was just nineteen. "I never..." Sam paused, trying to clear the cottony, scratchy feeling from her throat before she continued. "I never understood why you came after me all those years ago."

"I'll tell you why, my dear girl." He dragged the shovel menacingly behind him while he walked around the circle, careful to stay out of her reach. Then, throwing the shovel down next to a black, zippered duffel bag, he began to speak again. "You were just so beautiful and loved by everyone." He squatted down beside the black duffel bag and unzipped a side pocket, checking over his shoulder to see if she was at all curious about his actions. He smiled when he caught her trying to see around him. "I wanted that," he said, his words sounding more like the whine of a young child than a full-grown man to her ears. "What you had. Loving parents, supportive friends." After retrieving something from the bag before zipping it back up, he stood up, hiding whatever he'd taken behind his back before tucking it into the waistband of his pants.

"But why?" She coughed dryly into her hand. "Why take your anger out on me? I was not responsible for your circumstances."

"You represented everything I never had and everything I would never be."

"But you didn't answer me," Sam hoarsely barked, "Why me? From all of those girls in our town, you chose me. I never hurt you. We'd never really met before that evening," Sam said helplessly, lifting her hands into the air with her palms up, almost as a plea for understanding. "Sure, I may have seen you in the diner once or twice..."

"Try ten times, Sammy. I'd been in the diner ten times, but you never even gave me a second glance." He spit out the words as if they were poison on his tongue.

Shaking his head as if she were stupid, he approached the line. Then he lifted the chain on his neck to display the gold ring he'd taken from her so long ago—the trophy he'd kept against his skin all these years to remind him of her. When he saw the recognition in her eyes, he smiled broadly.

"Why does a dog bark, a bird sing, or a snake bite?" he asked as if it were all so elementary. "Because it's in their nature."

Her left hand began to shake uncontrollably—the hand he'd pulled that ring from so many years ago. A shiver of revulsion shook her entire body. She closed her eyes and took a deep, cleansing breath.

And then another.

When Sam opened her eyes, there was renewed determination shining in them, as if a switch in her brain had flipped. Years of training took over as she compartmentalized her emotions and pushed her fears aside.

"So, you are comparing yourself to a *dog*?" she challenged, attempting to push a few of his buttons. "Or maybe you are the snake? Which is it? By the way, what is your name? Since I am going to die today, I think it only fitting that I know the name of my killer since you haven't been exactly forthcoming with the reason I must die."

Waving his right hand and shaking his head as he absently stepped into the circle, oblivious to the boundaries he'd so carefully set up, he angrily spat, "You're twisting my words around. I simply mean that I act upon instincts." He leaned forward, momentarily pinching the bridge of his nose. Then, suddenly realizing that he'd stepped into her strike zone, he gave Sam a knowing smile and wagged his pointer finger at her before taking two steps back, out of her reach. "Ah, ah, ah. I see what you did there. You distracted me in hopes that I would make a stupid mistake, but I don't make stupid mistakes."

Sam scrubbed her hands over her face, trying to clear the cobwebs from her mind further. She had to think. Looking around, she determined that they were deep in the woods. Again, she tried to engage him. "So, your instincts are to kill people?" she said, looking off to the side of her. That's when she noticed the large claw marks on a nearby tree and froze.

Following her line of sight, he laughed when he realized Sam knew what the marks meant. "That's right," he said, snapping his fingers several times to draw her attention back to him. "Hey, I'm over here!"

Sam's breath caught in her chest and her heart began to pound so hard that she thought it would explode. For a moment, she couldn't hear anything but her own panic rushing to her head like a giant wave that was about to crash down upon her.

"Oh, now you've gone and ruined my little surprise for you." He attempted to sound disappointed, yet Sam could hear the glee in his voice.

"Is it a brown or a black bear?" she asked, bringing her eyes back around slowly to his. "Brown or black?" Sam screamed at him when he continued to smile at her.

"Why would you want to know that?" He chuckled as if the whole thing were a big joke.

"Brown or black?" she asked again, only this time Sam's tone was perfectly flat, almost calm.

"Oh, all right then. I'll tell you if you're going to be a party pooper. It's a brown bear."

"Male or female?"

Again, his joy could hardly be contained as he answered her. "Male."

Sam doubled over as if she had just been punched in the gut. He'd put her in the path of a male brown bear, who could weigh anywhere from eight hundred to twelve hundred pounds. They were one of the largest bears in the world, second only to the Kodiak bears from nearby Kodiak Island.

Adrenaline coursed through her bloodstream.

"I can see the wheels in your head turning, li'l Sammy," he taunted. "It's almost a shame to destroy someone as...well, beautiful and clever as you. So, I'll tell you what I'm going to do." He waited for Sam's eyes to come back and level with his. Pulling a nine-inch hunting knife from his waistband, he announced, "I'm willing to give you a fighting chance."

"A fighting chance," Sam scoffed, narrowing her eyes. "A hunting knife against a twelve-hundred-pound bear? You're nuts, buddy!"

Acting as if he was going to put the knife back into his waistband, he shook his head. "Well, I thought I was being generous, but if—"

"Wait. Give it to me," she demanded.

"Say please—"

"Pretty please," she quickly said before he'd even finished taunting her.

With a wicked smile, he threw the knife towards her feet. Sam jumped back just in time to avoid getting stabbed. She raised her eyes slowly to meet his and knew he was disappointed she had moved so quickly.

"Oops," he snickered. "I slipped."

Still looking at him, Sam took another deep, grounding breath, putting aside the expletives sitting on the edge of her tongue. "It could be days before your bear decides to come back around," she pointed out. "And my disappearance has certainly not gone unnoticed."

Pointing to himself, he said, "Do I look like someone who leaves anything to chance?"

"They will be coming for me."

"They will be too late," he dismissed.

"My partner will not waste any time. He will have sent out the dogs by now."

Stepping over to the black duffel bag, he gave it a kick. "Don't you mean dog?" he clarified. "Special Agent McLeroy, is it? He only has one dog. And have you forgotten? Your partner's in the hospital. I doubt that he will be in any shape to leave so quickly."

"It's a figure of speech."

"Of course," he said, giving her a sympathetic look. "But I'm afraid by the time they find you—*if* they find you—there won't be much left to identify, let alone bury. I know this bear's routine because I've spent a lot of time out here studying him." He picked up the duffel bag, hoisting it upon his shoulder. "That's where this comes in handy." He patted the side of the bag, then put it down next to the line and opened the main compartment to show her it was stuffed with cut-up pieces of fish.

Sam gagged and covered her mouth and nose but still dry heaved because of the smell. "Wow, you did think of every-thing," she managed to say between gags, her tone sarcastic and bitter.

"I've been feeding him on and off for months now," he said, pointing to the hunting blind he'd built up in the tree to Sam's left. "You see, that's where I sit and watch him. Oh, he's truly magnificent. But you will see him soon enough."

"Can't wait," Sam murmured under her breath, then no-ticed his grin widen.

"This is going to be fun," he added gleefully as he picked up the bag and headed down a path to Sam's right. "You just wait and see!" he called over his shoulder, practically skip-ping away.

Sam's mind was racing a hundred miles an hour as she looked up into the sky to determine the time of day and how long she had been unconscious. She guessed that it was now between seven and eight in the evening. Next, she mapped out the surroundings. The killer walked off toward the west, dropping fish pieces from his bag. Taking a deep breath, she resolved that she wouldn't let the feeling of helplessness overtake her. She was a fighter. She turned toward the east and took in the hunting blind to her left. Then she walked north towards the hole he'd been digging. Even though she couldn't quite see the bottom, it was clear to Sam that the hole was deep. He meant for her never to be found.

He must have been planning to get rid of his next victim here when he pivoted upon learning of Sam's location from the news conference.

Straightening her backbone, Sam decided that she would not go down without a fight. She picked up the hunting knife and then turned her attention to the stake in the ground— the stake that tethered her in place. Using the tip of the hunting knife, she began digging around the metal stake in the semi-hard dirt. Every so often, she'd stop to jerk on the chain and the stake, testing to see if there was any give to it before continuing to chip away. After digging for fifteen minutes, she began to feel frustrated. The stake wouldn't budge.

The sound of a happy tune being whistled signaled her captor was returning. Quickly brushing the dirt back into place, Sam decided she'd work on the stake again when she had a chance. Looking over her shoulder, she saw him coming around a tree and turned to face him.

"What have you been up to?" he asked, giving Sam a suspicious glare.

"Why don't you come over here and I'll show you," she invited.

"Perhaps I'll simply douse you in the remaining fish juices I have here in my bag," he said, suddenly throwing the contents in her direction and managing to get a little splash of the foul, odorous juice on her.

Jumping to her feet, Sam moved back a few steps to get out of his reach. He would have to step into the circle to get any more of that lousy muck on her. "Come any closer and we will see who wears the contents of your little bag," she dared him, gripping the hunting knife in her closed fist.

His lips flattened out and his humorous tone disappeared. "Maybe I will take you up on that offer later. But for now, I have preparations to make," he said, climbing up the makeshift ladder to his tree stand.

"Well, the offer is always open," Sam taunted, sitting back down and partly turning her back to him so that she could dig around the stake a little more while keeping one eye on him, so that he couldn't surprise her from behind.

"Say, what are you doing there?" he called down from high up in the tree.

Turning her head to the side while she continued to work, she said, "Come down here and find out."

"No, thank you. I like my vantage point from up here. It's no use, you know."

"What's no use?" she answered, still digging at the stake and hard ground.

"Trying to get that stake out of the ground."

"How would you know?" Sam replied. "Have you ever tried?"

He shook his head as he watched Sam pull at the chain again. "No, I can't say that I have."

"Then how do you know for certain that it's impossible?"

"You are wasting your time," he assured her.

"Well, it's my time to waste however I see fit." She glared back at him and continued to work to free herself.

After another twenty minutes of digging, Sam managed to get some slight back-and-forth movement from the stake, but movement nonetheless—a fact that she kept to herself as she kept digging.

Sam was startled by a sudden and exuberant expression of glee from the tree stand. Turning to see what had caused his excitement, she was momentarily paralyzed by fear. One of the largest brown bears she'd ever seen was slowly making his way down the path, clearly heading toward her. His enormous head was the size of a small child as he stopped to eat the trail of fish heads and guts left behind for him.

Sam began digging faster, frantically pulling dirt out with her bare hands before standing up and jerking on the chain. She tried not to move too quickly so that she didn't attract any undue attention to herself, but there was no time to waste. She was desperate to get to the hole dug for her grave. It was deep enough that she could likely stay out of reach of the bear's massive paw…if only she could get the stake out of the ground.

Her fear and desperation were now palpable as she looked up to see The Magician Killer watching her safely from above. "Sing for me, little bird," he screamed down to her, raising his hands as if conducting an orchestra. "Scream loudly!"

Her years of martial arts training kicked in. She had broken stacks of bricks with her bare hands for crying out loud. She would survive this. Spurred on to fight even harder to survive, she focused every bit of her energy on freeing that stake from the ground.

"There's no shame in screaming, my little songbird," he remarked, digging out his prized Sony Walkman and earphones from the bag he'd placed next to him earlier. "You could even plead for your life. It will only add to the dramatic ending of our relationship."

"We don't have that kind of a relationship, you psycho," Sam uttered between clenched teeth as she pulled furiously on the chain. "And I wouldn't give you the satisfaction of hearing me beg for anything, especially my life. I can't, however, guarantee that there still won't be screaming." Then, under her breath, she added, "Or *who* will be screaming when this is all over."

The bear stood up on his hind legs and began clawing at the tree to mark it before continuing his slow progression toward her.

Sam's body shook with adrenaline. She needed to focus all her energy on escaping; she couldn't do that if she was overcome with fear. "This is not going to be the way I die," she told herself just before dropping to her knees and chipping away at the dirt again. She now faced the bear, looking up at him every so often.

The bear stuck his nose up into the air again and sniffed. "Shit!" she exclaimed, speedily digging with the tip of the knife and scooping out the dirt before standing up to frantically yank at the chain again and again.

When she felt the stake move slightly more, Sam let out a sound of desperate excitement as she fell to her knees again and began to dig even faster.

"You will never make it," he taunted again from overhead. "He's caught your scent. He's coming closer."

Trying desperately to ignore his derisive words and mocking tone, Sam felt sick when she saw the bear was now only fifty feet away. The rush of blood and the pounding sound of her pulse in her ears was deafening. She knew she couldn't get to the hole if she were still tethered in place. "Dammit!" she cursed while struggling with the chain and stubborn stake.

When the bear was thirty feet away, it stopped and sniffed the air as if trying to determine if she was dinner.

Clenching the hunting knife in her right hand, Sam waved her arms in the air, shouting at the top of her lungs, "Get out of here, you stupid bear! There's nothing to see here!"

The bear stood on his hind legs again, letting out a terrifying roar before returning to all fours.

Sam swallowed, finding it hard to take a full breath now. Her limbs got all tingly, and she felt as if she might faint.

From his perch, her tormentor was cackling like a banshee. Sam gave a primal scream, yanking at the stake one last time. Slowly, ever so slowly, the ground gradually let loose of its grip on the stake.

The bear took another step closer to her.

Shocked to be 'free,' Sam took a step backward, menacingly holding the knife in one hand and the stake in the other. If nothing else, she could swing its chain and perhaps hit the bear in the nose, surprising him enough to find less troublesome prey. She swung it back and forth like a pendulum as she continued to back up toward the hole while eyeing the bear. Now she had the large, heavy stake going in a full circle.

She heard a horrifying noise coming from the man in the hunting blind as he screamed something at her that she couldn't quite understand. But he was not her main concern. The bear was quickly picking up speed. Facing him, Sam realized the chain was too short, and the bear would be on top of her by the time the stake hit, so she dropped it and made a mad scramble for the hole. The heavy metal chain and stake dragged behind her, slowing her progress. Taking a giant leap into the hole, she heard herself scream in terror, the sound deafening and strange to her own ears.

Her shackled foot pulled one way and she felt a shooting pain as she dove, hitting her head against the wall of dirt. Sam couldn't breathe for what felt like an eternity. The wind was knocked from her lungs when she hit the ground. Now she was writhing in pain from both her head and foot.

A ricocheting noise reverberated in Sam's ears and she recoiled, scrambling for the corner of the grave as she pulled her knees into her chest. The bear dropped partway into the hole, his enormous paw dangling above her head. She began to scream hysterically, realizing death had arrived.

CHAPTER TWENTY-FIVE

A Bear Skin Rug

STILL SCREAMING HYSTERICALLY, Sam stared at the bear, now so close she could reach out and stroke its fur. But pitched forward, it made no move to attack. A thin trail of blood trickled from the bear's head and mouth into the hole, dripping onto her still-shaking legs.

Sam looked up to see Nick standing at the opening of the hole. Shaking her head and blinking her eyes, she thought, *surely my mind is playing tricks on me.*

"Sam! Answer me! Are you hurt?" Nick yelled down into the hole as she remained mute. Jumping down, he squatted next to her and saw that she was shaking all over.

It wasn't until Nick put his hand on Sam's shoulder that she realized that he was real—and that she was indeed still alive. Looking around, she blinked, and relief came flooding into focus, along with a sharp pain that shot up her leg. Sam cried out and grabbed her foot.

Nick ripped off his windbreaker, wrapping the thin material around Sam's shoulders. "I thought you were dead," he said, then held her to his chest.

"Did you see him? How did you get past him?" Sam wrapped her shaky arms around his neck, hugging him. "Don't let him take me, Nick." Uncontrollable tears spilled from her eyes. "Oh, Nick, I can't believe you're here. I thought I would never see you again! Just hold me."

They could both hear Murphy barking frantically and men running and yelling orders somewhere above them.

"Murphy?" She cried.

"He'll be fine."

Then she locked eyes with Nick. "Honestly, how did you find me?"

"When I woke up in the hospital..." He let his words hang in the air between them for several long seconds. "I didn't think that I would find you alive, Sam. Using yourself as bait was a really stupid idea."

Brushing his criticism aside, Sam shook her head before admitting the truth, "I know, you're right, of course. I'm an idiot, Nick. But you didn't answer my question. How did you find me?"

They both froze when they heard Murphy yelp and begin barking ferociously. This was followed by a man screaming out as if he were being murdered. "See, I told you Murphy would be fine." He smiled broadly, looking back at her.

"Did you hear my question? Dammit, answer me, Nick."

"I did...I mean, I do," he insisted, pulling Sam against him. "I put a mini tracker in the necklace I gave you." He squeezed her tightly to him. "The size of a grain of rice. I told you I had your back. Besides, I'm here, aren't I?"

"You did what?" Her words sounded angry at first as she shoved him away. "Never mind, I don't care. You found me, and I'm alive," she continued, clasping him to her so tightly he could hardly breathe. "Oh, Nick, I was so scared I would end up like those other women and never be found again." She pulled back, grasping his face between her hands. "It was as if all of my nightmares had come to life and I was living them."

Nick smiled. "You're safe now, and that's all that matters in the end," he said, his face so close to hers that she thought he was going to kiss her.

"Do you two need a minute?" Jameson called down from above. "I brought you a blanket."

"Get me out of here," Sam insisted, pushing herself out of Nick's arms. She raised her arms into the air so Jameson could pull her out of the hole.

Then, a young ranger came behind him and lowered the handmade ladder he'd found into the hole.

Nick climbed out of the hole as Sam put her arms through the sleeves of his jacket and zipped it up with shaky hands.

Then Jameson draped a blanket around her shoulders.

"Don't worry, he's dead," the young ranger said, a large rifle resting upon his shoulder. "I can guarantee that when I shoot them, they definitely stay dead." The ranger offered his hand. "I'm Ranger Jack McAdams. Very pleased to meet you, Special Agent Stevens. We had a hell of a time finding you. We weren't even sure..." he started to say when Nick elbowed him in the ribs.

"Any chance I can get the skin of that bear when you are done with him?" Sam asked the young Ranger.

"I would have to ask my supervisors."

Reaching out her hand to steady herself on the young Ranger's arm, she pleaded, "See what you can do, Ranger Jack. It would mean the world to me."

With a large grin, Ranger McAdams gave Sam a wink, "I will need to fill out some extra paperwork, Special Agent Stevens, but I don't see why we can't do a favor for a local hero like you."

"All right, break it up you two," Jameson said. "We have a lot of paperwork of *our* own to fill out."

Nick and Jameson both reached out to catch Sam under her elbows as her shaky legs faltered. But Nick was the one who scooped her up into his arms. "It's a very long walk back to the vehicles. We are parked over that ridge," he justified, gesturing with his head when Sam looked as if she were about to protest. "And besides, you won't make it far on that ankle. You don't even have shoes on."

The heavy chain and metal stake rattled loudly as Jameson gathered it in his arms and stood beside them. "This thing weighs nearly as much as she does," he said. "Let me know if you need me to carry her part of the way."

Nodding his head, Nick said with a sly grin, "Seems to me I got the better end of this deal."

Sam looked around at the scene and everything going on as Nick began to walk back down the path leading to the vehicles.

The man who had tortured her dreams for decades was now handcuffed and in custody, leaning up against the very tree he'd taunted her from.

"Wait!" she cried. "I want to see him. And I want this thing off my ankle." She kicked her leg up in the air to emphasize her point while rattling the metal cuff and chain. "I've been shackled long enough, and I'm not just talking about this cuff and chain."

Nick stopped in his tracks and looked down at her for a long moment. "You're serious?"

Nodding, she said, "Of course I'm serious. Take me to him. Please."

"I don't think that would be a good idea at the moment—" Jameson began to say, then saw the look in her eyes.

Looking at her old partner and mentor, she said, "Sometimes one has to look into the depths of the abyss, or in this case, the eyes of the devil himself, before one can move on. Besides, he must have the key to this cuff on him."

Jameson placed a hand on Nick's shoulder and gave a quick nod, affirming Sam's logic.

Rolling his eyes, Nick acquiesced to Sam's request.

When the three of them reached the tree where the man sat on the ground, handcuffed and flanked by two large officers as guards, he looked somehow smaller than Sam remembered. Disheveled was the word that popped into her head. Blood dripped from wounds in his right arm and leg, and his pants and shirt were torn where Murphy had taken him down as he tried to flee.

The two guards looked at Sam. "We are glad to see you survived," the dark-haired officer said.

Sam smiled, but the lines didn't quite reach her eyes. "Me, too. And thank you for your efforts here today, gentlemen. Did either of you happen to find a key on him?"

The other officer reached into his pocket and pulled out a set of four keys, presenting the key ring to her.

Sam lifted her leg up to the man and smiled. "Jameson, would you mind?"

After two attempts, the third key turned in the cuff and the shackle dropped to the ground with a loud clank.

"Thank you," Sam said as she rubbed her swollen ankle. She then asked Nick to let her stand.

Nick considered her request for a moment before placing her gently on the ground. He held tightly to her left arm, lending her support as she kept her left foot off the ground.

Hopping forward, balancing on her right leg, Sam moved in closer to the man quietly sitting on the ground with his head bowed.

"Do we have a name yet? She asked, looking at the officers.

"No, ma'am. We are waiting for the forensic team to bring the portable fingerprinting device. Someone has gone back to the vehicle to retrieve it. But we will likely not find out his name until we get back to the station," the dark haired officer said. "The satellite coverage in the area is sketchy at best."

"Hey, you!" Sam said to her former tormenter. "Look at me!"

Jameson kicked the man in the foot. "Didn't your mother teach you any manners? You look a woman in the eyes when she's talking to you."

Sam waited for The Magician Killer to slowly bring his eyes up to hers. "Stand him up," she told the two officers with authority in her voice. The two officers lifted him to his feet and restrained him by holding onto his arms. "You're not so magical, now, are you?" she scoffed.

His eyes narrowed to small slits, and he looked as if he wanted to lunge at her until he saw Murphy come over and stand next to Sam's right side, giving him a low, menacing growl.

"There's that look," Sam said, deliberately taunting him with his own words. "That look you get when you suddenly realize that you're not the smartest person in the room."

"Make sure that he gets a good taste of our shackles, gentlemen," Sam insisted.

"Yes, ma'am," the officers answered in unison.

"Wait. Hold onto him tight, officers. He has something of mine I'm taking back right now." Reaching around the killer's neck, Sam untied the leather necklace Nick had given her. "Make sure this makes it into evidence. It seems I have a very smart partner," she smiled broadly, handing the necklace to Nick. Then she reached for the gold chain with her ring on it and gave it a swift yank, ripping it from the killer's neck. "I'll just take that back, too. Thank you for keeping it safe for me all these years. It belonged to my grandmother and I desperately missed it."

Forgetting about the dog, the man tried to lunge at Sam but was restrained by the two officers. Murphy also jumped to her defense, baring his teeth and snarling. "Keep that mangy mongrel away from me!" he cried in fear, shrinking back into the officers' restraints.

Sam scoffed deep in her throat. "That's what I thought. Not so tough when *you're* the one on the other end of an angry beast and his sharp fangs, now are you?"

Jameson stepped between them. "I think we've had enough for today," he said as he produced two evidence bags for Nick and Sam to drop the leather necklace and the ring and chain into.

Sam gave a satisfied smile as Nick picked her up in his arms, turned, and walked away.

"Well, did you see everything that you needed to see," he asked, "now that you've faced your devil?"

"We are all a product of our broken parts," Sam replied, looking back over his shoulder. "The only difference between me and him is that I came out on top."

Nick whistled and Murphy ran to catch up with them, his tail wagging.

"Good job, boy," Nick praised.

He carried Sam the half mile down the path to a waiting paramedic's bus and then placed her carefully on a waiting gurney. Leaning over her face, he whispered, "It's time to go home."

Placing her hands on either side of Nick's face, Sam nodded her head with tears shimmering in her eyes. "Thanks for having my back, McLeroy. You're the best partner an agent could ask for."

CHAPTER TWENTY-SIX

A Hero's Welcome

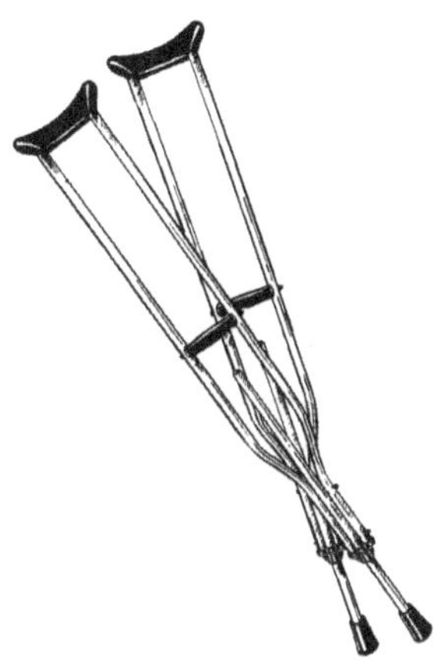

WHEN THEY ARRIVED at the hospital, several reporters were waiting for them as the bus doors opened. The flashing of lights from the cameras temporarily blinded Sam and she quickly covered her eyes.

Nick and Murphy were at the emergency entrance waiting for her to arrive.

The doors to the emergency entrance opened up and there was a line of officers, game wardens, and forest rangers along both sides of the corridor walls. They all stood at attention and saluted Special Agent Stevens as she was wheeled in on the gurney.

"Nick, what's going on?" she whispered so that only he could hear her.

Nick and Murphy walked proudly alongside her. "Everyone was called out to search for you, Sam. They are just showing their appreciation that you were brought in alive. Oh, and it's a hero's welcome for the entire team, and that includes you, Murphy."

Chief Mercer stood at the end of the line with his hand raised to her in a salute. "Special Agent Stevens, you are certainly a sight for these old eyes to see."

"And it is good to be alive, sir."

"I must admit, I wasn't sure if we would get to you in time."

"Frankly, I had my doubts as well," she confessed, letting out an emotion-filled sigh. "But all these officers...you are all making too big of a fuss—"

"We are just happy you were found alive, Agent Stevens," Chief Mercer said. "And hopefully soon all those families of the missing girls will have closure for all those years of pain."

"You guys are the real heroes to me." Sam looked over at Nick and then down at Murphy.

"Sir, we need to get her to triage," a stern-faced ER nurse said, stepping in to direct traffic. "Take her to bay nine," she ordered.

Due to a hairline fracture, Sam's ankle was immobilized and she was fitted with a black boot until the bone healed. As a precaution, she would be kept overnight for observation because of her dehydration and head injury.

Jameson, Nick, and Murphy entered Sam's room with a latte and a scone from the hospital cafeteria.

"You guys are the best. How did you know I really needed this?"

"Sam, we need to discuss something with you," Jameson said, sitting in the chair near her bed.

Nick sat on the edge of the bed and Murphy stuck his nose in her hand.

"Nick and I were talking, and well, I feel you need closure—" Jameson began when Sam cut him off.

"I have my closure, Jameson. He tried to kill me. He didn't succeed. I win, he loses. That is what I call closure!"

"Well, if you have closure, why is your left hand still trembling?" Jameson pointed out.

Sam slowly looked down at her left hand, then back up at Jameson. "You're the expert here, you tell me."

"Sam, in your mind you say you have closure, but you haven't received the answers to the questions that have haunted you for the past ten years. And yes, I've been filled in on the details. And before you ask me, no, I don't intend to report the unorthodox method in which you decided to proceed with this case—mainly because it would be a career-ender for you, and you're too valuable of an agent to lose."

"Jameson..." she sighed.

Holding up his hand, Jameson continued. "So, why not get answers, Sam? And put this thing to bed, for good. I'll get you in to see the still unnamed suspect as soon as possible," Jameson said.

"I think everyone should just take a beat here and sleep on it. Who knows, maybe we can see everything more clearly tomorrow," Nick insisted when he noticed Sam suddenly turn pale.

Jameson opened his mouth to say something more but quickly closed it again when he saw the look on Nick's face. "All right," he relented. "But this discussion isn't over. We still have a suspect to break in the morning."

"On a lighter note. I was told I will only need to spend one night here." Sam took a deep breath in and smiled as she adjusted her pillows.

"That's great news, Sam," Jameson said, reaching out and patting her on the shoulder. "Well, I lost the coin toss, so I get to fill out the reports tonight."

"Did you pull the two-headed quarter trick on Jameson to get out of doing the reports again, Special Agent McLeroy?" Sam joked.

Nick shrugged his shoulders. "Maybe."

"Wait, that coin was rigged?"

Sam jerked awake suddenly, then realized where she was, safe and sound in her hospital bed. Fresh tears dampened her pillow.

Nick, who had been lounging in a nearby chair after returning to her room, straightened his spine and came and stood over her bed, looking down into her eyes. "Can I get you a drink of water?"

"Oh, Nick," she gasped, trying to catch her breath. "I don't think I can face him again."

"Don't think about that right now, Sam."

"I'm taking my name back, you know," she said softly, with real conviction, turning her face up to look into his eyes. "Say my name—my real name. Call me Samantha."

Nick smiled. "Samantha," he said, testing the sound of it on his lips. "I like it."

"It sounds nice when you say it."

Leaning down, his mouth hovered near hers as the noise of the hospital just outside the door reminded him to be cautious. "It's a beautiful name, but to me, you will always be Sam."

"I just needed to hear someone say my name again to see if it made me shiver." She shook her head. "It didn't this time."

"And the world didn't end?"

"No, it didn't end," she repeated as a sad look crossed her face. "He has stolen so much from me, Nick. Things I can never get back."

"He can't hurt you anymore, Sam." Nick tilted her chin up and looked longingly into her eyes. "Everything is going to be good now, Samantha Stevens. I promise."

Swallowing hard, Sam cleared her throat as emotions threatened to overwhelm her. "No, he can't hurt me anymore," she realized. "This is going to take more than a few sessions with the shrink when I get back home. I honestly think I would have lost my mind if you hadn't been here."

"You're stronger than you give yourself credit for."

Placing a chair next to the bed so that he could be near Sam, Nick padded over to the bathroom to turn out the light before returning to her side. Then, reaching across her to turn off the light above the hospital bed, he put his hand over hers.

"What do you think you are doing?"

"I was planning on going to sleep."

"Here?" her voice sounded incredulous.

"Yes, here."

"But people will talk."

"Let them say I care deeply about my partner."

"But, Nick—"

"Murphy will stand guard. Besides, we both know I will be awake before the first light. Now stop worrying and go to sleep. I will watch over you."

CHAPTER TWENTY-SEVEN

My Job Here Is Done

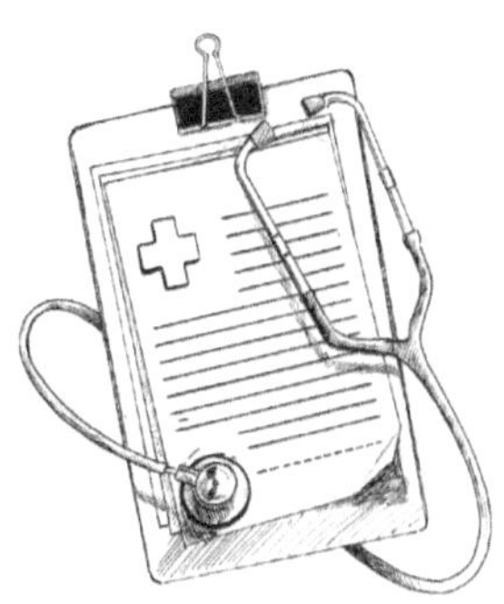

THE FIRST THING SAM NOTICED when she awoke was that Nick and Murphy were gone and there was an officer posted outside of her hospital room door.

Breakfast had been delivered while she slept soundly for the first time since she'd arrived in Alaska. And boy was she hungry.

Sam was looking at her horrible hospital food when Nick, Murphy, and Jameson knocked and announced themselves before entering her room.

"And how are you feeling this morning?" Nick asked, strolling over to her bedside.

Slapping the lid back down over her lukewarm oatmeal and toast, she gave him a grim smile. "Starving to death. Honestly, how hard is it to make something edible?"

"Then it's a good thing we smuggled in something from your favorite diner," Jameson said, producing a bag with an egg, bacon, and cheese breakfast burrito and a cup of coffee.

"You are really starting to wear on me, Jameson. In a good way."

This made him laugh out loud as he handed her the bag and took a seat in the nearest chair.

"I told you a proper meal would do the trick." He winked at Nick.

Nick sat on the edge of her bed while Murphy put his front paws on the bed to greet her. "How are you, boy? I missed you." Sam patted his head. "So, tell me, what's happening with the case?"

"I'm afraid I have some—" Nick started to say as he looked over at Jameson.

"Sam, we need to tell you something," Jameson said, cutting Nick off. His tone was solemn as he stood up.

Nick gave Jameson a sharp look, "I thought we agreed to tread lightly."

Shrugging his shoulders and looking properly chastised, Jameson sat back down.

"Maybe this should wait until I've eaten," Sam said, taking a bite of her burrito and then sipping her coffee. "You don't want to give me indigestion.

"Good idea," Nick consented. "I guess it can wait."

Taking one more bite, Sam looked up at both men, then put it down. "Fine. I think you better give it to me straight," she said, still chewing. "No. Wait, on second thought." She held up a finger to forestall any bad news as she took another large bite of the burrito and chewed, relishing the taste of everything mixed together in her mouth. Then she took a sip of her coffee to wash it down. Sam gave a satisfied sigh after swallowing. "All right, I'm ready. Hit me with it," she said, bracing for the worst.

"The prisoner escaped custody shortly after our conversation last night—"

"You are joking, right?"

Standing back up, Jameson quickly approached the other side of the bed. "This is no joke, Sam. Honest. He managed to free himself from his handcuffs, disable one officer, and fatally strangle the other before dumping them both on the side of the road and making his escape in their vehicle."

Sam couldn't believe what she was hearing. "This is unbelievable. This is all your fault. I barely survived my last encounter with this guy," she said, shaking her head. "Get me out of here," Sam insisted, throwing the covers back and pulling the hospital gown around her to cover her backside as she stood up.

"Now hold on there, Agent Stevens," Jameson began to say.

Pushing the button to call the nurse, Sam glared at him. "Don't you, Agent Stevens me, Jameson Fitzgerald Scott, or I will put you down on the ground, and it will take three nurses and a doctor to get you up again! That is a promise!" she bellowed, looking around frantically for her clothes.

Holding up his hands in front of himself, mainly to make sure he could get out of her way if she came at him, Jameson recanted, "I didn't mean anything by it, Sam. I just want you to think about what you are doing before you go off half-cocked. And my middle name isn't Fitzgerald!"

"Well, it should be," she growled back, ripping the IV from her right arm because a nurse hadn't arrived yet. Sam grabbed the bed sheet and applied pressure to her arm.

When the nurse entered the room and saw the chaos, she immediately picked up the room phone and called a code. In moments, the room was flooded with another nurse and a doctor.

"I need you to get back into bed," the first nurse ordered, trying to push Sam back into bed.

"Lady, if you don't want to lose that hand, I would suggest that you remove it from my person before I separate you from it," Sam said in a low, menacing voice.

"I'm serious, Miss Stevens. You must return to bed," the nurse said, still holding Sam's arm.

Murphy came around to stand next to Sam and gave a slight growl of warning.

"Get that dog out of here!" the nurse yelled as she contin-ued to hold staunchly to Sam's arm." Murphy began to bark.

"That's Special Agent Stevens to you, Nurse Ratched!" Sam exclaimed.

Nick stepped in, gently touching the nurse's hand. "Spe-cial Agent Stevens has asked you to remove your hand once.

I would strongly advise you to do so."

"If I had a nickel for everyone who didn't heed Stevens' warning, I'd be rich," Jameson chimed in before whistling between his teeth.

"And Officer Murphy is no ordinary dog. He's a highly decorated officer of the law. Can't you see that by the halter he's wearing?" Nick added, looking straight at the nurse, who quickly removed her hand and took a step back.

"Now, if you will be so kind as to fetch a bandage for my arm and give me my clothes, I am leaving here. Today!" Then, seeing the disapproving look on Nick's face, Sam added, "Please," in a sweet but slightly sarcastic tone."

"Murphy!" Nick commanded, causing the dog to fall silent.

The doctor who just entered the room moments before cleared his throat before speaking. "We certainly can't keep you here if you truly wish to leave, Agent Stevens, but I wouldn't advise leaving just yet."

"Get me the appropriate paperwork to sign, Doctor—" Sam squinted to read his name tag, "Reid. Because with or without your permission, I am leaving this hospital."

"You heard the woman," Jameson said.

Nick narrowed his eyes at Jameson.

Shrugging his shoulders, Jameson said, "Whaaat?" Then he added, "You haven't known her as long as I have, friend. Nothing changes her mind or gets in her way when she uses that tone. If she says she is walking out of here, you'd better believe she is walking out of here!"

Doctor Reid nodded to the second nurse standing next to him, and she rushed from the room to get the paperwork.

"Where will you go, Agent Stevens?" the doctor asked calmly, trying to defuse the entire situation as he reached into a cabinet to retrieve some gauze and a bandage for Sam's arm.

"I'm catching the first plane back to D.C.," she said to everyone in the room as she sat on the edge of the bed to wait for the doctor to treat her arm. "My job here is done. I completed what I came to do." Then, darting her eyes toward the ground, she grumbled under her breath. "It isn't my fault if some inept officers let the prisoner go after all the hard work we went through to capture this psychopath." Bringing her eyes back up to make eye contact with everyone in the room, she declared, "But now it's time to go home."

"We'll get this guy, Sam. There is no way he's getting around all of our roadblocks. He will be caught," Nick insisted. "We can keep you safe."

"We already tried that once, Special Agent McLeroy. I nearly lost my life in the process. Remember? I certainly will not be sticking around here to repeat this fiasco and give this guy another crack at ending me for good!"

Running a shaking hand through his hair, Nick didn't know what else to say to convince her to stay.

"You and Agent Scott can handle this from here on out. He's one of the best at what he does. After all that's happened, I'm too close to this and too emotionally invested to see straight right now."

"Special Agent Stevens is right, McLeroy. We can run this show and catch this guy. It's for the best."

"I'll take you back to the hotel to get your things, Sam," Nick said, knowing there wasn't anything he could say at this point to change her mind.

CHAPTER TWENTY-EIGHT

Saying Goodbye

THE CAR RIDE BACK TO THE HOTEL was somber. No one spoke. They were lost in their own thoughts.

The only one communicating was Murphy. He kept putting his nose under Sam's arm and nudging her until she reached over and scratched his head and ears.

Nick jumped out to retrieve Sam's crutches when he put the car in park. Murphy followed him, standing at attention at Sam's right side. He stayed by her side up the elevator and down the hallway as she walked to the room.

"Sam," Nick began, placing a hand on her shoulder. "Are you sure you won't stay?"

Turning to face him after they entered the room, Sam explained, "No, Nick, I can't, and you know why. My head is in the wrong place at this point. I can't even think straight right now. We both know I will likely catch hell for my part in it when I return to DC. The facts will come out and it would no longer be ethical for me to remain on the case. You know this," she said, shaking her head.

"I know, but—"

"But nothing, Nick," she interrupted. "We have to do this one by the book from here on out. No exception. If Hagen gets even a whiff of any impropriety, I will be on desk duty until the day I die. You know it's true. Not to mention the fact that I want to ensure that the perp doesn't get away on a technicality. That is, if you can manage to catch him again."

"You're right, Sam, but I hate to see you leave this way. I feel that there are still some unresolved issues to work out."

"Maybe for you, but I am all set. Besides, I'm not—" Sam continued, turning around when she heard the hotel room door open.

Then she saw Thea, standing in the doorway.

"How...? Why...are you...here—?" Sam stammered, then laughed, reaching out to put an arm around her friend and hug her tightly.

"I heard things got a little crazy yesterday, so I asked to be allowed to join you."

The truth was that Thea had taken emergency leave and purchased a ticket to Alaska because she knew Sam would need her.

"Well, you wasted your time. I'm going home," Sam said as she stepped into the living room area and stopped. She stared at the spot where she had fallen unconscious and felt a shiver crawl up her spine, then hobbled towards her room.

"Then it looks like I've arrived just in time to be your escort. And by the looks of it, you're going to need all the help you can get," Thea said as she scrambled to catch up with Sam.

Thea gave Nick and Jameson a sympathetic look before shutting the door behind her.

"Here, let me help you with that, Sam," Thea insisted, taking the suitcase from Sam's hands as she teetered precariously on one foot, trying to cross the room with the bag and crutch simultaneously. "I will pack this for you while you sit on this bed and put your foot up. I insist."

Taking a deep breath and blowing it out, Sam felt anxious. "You really are a good friend to come all this way, Thea. And I could really use a friend right now."

Crossing the room with an arm full of clothes, Thea smiled. "I wouldn't do this for just anyone, you know."

"Supervising Special Agent Tom Hagen didn't send you out here, did he?"

"You calling me a liar, Special Agent Sam Stevens?"

"I wouldn't dream of it, Agent Thompson. That would be wrong on so many levels. I suspect that you paid out of your own pocket for this little expedition." Sam smiled warmly at her friend.

"Hey, by the way," Thea said, nodding her head towards the door, "you failed to mention how handsome Special Agent McLeroy is."

"I thought I told you he's a very capable partner."

"Is that supposed to be some strange code for smoking hot?"

They both laughed as Thea gathered another arm full of clothes, depositing them into the suitcase before heading to the bathroom to gather toiletries. "So, I guess you can fill me in on all the sordid details while we fly home."

"There isn't much to tell, Thea. Nick…I mean, Special Agent McLeroy and Murphy are the best partners I've ever had. I couldn't have asked for anyone better to have my back. They saved my life. End of story."

"Liar," Thea whispered as she deposited the toiletries in the suitcase and closed it up.

Sam wanted to confide in Thea, the one person she knew would do anything for her. But a part of her still didn't trust anyone with her personal life.

"I think he's gay. He hasn't said anything to me, but I got that vibe from him," Sam insisted, hoping that she sounded convincing.

"Really?" Thea pulled a face. "Because I didn't get that vibe from him at all." Thea put her hands on her hips and looked puzzled. "I can usually tell with men. Oh well, live and learn.

"Oh, by the way, granny sends her regards. She wanted me to let you know that she did put a protection spell on you."

"Be sure to thank your granny for me. I definitely needed all the protection I could get."

Thea picked up the suitcase. "I think we are set. Are you ready?"

"I've been ready to go home since the day I stepped off the plane. Let's get out of here." Sam stood up, grabbed the crutches, and hobbled toward the door.

CHAPTER TWENTY-NINE

The Hunt Goes On

NOT EXACTLY SURE HOW HE'D managed to escape, the man they'd dubbed the Magician Killer stood behind a tree watching a campsite, pondering his good fortune. He truly felt magical. As a large smile rested on his lips, he continued to watch for movement from the tent while he attempted to stay concealed from anyone who might happen to pass by.

He'd managed to escape those incompetents, disappearing once again into the wilderness, where he was most at home. But he still had not accomplished what it was he had come to do—make Samantha Stevens disappear for good this time.

The campsite appeared deserted. The occupant was most likely out for an early morning hike or fishing for his breakfast. He didn't waste time. Opening the tent flap, he searched for a change of clothing and found a pair of worn jeans, an old T-shirt in his size, and some protein bars. Stuffing two bars into his pocket, he meticulously put everything back in place, closed the tent flap, and walked away. The unsuspecting camper would never know that he'd been there.

"This is your lucky day," he said to himself, just to hear his own voice as he left the campsite. "Lucky day indeed."

Nick and Murphy flew their two passengers in the float-plane to Lake Hood, where they had started their journey near Anchorage, in complete silence. After all, there wasn't much to be said.

They grabbed the Jeep Nick had arranged to be waiting for them and drove to the airport. Thea was the first to exit when he pulled up to the curb. "I'll get our luggage," she called out.

"Sam, wait," Nick said as he laid his hand on Sam's arm. "There's so much I still want to tell you."

"I know, Nick," her voice was sympathetic as she gave him a sad smile. "Me, too. But right now—" Sam simply let the words hang in the air between them.

Mustering up a smile, Sam changed the subject. "Be sure to place roadblocks in strategic locations, and flood the television with round-the-clock reports."

"I know, Sam. I'm not a rookie."

Sam noticed Thea waiting behind the Jeep with the luggage, giving her and Nick the privacy to say goodbye. "Oh, and don't forget to lock down the border. If he's as smart as I think he is, he will find a way to get across and into Canada. And be sure the reports make their way into Canada."

"We have already done that, but I will make sure that they continue to reinforce that order and don't get lax," he said, wanting to reach out and pull Sam into his arms and kiss her one last time.

"Jameson and I will get this guy," was all Nick could think of to say to her as he smiled and nodded his head to Thea, feeling very awkward all of a sudden.

"I know you will."

Murphy stuck his head between them and looked back and forth. "I'm going to miss you so much, boy," Sam said, scratching his head, hoping Nick understood her cryptic message.

"He's going to really miss you, too, Sam," Nick said, waiting for Sam to look at him again. He could feel her anxiety and see the stress in her eyes. "Are we good, Sam? I mean, will you be glad to see me again someday?"

"I would be happy to see you any day of the week, Very Special Agent Nicholas McLeroy. And don't go getting yourself killed tracking this psycho down. You hear me?" she added, as tears shimmered in her eyes when she looked up at him.

Crossing his heart, Nick said quietly, "I promise I won't die." His eyes locked on her lips.

"I'm going to hold you to it. But right now, I have to go or I'm going to miss my flight home."

Then, reaching out to him, Sam gave Nick a quick hug. "You've been a really great partner, and I'm going to miss you very much." Then, looking into the back seat again, she scratched Murphy behind the ears one last time. "You too, boy. Keep an eye on this guy. We both know who the responsible partner is between the two of you."

Murphy barked in answer to her as if he understood exactly what she had said to him and it made her smile as she stepped out of the Jeep.

"Keep me updated. I still want in on the credit for this capture," Sam turned and said before saluting Nick with two fingers to her forehead. "I'll see you on the other side, Mc-Leroy."

"Not if I see you first, Stevens," he answered back before she closed the door.

He started the Jeep, then waited for Sam to step onto the curb and head into the terminal before he drove away.

Sam turned and watched his tail lights as they disappeared from sight.

"Are you ready to go, partner?" Thea asked, suspecting what the strange look in Sam's eyes meant.

In the last three and a half years since Thea had known Samantha Stevens, she'd never seen her become attached to anyone.

"Yes!" Sam said, with a little too much emphasis on the word 'yes.' "I thought he'd never leave." She turned and hobbled on her crutches toward the sliding glass doors. "I can't wait to get home. I've been craving some good Thai food."

"I promise, that will be the first take-out I will get for you when we get settled."

"My mouth is already watering. Personally, I'm just praying for a tailwind and no mechanical or weather-related delays," Sam said over her shoulder.

CHAPTER THIRTY

TWO MONTHS LATER
Settling into a New Normal

S AM SAT AT HER DESK FILING reports when Supervising Special Agent Tom Hagen called out to her, "Special Agent Stevens, my office."

Standing up at her desk, Sam slipped on her coat and buttoned it. It felt wonderful to have that big black walking boot off her foot.

She was now wearing regular shoes even though her foot was still sore when she walked long distances. She refused to use the cane the doctor suggested. It was a vanity thing for Sam.

Thea poked her head over the partition, "What do you think that's about?" she inquired.

"No idea. I'll fill you in when I get back."

With a wink and a smile, Thea nodded her head towards Hagen's office when she saw him standing in the doorway. "Better hurry."

"You know I don't hurry anywhere these days."

"Special Agent Stevens, take a seat," Hagen said, waving her to one of the leather chairs in the sitting area of his office and closing the door behind him. "Can I offer you coffee, tea, perhaps something a bit stronger?"

"No thank you, sir. I just came back from lunch."

"Are there any updates on the Magician Killer Case?"

"It's as if he simply vanished, sir. There hasn't been a confirmed sighting of him since he escaped. Of course, there are those crackpots looking to get in on the reward money offered. But nothing credible yet, sir."

"How are you doing, Sam?" Agent Hagen asked, his voice uncommonly sympathetic.

"I'm fine, sir." Sam was surprised by his question. "I'm doing my required sessions with the therapist."

"But how arc you sleeping?

"Never better, sir. Thank you for your concern," she answered, knowing this was normal procedure for her supervisor to check on her on a regular basis after a traumatic event.

"Because you are entitled to more time off if you need it. Considering all that you've been through—"

"Your concern is touching, but I'm fine, sir."

What she really wanted to say was that the work here actually distracted her from thinking about the man who wanted her dead and was still roaming free, and that she was paralyzed by fear when she went home alone each night to an empty house. But admitting something like that was a career-ender, and Sam knew it.

"You know you can confide in me. I'm here for you, Special Agent Stevens."

"Thank you, sir, and I will be sure to keep you updated on any developments," Sam said, itching to get out of what she perceived as an interrogation seat.

"Very good, Stevens." Hagen stood and walked around the desk to his high-backed leather chair. "It's getting late. Why don't you knock off early tonight, and I'll see you in the morning. That's an order, Stevens."

"Yes, sir. I'll just wrap up what I'm doing and go home." Sam felt a tremor in her left hand at the mere thought of going home to an empty house.

The only thing that made going home bearable was the fact that the bureau installed a sophisticated security system throughout her condo when she returned from Alaska. Any time a package was delivered, or a bird flew into the window, Sam received a notification on her phone. The police were on speed dial and she lived in a gated community with guards who patrolled the area. If she hit one of the three panic buttons placed throughout the house, the guards would be activated and at her door within three minutes. The only problem was she would have to be able to get to one of the panic buttons.

That, coupled with the fact that Thea lived in the same condo complex and had been staying over at her place to help Sam through the difficult, long nights, was the only reason Sam hadn't lost her mind.

Thea was turning out to be a true and loyal friend—something Sam didn't have much experience with. She never said anything when Sam insisted the lights stay on all night or asked her to stand guard as she took a shower.

"If there isn't anything further, sir," Sam began as she got to her feet, "then I will be going."

Shaking his head, he said, "That will be all," giving Sam a pleasant smile. "Have a nice evening."

"So, what did he say?" Thea asked, sliding around the cubical the moment Sam reached her desk.

"He's feeling generous and said I should knock off early tonight. And since you are my ride, that means you get to knock off early, too."

"Yay," Thea cheered, quickly rolling her chair back to her own cubicle to shut off her computer and grab her coat and purse. "Where shall we eat tonight?"

Placing a sticky note on a file so she would know where she had left off and locking it in her desk, Sam smiled and looked up at Thea. "Something with carbs."

"I know just the place. You're going to love it."

"As long as we can get it to go, I'm all in. I'm feeling a bit worn out and I want to put my feet up, zone out, and watch something good tonight."

"Want to come to my place tonight?"

"No, I need a good night's rest in my own bed," Sam replied as they stepped onto the elevator.

"Oh, I almost forgot. Check your phone. It went off while you were talking to Hagen."

Pulling her phone out of her pocket, Sam saw that Nick had sent her a text telling her that he and Jameson were landing in D.C., and asking if they could come over later. Sam smiled.

"What's that about?"

"What are you talking about?" Sam feigned innocence as she texted back her reply.

"All right, I see how it is," Thea said. "You have a secret man."

"No. It's just Nick. He and Jameson are landing soon and wanted to stop by later. I told him they could stop by around seven-thirty for a few minutes, but that I had to get up for work early in the morning."

"I get it. That boy's about as gay as a—"

"It's not like that, Thea. I think he just wanted to see how I've been doing. That's all."

"Uh hum. Sure." Thea gave Sam a side-eye. "I see you, and I will say no more. Your secret is safe with me." She winked, making Sam smile even wider.

Thea said goodbye to a few people they passed coming off of the elevator, and they, in turn, made a conscious effort to include Sam in their farewells. After all, she was the returning agent who had survived a near-death experience and lived to tell the tale.

They ordered 'to go' from their favorite Italian restaurant, Filomena's on Wisconsin Avenue. Sam ordered the Mama Mia Shrimp with pasta while Thea had the Linguini Cardinale. They decided to split a classic Caesar salad and splurged a bit by ordering two slices of chocolate truffle cake for dessert, picking it all up on their way home.

Sitting in Samantha's condo leisurely eating their meal, Thea noticed a bear skin rug in front of the fireplace. "When did *that* come?"

"I've had it in a box in the closet for a few weeks now. I wasn't quite sure how I felt about it, but I decided it was a symbol of my survival, so I just put it out this morning. What do you think?"

"I think it's gorgeous. And man, it is huge! Did you think that thing was going to eat you?"

"Yea, it sure was looking like that for a while."

The two continued chatting while enjoying their savory meal and the wine pairing Sam had found in her cupboard.

Thea leaned back in the upholstered dining chair while patting her stomach. "I am stuffed," she exclaimed. "I'm going to need a break before I dig into that chocolate cake."

"Me, too. I'll clean up while you run back to your place and get some clothes for tomorrow."

"I need to water my plants and feed the cat, too. It shouldn't take me very long." Thea placed her dishes in the sink before heading toward the door.

"Take your time, Thea. No rush. Oh, be sure you grab your workout gear. I'm feeling like a quick stop at the gym in the morning. I may not be able to run, but that doesn't mean that we can't lift some weights and keep in shape. That is, if that's alright with you."

"You are a real taskmaster, Samantha Stevens, and I like it," Thea called over her shoulder before shutting the door and walking across the complex to her place.

The Unthinkable

S AM WASHED THE FEW DISHES they'd used by hand and left them to air dry, then went into the bedroom to put on her sweatpants and Rolling Stones T-shirt.

She heard the front door open and then close. Sam walked through her bedroom door as she called out to Thea, "That was fast." She walked slowly down the hallway with a lightness to her mood that she hadn't felt in a long time. "I'm going to have to name you Lightning McQueen from now—"

The rest of Sam's words froze in her throat. The man from her nightmares stood in the middle of the living room.

"Miss me?" he asked, a sardonic smile curving his lips. "I like it." He nodded, indicating the room and décor, and added with a menacing grin, "I think it really reflects who you are."

"How...Why...?" she stammered, trying to put a coherent thought together as her mind seemed to freeze.

"The bearskin rug is a nice touch. Is that who I think it is?"

So many things flashed through Sam's mind all at once. *Could she reach her service revolver sitting on the nightstand before he stopped her? How did he make it to Washington, D.C., without being spotted? Where was Thea, and did this madman do something to her? Would she be able to walk away from this man a third time, alive?*

Her entire body buzzed with fear and adrenaline. Then she took a deep breath. And then another. She felt the adrenaline take over and everything changed. She now knew what she needed to do.

"I hadn't really given you much thought to tell you the truth," she lied with conviction.

"Oh, now, that truly hurts my feelings, Sammy, my girl." He moved slowly around the coffee table towards her.

For every step he took forward, Sam took a solid step backward. "So, what have you been up to? You know, since the last time we were together," Sam asked casually, grimacing when she stepped down on her left foot wrong.

"I stashed away in a sweet couple's trailer and they unwittingly helped me across the border. Then I worked my way through Canada and dropped down into D.C."

"But how did you know where I lived?"

"You know, when you did your first news conference, your name and where you were from scrolled across the bottom of the screen. The rest was easy. I've been watching you for days," he answered with a wicked smile.

Sam felt her dinner and stomach acids rise to the back of her throat and swallowed hard to keep them down. "You never did tell me much about yourself the last time we were together. It's really poor form not to disclose more details about yourself to someone you've had a long-time obsession with."

"An oversight on my part." Feigning an apology, he brought a hand to his heart and tried to look pained. "Please forgive me. Well, since you asked so nicely, allow me to correct my poor manners. I was given the Christian name Zebedia, but my family called me Zeke. Zebedia seems so..." he said, looking up, searching for the right word, "pretentious. Don't you think?"

"I can see how that might be to a young boy," she agreed while continuing to back up towards her bedroom.

Her hand hit the silent alarm as she stepped through the doorway. She hoped that all of his attention would be on her so that he wouldn't notice the panel on the wall.

Sam didn't need to look where she was going. She always kept her gun on the nightstand, farthest away from the door. The back of her leg hit the bed and she quickly glanced over her shoulder to make sure her weapon was still there.

Zeke saw her gun sitting on the nightstand the moment he entered the room. "Do you think you can reach it," he nodded his head toward the gun, "before I get to you?"

"That was my hope," Sam said, trying to slow her breath and steady her nerves. She needed all of her concentration and precision if she was going to come out on top and alive when this was all over.

Then, in a split second, she dove over the bed, reaching out her hand. At the same time, Zeke landed on top of her, pulling her hand out of reach of the weapon.

Sam flipped over onto her back and fought him with everything she had, throwing punches and trying to kick him off of her. Unfortunately, he had the tactical advantage of being on top.

Using his knees, he pinned her arms down to her side while sitting on top of her chest, pressing the air from her lungs.

She tried to get her good leg up and around the front of him, but he had anticipated that move and countered it by leaning forward and punching her in the face.

Momentarily stunned, Sam quickly recovered and began to buck, kick, and move every which way, trying to dislodge him from his perch.

Zeke wrapped one hand and then the other around her slender neck, slowly, methodically, choking off her airflow. Then he loosened his grip until she recovered consciousness before beginning his sadistic game of choking her all over again.

He leaned down to whisper in her ear as the blood flowed back into her brain. "I could end it all instantly, Sammy, my little bird."

Coming to, Sam felt fuzzy and light-headed as stars danced in her peripheral vision. Her limbs felt light and rubbery. She knew she was experiencing hypoxia from the lack of oxygen to her brain.

She was truly scared and wondered if this would be it this time.

Her mind was still muddled, but Sam retaliated with the only thing she could—her words. "Then get on with it, you worthless piece of—"

Viciously squeezing her throat tightly with his long, slender fingers, Zeke watched Sam's face turn a gruesome blueish-red color, cursing her name as she once again passed out.

As he watched the life leaving her face, Zeke was so engrossed with his all-consuming hatred for Sam that he failed to hear the front door open and a man's voice giving the command, "Fass."

Seconds later, he felt searing pain shooting through his arm and back simultaneously as Murphy bit him everywhere at once.

Letting out a blood-curdling scream, he jumped off of Sam as his four-legged attacker growled in his ear and attempted to bite it off.

Zeke scrambled for the corner of the room, curling into a protective ball to try to stop any further attack, and let out another ghastly scream as if he was being murdered. "Stop! Make it stop! Please, I beg you."

Nick gave another German command and Murphy stopped biting. He stood at attention over the cowering figure in the corner while growling menacingly at his prey.

Nick reached Sam first, followed by Thea. Jameson headed to the man cringing on the floor beside Murphy.

"Make sure you cuff him," Nick yelled at Jameson as he leaned over Sam, trying to find any signs of life. "Damn it," he cursed out loud, pulling her seemingly lifeless body onto the floor. "Thea, call 9-1-1, now! And tell them to put a rush on it. And Jameson, get him out of here!"

Nick thumped Sam on the chest hard with his fist, then began CPR, his mind racing. *If the plane hadn't been late and they had arrived twenty minutes earlier, could they have prevented this? If Sam didn't make it, would he ever be able to forgive himself?*

"Sam, open your eyes. Breathe, damn you!" His words came out in short, desperate gasps of air as he pumped up and down on her chest. "Don't you die on me, Stevens!"

Thea quickly finished her call, keeping first responders on the line as she leaned down to help by breathing into Sam's mouth every fifth pump. "What did you do with him, Jameson?"

"Handed him off to the Security Guards. But don't worry, they are in the next room, and I made sure there were four of them before I left.

"Well, don't just stand there with your hat in hand, Scott. Call for back-up! Get more Fed's down here!"

They were both working on Sam when Nick called out, "Stop," as he felt the crook of Sam's neck while leaning close to her face, checking for any signs of volunteer air coming out of her mouth.

He was about to begin CPR again when Sam suddenly opened her eyes and clutched at her chest, rolling to her side in pain. Looking at Nick, she quickly surmised what had happened as she gasped for air.

"I think you broke my ribs," she whispered, her words barely audible. But Nick heard her and let out a grateful sigh. She was alive.

Nick pulled Sam to him, "Stevens, I have never been so happy to hear you complaining at me. And the proper response would be, thank you, Nick and Jameson, for saving my life."

In a hoarse whisper, she rasped out, "Did I forget to say that? I'm sorry, I was just over here dying. Can you ever forgive me?"

"There she is!" he announced. "She's back." Whispering in her ear and pulling her close, Nick continued, "And I'm so very grateful."

"You're crushing me."

Thea wrapped her arms around them both and cried, "You're alive."

"Did you get him?" Sam whispered, trying to see around her friends.

Jameson assured her they had just as two D.C. police officers came through the door with a pair of paramedics directly behind them.

Then he stepped into the next room that was suddenly flooded with officers. "I want our escapee shackled and chained before you transport him. And there are to be no less than three men on him at all times. Preferably four, if you can spare the manpower," Jameson said to the officers. "He's escaped before. Don't let him escape again."

"Yes, sir," the young officer said. "We will take him to lock-up, Special Agent."

"I'll send someone by with the paperwork later and take him off your hands just as soon as we are finished here," Jameson insisted, before ducking back into Sam's room as the paramedics were finishing up.

"Okay sir, we are about done here," the senior EMT said as he picked up his bag and slung it over his shoulder. Then he called down the hallway, "Clear the way, we're ready for transport."

"We will meet you at the hospital, Sam. We will be right behind you," Nick said, standing next to Thea, the two of them trying to get out of the way.

The younger paramedic saw the dog who was now sitting beside Nick. "Sir, they won't allow animals at the hospital. Service dog or not."

"Can no one see his vest? This is not a service dog. He is a highly decorated law officer who just saved her life."

Sam put her arm around Murphy and buried her head in his fur, "Thanks for saving my life, boy," she managed to squeak out.

"Sam, you have to go now," Thea said.

Nick and Sam's eyes locked on each other as Sam mouthed out the words, *thank you.*

The senior paramedic sighed and shrugged his shoulders. "Hey. It's up to the hospital what they do with the dog entering. We are just here to transport."

"Hold up just a second," Sam whispered, with a grimace that showed off her perfectly even, white teeth, even though the pain was unbearable.

Gesturing to Jameson to come close to her, she croaked out, "And Jameson, see that Zebedia doesn't escape this time."

"Will do," he said, saluting Sam. "I will meet you at the hospital as soon as the prisoner is secured," he called over his shoulder on his way out the door, following behind the four officers transporting the prisoner.

CHAPTER THIRTY-TWO

Déjà Vu

S AM SAT IN HER HOSPITAL bed with a sense of déjà vu as her lunch was delivered. She lifted the cover from the plate and pulled a face. "Honestly, how hard is it to make turkey, mashed potatoes, and gravy look appetizing?" she croaked hoarsely.

Jameson walked into the room with a bag in his hand, "Who's your favorite special agent ever?"

Sniffing the air, Sam said, "Bacon cheeseburger with the works?"

"Of course. With fries and a chocolate shake, just the way you like it," Jameson added.

"I don't care what others say about you, Jameson, you're alright."

Nick sat at the foot of the bed while Thea occupied a nearby chair.

"So, where's our lunch, Scott? You know the golden rule about sharing with the entire class," Nick said.

"I learned how to be the teacher's pet early in life, McLeroy, and it didn't include sharing with the entire class."

Sam offered up her french fries to anyone who wanted them and attempted to eat her hamburger, managing to get half of it down. But the chocolate shake was her favorite since it was easier to swallow.

"So, how did you two know I needed help?" Sam eyed Nick and Jameson.

"We had just flown in and were on our way to your place to check in with you. That's when I got a call from headquarters that there was an emergency call coming from your residence," Nick said. "Luckily, we were just around the corner."

Sam was sipping on her chocolate shake when Jameson cleared his throat.

"Did you enjoy your meal?" Jameson asked.

Nodding her head, Sam continued sucking on the straw of her shake. "Most definitely," she answered, as a satisfied sigh escaped her lips. "Hey, did you hear the good news?" she whispered as her voice faded. "I'm getting sprung from here this afternoon. The doctor said there was no permanent damage. Just a couple of broken ribs, a bruised throat, and, of course, my ego. Nothing that won't heal over time."

"I need to broach a sensitive subject and I don't want you to bite my head off, Sam," Jameson said.

"Uh-oh. This must be serious," Sam narrowed her eyes at him. "You plied me with food, and now we need to have a grown-up conversation. Why do you need to spoil a perfectly good meal and kill the moment, Jameson?"

"My apologies, Sam."

"This isn't funny anymore, Jameson, and I don't wish to play along," she said, putting down her shake. "The last time you looked like that, our killer escaped," Sam narrowed her eyes at Jameson. "Tell me he didn't escape again," her hoarse voice cracked.

"No, nothing like that," Jameson assured her. "We haven't been able to get anything out of the man you named The Magician Killer. The only thing he will say is, 'I need to speak with Sammy. I will only talk to Sammy.'"

Sam grew very still while the blood drained from her face. She felt her left hand begin to tremble. Her heart began to pound rapidly in her chest and the monitor she was hooked up to started beeping loudly.

"Could you hand me a glass of water, Nick? My mouth seems to have gone suddenly dry."

"Sure, Sam."

"We need you to talk to him, Sam, for no reason other than to gain vital information and maybe get closure for yourself," Jameson said, standing next to her.

"You really need to stop saying that Jameson. I'm not one

of your subjects you can manipulate. I got my closure, and I am finished. Truly finished. Why can't you see that?" She emphasized her statement by shoving her trash in the bag, crushing it, and throwing it at the trash can in the corner.

"But the case isn't finished, Sam. We need you to speak with the prisoner."

"His name is Zebedia, but he likes to be called Zeke," she said, narrowing her eyes. "And that's as much as I care to know about the man!"

There was a knock on the door. It was Sam's doctor. "Knock, knock," he said, poking his head into the room before he entered. "It looks like my invitation to the party got lost in the mail," he joked.

"Hello, Doctor. Have you come to spring me from this place?" Sam rasped out the words.

"Sam, we'll be just outside the room if you need us," Nick said, opening the door as he waited for the other two to exit before shutting the door behind him.

Nick volunteered to drive Sam home while Thea and Jameson returned to work.

"So, are you going to do it?" Nick asked, looking at Sam out of the corner of his eye as he drove.

"I haven't decided yet. I need to sleep on it."

"Mind if Murphy and I crash with you tonight?"

Sam smiled. "Of course. What are partners for if not to crash at each other's place from time to time?" Sam was glad that she and Thea had already decided that it was time to rip the Band-Aid off, so to speak. Since the man who had haunted her nightmares was behind bars, Thea was no longer needed as her house guest to help her sleep at night.

"I was hoping you'd say yes. So I packed a spare bag and food for the big guy, just in case."

"I can always count on you to be prepared. You are a regular Eagle Scout, Nicholas Emory McLeroy."

"Hey, I told you that my mother is the only woman allowed to use my middle name. I don't like it."

"But you were named after your grandfather and I think it is a perfectly lovely name."

Pulling up in front of Sam's condo, Nick hurried around the car to help her out and up to the door. Murphy followed Sam into the house while Nick retrieved his bag from the car and settled into the guest room.

After work, Thea picked up food for everyone at the Mexican restaurant down the street and they all enjoyed one another's company. They even played a rousing game of Catan before calling it a night.

As Sam was settling down for the night, Nick knocked on her open door and casually leaned on the door jam, "Sam, do you have an extra toothbrush? Murphy forgot his and he won't go to bed without brushing his teeth."

"Just a minute," she called out. Sam smiled and handed Nick a new toothbrush she hadn't opened yet, "I don't blame the guy. Personally, I could never go to bed without brushing my teeth either," she teased.

"Oh, and Murphy wanted me to ask if he could sleep in here with you tonight. After he brushes his teeth, of course."

"I'll leave my door open for him," Sam said with a wink. "He can keep me company in case I have a bad dream."

"You've always been a very considerate partner," Nick laughed as he headed back down the hallway to brush his teeth. "You're the best, Samantha Stevens. I don't care what anyone else says about you. I would defend you to the end."

"Thanks, partner, you're the best too," she called back, climbing into bed with a book in her hand.

Sam was in bed reading when Murphy scrambled into the room, jumped up onto the bed, and crawled up next to her. "Hello, boy," she laughed as he licked her cheek. "I've missed you." Sam hugged his neck. "You can stay as long as you don't hog my blankets."

"Do you have room for one more?" Nick asked, leaning against the doorjamb.

"It's a good thing I have a king-size bed."

"We both know you didn't really want to read that dry, boring book tonight." He crawled into bed and pulled Sam close.

Nick gave the command "Platz," and Murphy jumped out of bed, settling down where he could keep an eye on Sam and Nick.

"You're going to have to teach me that trick someday," she said, placing the bookmark between the pages.

"I will teach you all my tricks if you like," he confided with a sly grin just before he turned out the lights on his side of the bed and leaned over to kiss Sam on the lips.

"Why, Special Agent McLeroy, I do believe you just might be a bad influence on me." Sam put down her book and turned out her light, snuggling closer to Nick.

"Is that truly a bad thing?"

"Not if you keep that up," she offered, her voice laced with desire.

Face-To-Face With the Devil Himself

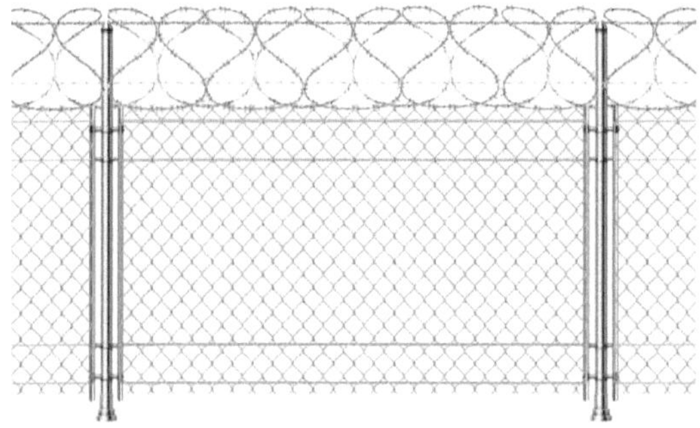

NICK BARELY STIRRED next to Sam when she awoke with a start at four-fifteen in the morning.

Sam had been having another one of those dreams. Her hair and shirt were damp with perspiration while her heart still beat erratically. Sam felt like a scared rabbit who had been running from a predator.

Quietly, she climbed out of bed, hobbled to the bathroom, and shut the door while flipping on the light. Splashing cold water on her face, she took a moment to simply lean on the counter and regain some composure.

Standing, Sam looked at herself in the mirror, seeing the water dripping from her chin, the bloodshot eyes, and the beginning of dark circles forming beneath them from lack of sleep. She felt as if she'd aged overnight.

She popped a pain pill into her mouth and swallowed it down with some water from the sink. Her ribs were beginning to ache.

A rush of anger tensed every muscle in her body. Gripping the sink in front of her, Sam moved her head in a circle and then leaned back, hearing her neck popping like bubble wrap. Tears of frustration ran down her cheeks and she wiped them away with shaky hands as a sob caught in her throat, making her want to scream with rage. Sam dropped to her knees on the cold, tiled floor. Balling up her shaking left hand, she banged it against her thigh.

How could she have come to be this pitiful, frightened mess she'd seen in the mirror this morning? For too many years, to further her career, Sam had channeled all that pent-up anger and fear. Now, the man who'd haunted her dreams was behind bars, yet, somehow, he still managed to reach out into the world and mess with her mind, even in her sleeping hours.

Sam heard a knock on the bathroom door. "Are you all right?" Nick asked from the other side.

She paused a moment, then got to her feet. "I'm fine, Nick. I'll be right out, just give me a second."

That small, determined voice inside of her would somehow make her words true.

Nick could hear the fear and pain in her voice. Even though she tried to sound fine, he knew she wasn't fine. But he would respect her right to privacy until she stepped out of the bathroom and into his arms. He would do anything he could to help her heal. Anything.

It was eleven-twenty in the morning, and Sam was in a car, headed to see the man who had haunted her nightmares for years.

No one said a word about Sam's red-rimmed eyes as they left her condo and drove to the site where *he* was being housed, forty minutes away at a maximum-security facility. Furtive glances passed between Nick and Jameson, yet nobody tried to engage Sam as she stared out her window from the back seat, lost in her own thoughts.

When they arrived at the facility, Nick immediately got out of the car and opened the door for Sam. He stood holding the door open for a full twenty to thirty seconds before Sam moved to get out. When she did, she moved slowly, almost unsure that she could actually go through with it.

"Remember, when you talk with him, don't let him get the upper hand by rattling you," Jameson advised. "And whatever you do, don't let him see that you are scared."

"This isn't my first rodeo, Jameson," Sam said crossly. "You don't have to treat me as if I'm still your student."

"No, that's not it at all," Jameson said gently. "Sam, I'm sorry this happened to you, and that you have to go through this now. But I'm not the enemy here."

Suddenly feeling bad for snapping at her old mentor, Sam looked down at the ground and took a deep breath. "I know you aren't, and I'm sorry for snapping at you. None of this is on you. I'm just feeling a little prickly today."

Noting the dark circles that showed through her makeup, Jameson felt guilty for asking her to do this so soon after her trauma. "If you want to cancel today, we can try questioning the prisoner next week."

"Jameson Scott, have you gone soft on me?" she asked. "Because last time I checked, we were still the FBI, and I am still an agent of said department. I know how to do my..." Sam paused, taking a deep breath to calm herself. Then, placing a hand on Jameson's arm, she looked him in the eyes. "I'm sorry for getting so riled up. None of this is your fault, Jameson, and I don't mean to take my anger out on you."

"Are we good?" he asked.

Nodding her head, Sam replied, "We're good. And you're right—I will never be free of him if I don't see this through."

The three of them walked the rest of the way in silence as Nick's hand brushed up against Sam's for just a split second. He wanted to hold her hand, comfort her before she had to face *him*, and let her know that he supported her. But he also knew that it would be awkward and send a clear message to Jameson that they were romantically involved. Besides, Nick still didn't fully trust Jameson.

Turning in her service revolver and showing her identification to the guard on duty at the visitor's desk, Sam stepped through the screening area first. They were all met by Officer Diaz, a rather large man who looked as if he spent a lot of time at the gym.

"Is Zebedia Lyman ready for interrogation, Officer Diaz?" Sam asked, reading his name badge before he led them down the maze of corridors.

"Yes. That must make you Special Agent Stevens."

"Yes, sir, that would be me," she replied. "May I see the report? I need to prepare myself before I interview our prisoner."

"Of course. It's waiting for you in the ready room," he said, stopping in front of a door and then opening it for her. "I heard what he did to you, and I want to say that I respect the fact that you are going to speak with him. That takes a lot of guts, ma'am."

Sam tried to smile, but it didn't quite reach her eyes, "Thank you, Officer Diaz. That's kind of you to say."

Sitting down at the desk, Sam opened the thin file and began reading the report. Afterward, she stood up and wandered over to the corner of the room to digest everything she had just read and to observe the prisoner through the one-way glass. "I need more papers to make the file look thicker," she said to Nick and Jameson as they sat reviewing the files after her. "I want him to think that we know everything there is to know about him."

Officer Diaz returned. "When you are ready, ma'am. The prisoner is restrained and will not be able to touch you, but I would still suggest that you maintain your distance. The table is not bolted to the floor, but the prisoner's legs and wrists are shackled. I will be directly outside the door."

"Perfect," Sam said before requesting Officer Diaz to bring her more papers to fill the slender file. Without Sam saying it out loud, the officer understood the reason for this and returned with a stack of papers just the right thickness and placed them at the back of the file.

Then, with a nod, Sam walked back over to the table, picking up the newly enhanced file and two small bottles of water. "Don't worry, I've got this," she said, ignoring the stir of fear in her heart.

Stepping into the grim interrogation room, Sam tossed one of the water bottles to Lyman to see if he was paying attention. Catching the bottle in mid-air, he smirked, "You brought me the good stuff. And here I thought maybe you would hold a grudge."

Without missing a beat, she looked directly at the man who had haunted her for so many years and took the seat opposite him, dropping the newly thickened file upon the table with a loud thud. Sam allowed a wicked smirk to cross her lips. "Shall we start with something easy? Where are you from?"

He studied her intently for a silent moment, then leaned back in his chair. "Seems to me you already know the answer to that question by the size of that file."

Mimicking his move, Sam leaned back as well and looked confidently at him before replying. "We do, most definitely, know quite a few things about you, *Mr. Lyman.*" Smiling, she continued. "May I call you Zebedia? Oh that's right. You prefer Zeke."

He looked irritated by the question. *I wonder how many buttons I can push that will keep him off balance,* she thought.

"Whichever you prefer, *Samantha,*" he sneered. "As long as you don't mind me calling you *Sammy.* I'm so glad we are having this little talk. It gives us an opportunity to get to know one another even better."

"So, where would you like to start, Zeke?" Sam said, noticing that he didn't flinch this time. "Your childhood or when you decided to start killing people?"

"My childhood was so boring—"

"Excellent, your childhood it is, Zebedia."

Bringing his fist down hard on the table, Lyman roared, "I told you, my childhood is off-limits!"

Zebedia looked extra rattled, so Sam continued pushing the same button. "No, Zebedia. You told me that your childhood was *boring.* You said nothing about it being off-limits."

"Stop calling me that. I hate that name," he spat. "You're just like the rest of them, twisting my—"

"Just like who, Zebediah?...Sorry, I mean, Zeke," Sam interrupted, noting his increased agitation. She'd definitely found his weak spot. "What others are you referring to? And tell me about the reason your given name irritates you so much."

Leaning back in his chair again, he brought his right hand up to rest under his chin. "I see what you are up to," he said, wagging a finger at her. "You think you are very clever. But you're not."

"Oh, I don't know about that, Mr. Lyman. I've been told by many people that I'm very clever." Sam leaned forward and flipped open the file. "Did you start with small animals? I mean, before you switched over to people. Or maybe your mommy didn't love you enough?"

"You sound ridiculous," he scoffed.

"Do I? Or is it the fact that I am hitting so close to the mark that it makes you uncomfortable?" Sam taunted. "Perhaps you don't really know what set you off in the beginning. Don't feel bad. Not everyone is enlightened. I mean, really—"

"You're trying to push me, Sammy. But I won't be pushed," he said with a sly smile, opening his bottle of water and taking a long, slow drink.

"Why don't you want to discuss your childhood and share the reason that your given name upsets you?"

Putting the bottle of water down on the table, he narrowed his eyes at Sam. "Tell me, Sammy, how have you been for the last ten years? Do you ever think of me late at night?"

Sam froze. The tremor began in her left hand as she slowly scooted her chair back and stood up. Retreating to the back wall, next to the one-way mirror, she took a moment before turning back around. Slowly, she brought her eyes up to meet his.

He was smiling as their eyes met. "You have triggers as well, I see. I'm glad you think of me."

Flip the script, flip the script, her mind screamed as her mouth suddenly went very dry. Sam's eyes traveled over to the second bottle of water across from him on the table.

"Don't worry, I didn't spike it," he said.

With a chuckle, she walked back to the table, twisted off the bottle top, and swallowed deeply. "That's a good one, Zeke. I almost forgot to laugh." Then, taking her seat, Sam leaned back and crossed her legs. "Getting back to you. Shall we? When did you decide to start killing people?"

Lyman tented his fingers and rested his chin on the point. "When I met you."

Sam found it difficult to keep her expression the same, so she used her pen to make an unnecessary note in the file in front of her. Lyman leaned forward, trying to see what she was writing, so she deliberately closed the file. Bringing her eyes back up to meet his, Sam braced herself to meet his evil gaze. "Can you confirm that you were abused by your mother as a child?"

Lyman looked shocked by her question. "Why are you still harping on my childhood? I told you I'm not going to talk about it. Besides, I didn't do anything. I'm innocent."

"Of course you are, Zeke," Sam said, her words falling between them like a flat note. "You requested to speak with me. So, please, tell me what it is you wanted to talk about."

"I unnerve you, don't I?" He smiled, showing off a row of uneven, yellow teeth.

Leaning back in her chair, Sam laughed. "You give yourself far too much credit."

"Ha!" He snapped his fingers, looking smug. "I'm right."

"Tell me about the victims, Zebedia. Where are they buried? How did you kill them? Why have we not found more of them?"

"I told you, I've done nothing wrong," he smiled innocently.

"If you wanted to get into a pissing contest, you should have requested to speak with someone else," she said, scraping the chair legs against the concrete floor as she stood up to go.

"Wait!" Lyman yelled.

Sam ignored him as she gathered the folder and bottle of water into her hands. "You are wasting my time, Mr. Lyman."

"I liked it better when you called me Zeke."

"I will make a note of that. Good day," she said dismissively as she took another step toward the door.

"Wait, dammit! Did you merely come to stare at the caged animal in the zoo? Or maybe you came to find out what makes Zeke Lyman tick?"

Turning back around, Sam placed the file back down on the table. "Stop wasting my time! I came for the magic show.

So, show me some magic!" she yelled, slamming her hand down on the table between them and startling him. "I'm warning you, if I walk out of this room, I will not come back, and I will never think of you again. Do you hear me? Never!"

"My mommy didn't hug me enough. My daddy doubted my legitimacy, so he beat me regularly. I didn't make the football team." His voice quickened, and his tone raised to a fevered pitch as he rushed onward like a madman. "Maybe it's simply the fact that, at the moment, nothing matters more than Zeke Lyman. When I hold their lives in my hands, I mean. Is that what you wanted to know? Is that the kind of complex psycho-babble crap you wanted to hear, Sammy?"

Unperturbed, Sam leaned forward with her hands on the table, giving him a steely-eyed glare. "No, Zebedia Lyman, because we both know none of those reasons are why you kill." Shaking her head and looking disappointed, she continued, "Do you even know when this all began for you? Are you in touch with what truly makes you tick?" Sam scoffed. "And all this time I believed you to be this intelligent, complicated individual, like some rare, white unicorn. But you're not a rare white unicorn or some anomaly at all, are you, Zebedia Lyman?"

"I'm not?" He looked shocked.

"No, Zebedia, you're not. Because as I got up close and personal with you and your handiwork, I realized a different truth." Sam paused for dramatic effect, looking him straight in the eyes. "Are you listening? Because this is important to understand," she said while tapping the side of her temple with her pointer finger. "Some toys come down the assembly line broken. They're defective from the get-go. Plain and simple. *You're* nothing more than a broken, insignificant toy, Zebedia." Sam stood up, taking another drink from her bottle of water before picking up the file, as if she had all the time in the world. Then she smiled pleasantly and took a few steps toward the door, pausing as if she'd just had an afterthought. Slowly, she turned around, careful to hide the fact that her left hand had begun to shake again. She felt as if her knees were knocking together. "Say something interesting or important to this case, or so help me, I will walk out this door, and I won't come back."

"You look like her," Lyman said quietly, diverting his eyes away from Sam.

"Like who, Zeke? Your mother? Do I look like your mother?" Sam came back and stood in front of the table. "Is that why you picked me?"

He sat mutely, staring at the table until Sam slammed her hand down hard onto the tabletop again, startling him out of his daze. "Answer the question, Zebedia. Do I look like your mother, and is that why you picked me?"

"Yes!" he shouted, his eyes narrowing as he glared menacingly at her.

Sam was taken aback by the raw hatred she saw in his eyes at that moment, and her breath caught in her lungs as she took a step backward. An involuntary shiver traveled up her spine. "Will you tell me where you buried the bodies?"

"I will be happy to *show* you where I buried the bodies."

"I am afraid a road trip is off the negotiating table, Zeke. You will not be going anywhere for a very long time." Sam's voice was unyielding. "The best you can hope for is leniency by cooperating with us."

Sam pulled out a map, laying it out before him, and Lyman began talking. When they were finished, there were eighteen marks on her Alaskan map. Her job here was done. Standing and gathering up her paperwork, she brought her eyes up to meet his for what she knew would be the last time, which she was eternally grateful for. Of course, she knew she would have to face him again in a courtroom setting, but the circumstances would be different than one-on-one.

"Thank you for all your cooperation, Mr. Lyman. Your help will bring closure to a lot of families."

"When will I see you again?" he said. His eyes traveling up her body repulsed her.

Pausing for a long moment, Sam felt like a fly with its wings pinned to the wall. Swallowing hard, she licked her lips before speaking.

"Mr. Lyman, I feel that you were given the wrong impression. My being here does not in any way mean that you and I will continue any kind of relationship after today." Her voice was cool as her eyes frosted over. "This will be the one and only time you and I will ever be in the same room together, except for the day you go to court and I testify against you."

Without warning, the prisoner slammed his fist down on the table with a loud bang. Startled by his reaction, Sam jumped back.

"No! No, no, no, no. This can't be!" Lyman screamed. "I will not have it."

"I will make note of your objection," she interjected, her tone coolly detached. "But I am afraid it's true. We will not meet again, Mr. Lyman, nor will I have further contact or interaction with you. It appears that your magic show has come to an end."

Lyman shook with rage, jerking at his chains like a madman in an attempt to break free.

Taking two steps backward, Sam pounded on the metal door. "Officer Diaz, we're done here," she announced, flinching with each jerk of Lyman's chains as he screamed profanities at her, spittle flying with each lambasted word.

Officer Diaz opened the door and jumped out of her way as she hurried through the doorway.

"He's all yours. I'm ready to go home now," Sam said as Officer Diaz slammed the door closed behind her.

She did not stop as she quickly made her way toward the exit. Nick and Jameson exited the room next door and had to run to catch up to her.

"Sam, are you all right?" Nick asked when he reached her at the visitor desk where she stopped to retrieve her sidearm.

Turning to look at him and Jameson, Sam smiled through the tears that had escaped from her eyes. "Never better," she said, swallowing hard. "I've come to the realization that I've allowed him to rob me of so much of my life. And I keep asking myself, why? Why have I let him take over my life in that way?"

"Well then, what are you going to do about it?" Nick asked.

"I'm going to take my life back."

Coming closer to Sam, Nick put his arms around her and hugged her. "I'm so proud of you, Sam. But I'm especially glad you didn't let him kill you."

"You and Murphy saved my life twice," Sam said, letting out a heavy sigh as she pulled away, then stuck out her hand, "Special Agent Samantha Stevens. It's a pleasure to meet you, Special Agent Nicholas McLeroy."

Giving Samantha a broad smile, Nick gripped her outstretched hand. "It's a pleasure to finally get to meet you, Special Agent Samantha Stevens. Now, how about we go out tonight to celebrate? You, me, Jameson, and your friend Thea."

"That sounds great. But first, let's get out of here. This place gives me the creeps."

"Me, too," Jameson chimed in.

CHAPTER THIRTY-FOUR
EIGHT MONTHS LATER
Washington, D.C.
Federal Bureau of
Investigation Building

SAMANTHA SAT AT HER DESK, lined with replicas of tiny robots, combing through a cold case file and feeling confident she had just figured out who the perpetrator was when Supervising Special Agent Tom Hagen stepped out of his office and called, "Special Agent Stevens. My office. Now, please."

Looking up from her work, Sam winked at Thea, sitting across from her. "Well, it seems my supposed hero status is already on shaky ground," she joked.

"Honestly, your hero status lasted longer than I thought it would," Thea quipped.

Finding a sticky note, Sam scribbled, 'Look into the night watchman,' then attached it to the front of the file.

"Even the mighty must fall at some point," Thea joked, jutting her head toward Hagen's office. "You'd better get in there before he calls you a second time. You know how he hates to be kept waiting."

Sam put on her blazer and buttoned it, then smoothed out any wrinkles with her hand. "How do I look?"

"Perfect."

"Thanks, Thea. Wish me luck," she added before taking a drink from her thermos.

"Best of luck."

Walking quickly to her boss's office, Sam knocked on his closed door.

"Come in."

"You called for me, sir?" Sam stepped in, closing the door behind her.

"I believe you know Special Agent McLeroy," Hagen said, waving his hand in Nick's direction.

"Yes, we know one another very well, sir. It is a pleasure to see you again, Special Agent McLeroy," she added before bending down and addressing Murphy at his side. "And it is so good to see you again, Officer Murphy. I see you got your third gold star. Good for you." She scratched him behind his ears.

"Agent McLeroy has transferred to our office and I have decided to make the two of you partners," Hagen announced.

"Oh?"

Nick stepped forward, his blue-green eyes sparkling. "Only if that would work for you, Special Agent Stevens."

"Partners? That's so unexpected," she said, standing at her full height. Sam looked up into Nick's eyes. "It would be my honor to partner with you, Agent McLeroy. But only because I really like your dog, and you both saved my life not once but twice."

"Excellent," Hagen said, leaning back in his chair. "You'll need to have a desk brought up from the basement. The two of you can decide where you want it put."

"Thank you, sir." Nick shook the director's hand.

"You will make a nice addition to our team, McLeroy. Dismissed."

"Yes, sir," Nick and Sam said simultaneously, standing erect.

Nick reached the closed door first, opening it for Sam. "After you."

Murphy stood close to the both of them as they exited the office.

"Thank you," Sam said quietly, smiling at Nick as their hands touched. "You realize Murphy likes me better than you."

"He's a very fickle partner," Nick added, looking down at his faithful companion. "And he has excellent taste."

"Come with me," Sam said. "I'll show you where the basement is. You can pick out a desk and chair."

Sam caught Thea spying from down the hall and offered a stealthy thumbs up.

Sam, Nick, and Murphy walked to the elevator in silence, maintaining some distance from each other. But once the elevator doors closed behind them, Sam pushed the button and stepped back to stand next to Nick in the otherwise empty car.

Sam spoke first. "So, is your new place everything I said it would be?"

"Everything and more." Their hands brushed as they gripped the railing, cognizant of the cameras in the car. "Want to help me finish unpacking?"

"Only if you have steaks and a barbecue," she laughed. "I have been in the mood for a thick, juicy slice of rare beef."

"You're in luck. I just purchased a brand-new grill and some charcoal for grilling. Anything else?" he asked.

"So, when did this turn into us being partners? I thought we were just going to work in the same office."

The doors opened, and Nick stuck his hand out to hold them open. "Let's talk about it later."

Sam nodded and gave him a broad smile. "I'll bring the wine tonight," she said as she stepped off the elevator. Her voice changing to a business-like tone, she continued, "And this is the basement. To our right, you will see chairs, and to our left," she added, stretching her arms open wide, "are the long-forgotten desks from years gone by. I will let you in on a little secret." She cupped her hand and leaned in. "If you want one that isn't too old or beat up, you will have to butter up Vera. She is a real sweetheart. And by sweetheart, I mean you'd better watch your step with her. Of course, if you bring her a pastry and a latte, you can get anything you want. Fortunately for you, I have an in with Vera and she genuinely likes me."

"Good to know," Nick chuckled.

"What's more, she is an animal lover, so Murphy's a shoo-in," she said, stopping at the open door that read 'Acquisitions Coordinator: Vera Stromberg.'

Sam knocked on the doorframe, opened the door, and stepped into the office, seeing a short woman who stood only five-feet-three inches tall. Vera was in her sixties with dirty blond hair cut into a short bob with too much hair spray and back combing. She always wore her pencil skirts just below the knee with a coordinating blouse and sweater. Her glasses had a gold chain attached to them so she could never lose them. To say that Vera was stuck in the past would be an understatement.

"Vera, how are you doing today? I brought you some customers." Gesturing toward the two who followed her into the room, she continued, "I wanted to introduce you to my new partner, Special Agent Nicholas McLeroy."

"And this is Officer Murphy," Nick added. "I would be careful around him. He's a real dog. He likes the ladies."

Vera chuckled and winked at Sam, "I like him already."

They spent thirty-five minutes finding the best desk and ergonomic chair for Nick and called it a day.

After work, Nick met Sam at his place, which just so happened to be next door to Sam's.

"I plan to put in a discrete gate over there next week," he said as he pointed out the exact spot he'd picked for the new gate.

"That will be convenient. Good thing those bushes will hide the fact that there is a gate there."

"That's what I was thinking," Nick's smile widened. "It will be even more discreet when I stop trimming those shrubs. Say, we can take one car to work and shop for groceries together."

"Of course. We will start a carpool with other agents," Sam said. "You know Thea just lives across the complex from us," she pointed out.

With a wink, Nick added, "Discretion is my middle name."

"I would have sworn your middle name was Emory."

Nick laughed. "Hey, I told you only my mother gets to call me by my middle name."

"Well, someone has to keep you humble."

"Speaking of being humble, let me explain what happened in Hagen's office today. When I applied to work in the D.C., office, I was intent on working in a different department, but then Hagen surprised me by saying that he had decided to make us partners. What was I supposed to say? He felt that we had done such an excellent job on The Magician Killer case."

Sam adjusted her stiff neck, "I totally get it. How would you turn him down without giving our secret away?"

"Exactly."

"But Nick, we are going to have to be very careful when in public. Neither one of us can afford a slip-up. It would be career suicide.

"I know, Sam. And I will."

They looked at each other, each realizing that they had a challenge ahead of them, keeping their relationship hidden from their coworkers. Then Nick changed the subject.

"Did I tell you about this possible case in Vermont I've been analyzing?"

"No, but you can tell me all about it over dinner. And speaking of dinner, hadn't you better get the steaks on while I make the salad?"

"Right away, partner," he said with a salute. "I believe this is the beginning of a beautiful partnership, Samantha Stevens."

"You took the words right out of my mouth, Nicholas Mc-Leroy."

Follow me for more great novels by me at:

https://www.amazon.com/author/dianemerrillwigginton

https://frankly.franklinpublishers.com/v2/preview/8cJRD9R-69n1kS8mtEeBr

And remember, authors work hard to bring you quality stories, so if you would like to thank an author, be sure to leave a kind review on Amazon and the other websites where books can be found. It would really make me smile.

Other places you can follow me and keep in touch to get updates include:

Bookbub: https://www.bookbub.com/profile/diane-merrill-wigginton?follow=true

Amazon: https://www.amazon.com/author/dianemerrillwigginton

Facebook: https://www.facebook.com/diane.fraiserwigginton/

Twitter: https://twitter.com/wiggintondiane

Goodreads: https://www.goodreads.com/author/show/8355606.Diane_Merrill_Wigginton

Linkedin: https://www.linkedin.com/in/ diane-merrill-wigginton-926b89159

dianemerrillwigginton.com

dianemerrillwigginton.com/my-books